Starting Over

Kat Ryan

STARTING OVER

Published by Red Rims Publishing

ISBN: 978-1-7376748-8-7 (eBook) ISBN: 978-1-7376748-9-4 (Paperback)

Developmental editing by Sue Brown-Moore, SueBrownMoore.com

Proofreading by Victory Editing

Cover Design by Elle Maxwell of Elle Maxwell Designs

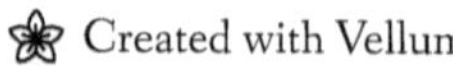 Created with Vellum

Dedicated to my therapist, Molly, and all the amazing therapists out there.

Thanks for the work you do.

Chapter 1

Piece of Cake

Drew
    I gasped as I sat up in bed, heart racing. My breaths came in short puffs.

Glancing around the room, I worked to relax. There was no smoke, no shouts, no chaos. Instead, peace surrounded me. Moonlight shone through the window, illuminating the sparse amount of furniture decorating the Airbnb I'd been renting for the past few months.

Kicking the covers off, I moved to the edge of the bed and got up. The room felt too tight as I paced with a glance at my watch, then moved back to the window. Only a little after midnight. Fuck.

Frustration filled me up as I grabbed at the hem of my sweat-drenched T-shirt and tore it off, tossing it onto the floor. This was getting out of hand. I'd moved to this small town of Highland Falls two months ago. My brother had been here for years, and I'd been certain that it was the medicine I needed.

Clearly I'd been wrong.

Jesus.

My skin felt like it was crawling, and my heart was still racing. Sleep wouldn't be coming anytime soon. The past six months had taught me a lot, and one of those lessons was that this shitty feeling wasn't going away by lying in bed. If anything, it would make it worse.

Briefly I considered some relaxation music. Revisiting the time, I reconsidered. The guys I was renting this place from were pretty great and didn't deserve to be woken up because of me. Mental note: get serious about finding a rental. Yesterday wasn't soon enough. This small town wasn't swimming in options, but there had to be something. At any rate, it didn't matter now. What I needed at the moment was some type of distraction. I walked a lap around the studio space. Again. The small square footage did nothing to get rid of the anxious feelings pervading every inch of my body.

I dropped to the couch and grabbed my phone from the side table where it was charging. My finger hovered over my brother's name in my messages. I desperately wanted to tap out a text to him, find my way back to normalcy while giving him some shit. However, as much as I wanted to talk to Jake, I couldn't text him this late. He and his fiancée, Ivy, had likely been sacked out for hours.

I wouldn't do that to him.

Couldn't.

Ditto to our sister, Steph.

Scrolling through text messages, my last text with James, otherwise known as Murph to his friends, called out like a beacon from some distant lighthouse. He'd sent a text today that I'd missed until now:

Murph: *Talk. Soon. Like yesterday.*

The texts before it were all similar in nature, all unanswered until I hit the one from May.

Me: *Running late. New recruits are green. Meet you at the brewery.*

Murph: *You're buying the first round then. See you there.*

I stared at the message as the screen grew blurry. Two hundred and thirteen days, and it hadn't gotten any fucking easier. I was spiraling and I damn well knew it, but I had no idea what to do. I'd lost any faith in myself last spring and seemed to have no way to get it back.

Fuck it. January in central Illinois be damned, I needed to run.

After scrounging up some winter running gear, I was out the door and into the moonlit night within minutes. Snow blanketed the grass, and a layer coated the road, but there was enough give that I didn't wipe out on my ass with my first stride.

Within the first block, my lungs had already begun to open up. The tension left my body in waves with the pounding rhythm of my feet against the road. I ran past Jake's brewery, the Homestead, that he'd started with his friend Sully.

I was still getting used to the fact that places around here closed up at a reasonable hour, especially during the week. A Tuesday in January at half past midnight found the brewery and everything else in town shut down for the night. If I was still in Boulder or Fort Collins, the evening would be young and the nightlife plentiful.

I'd left that all behind months ago. It might as well be another lifetime.

Turning the corner from the brewery, I headed toward the center of the business district in Highland Falls, the town square that surrounded the courthouse. Even late at night, the white lights that were strung around acorn lampposts and small trees around the square were lit. Streets were bathed in their warm glow, and they reflected off the snow. The air was still and crisp.

As I passed Pages, Ivy's bookstore, I stopped. The place on the corner, next door to the bookstore, had floor-to-ceiling windows lining the front and side of their space, though there was a light gray vinyl design on the lower half of the windows to give some privacy. Warm white lights flooded the room, giving me the opportunity to check out the interior.

Stepping up to the glass, I looked inside. Brick walls formed an *L* at the back with a portion of the exterior wall. It looked like mirrors lined the space opposite the windows and bricks. Dark wood floors gleamed in the low light, and there was a counter near the front as well as a decorative screen in the corner and a narrow hallway on one side headed to toward the back. Otherwise the space was open.

Thinking back, I recalled Ivy had mentioned a yoga studio opening here shortly before Christmas. I think she and her friends had taken the classes, but she'd said something about the location being new. If I was remembering our conversation correctly, the classes might have moved around town before, like some type of nomadic traveler, but now they stayed in one place.

As I moved to the door, I found myself laughing at the name of the business, NOMAD YOGA. Seemed to fit. Their schedule was listed in the window. Looking it over, I noted that at eight on Wednesday mornings they had something called *power flow*.

Yoga. I hadn't tried that before. Couldn't hurt, right? Maybe it would be exactly what I needed. I turned from the window and ran toward home, if I could call it that. A plan in place, my heart beating smoother, maybe it was time to try to get some rest.

* * *

The next morning after a night of fitful sleep—I might have gotten five hours if I was lucky—I was up and out of my place by a quarter till eight. The feeling of anxiety humming through me had become a daily occurrence. I had to do something, and at this point, I was open to anything. I thought back to my former chief's recommendation to see a therapist who he knew had worked with former Hotshots. I added a call in to him to my mental to-do list to get the name. It was time.

Leaving the Bronco at home, I decided to jog to the studio. Exercise was the only thing I found to keep the crawly feelings at bay, but it was typically a temporary fix. Still, the jog would be a way to squeeze in a version of my daily workout. My guess was yoga wouldn't provide the level of activity I craved. However, I was hoping it could ease the swirling emotions inside. At the very least, I assumed I'd be relaxed afterward.

Once I reached the town square by the studio, I noted that most of the parking was taken. Guess it was a good thing I'd left my vehicle at home.

I skidded to a stop in front of Ivy's bookstore, Pages, looking to see if she was there. I didn't think they opened for another couple of hours, but it didn't hurt to check. However, there were no signs of life to be seen.

Instead, I opened the door to Nomad Yoga and ducked inside. The scent of something hit me immediately, though I couldn't place it. The lights were low, and I saw several mats rolled out. A handful of them were taken with some women in the front talking to each other. An older man was in the back corner, stretching on his own. Glancing in his direction again, I noted that he appeared to be the age of my parents.

I'd wondered how busy this class could be, during the workday and all. My hours working at the brewery were pretty flexible and typically didn't start until lunchtime on days I was scheduled, so no issue there if I wanted to make this a regular thing.

A glance toward the front again at the group of women talking. Was the instructor in that group? With a nod to the guy in the back, I claimed a mat as I debated how to figure out who was in charge. I mean, this class had to cost something, right? Who did I pay? How much was a session anyway? Was there somewhere I needed to drop my money or did you pay by an app?

Before I could decide who to ask, a movement from the back of the studio caught my eye. Two women came around the corner. One I knew well. Ivy. My brother's fiancée looked like she belonged to the Woodstock generation. Even in yoga clothes, her hippie-chick vibe was going strong.

The other woman had on yoga pants and a loose tank that allowed you to see her sports bra underneath. Her brown hair was piled on top of her head in some type of bun. I briefly wondered if I'd seen her in the brewery before but felt sure I'd remember her if I had.

As they came to a stop at the front of the room, I caught a glimpse of a chocolate-colored polish on her toenails, which somehow seemed like a private fact I shouldn't know. My mystery woman laughed at something Ivy said and rolled out her mat at the front of the room. *My mystery woman?* What was happening to me? I felt an unfamiliar sensation in my gut that I didn't know what to do with.

Ivy turned, and her eyes met mine, her face brightening. "Drew! What are you doing here?"

So much for staying under the radar.

She moved quickly to where I stood frozen to my mat as she gave me an incredulous expression. Yeah, I wouldn't have thought I was the yoga type either. Her arms slipped around my waist, and she squeezed, bringing me back to myself.

I cleared my throat. "Hey, Bookstore, thought I'd give yoga a shot. Didn't know you'd be here."

"I'm always here—well, when I can get away, that is. Kate and Kristine have amazing classes that leave me centered afterward no matter what stress I have at home or at work."

With that intel, I was putting my money on the mystery woman being Kate or Kristine. "Who do I pay?" I said, figuring she'd know the drill.

Ivy took a step back from me and looked toward the front of the room. "Kate, we have a guest."

And just like that, I had a name for my mystery woman. The floaty feeling of nerves in my stomach increased as Kate headed back our way. My eyes tracked her soft curves, her lean muscles, and the twitch of humor I saw in her eyes. As she got closer, I noted those brown beauties were watching me with more than a little amusement, like she was waiting for something to happen. Was I staring? Hell, I was staring. Jesus, I needed to get my shit together.

"Hey, I'm Kate," she said, hand outstretched. Her voice was warm, friendly. Sure as shit, that wasn't something I'd ever noticed in someone before.

"Drew." My hand grasped hers, and I fought the urge to tug her to me as my hand tingled in her grasp. "Um, so"—I looked to Ivy, who was watching this exchange with far too much enjoyment—"you know Bookstore?"

Kate raised an eyebrow. "Bookstore?"

Hell. I started to interject when Ivy apparently decided I'd botched this whole situation enough for now and she was charging in to rescue me.

"Drew nicknamed me Bookstore when Jake first started talking about me to his brother"—she nodded in my direction—"months ago." Ivy slipped a hair tie off her wrist and twisted her long waves up in a style similar to Kate. "I've decided to embrace it. Anyway, Kate, can you punch my card for two classes today? I'll get Drew's."

"No, you don't have to do that." I protested, pulling some cash out of the pocket of my joggers. "I've got this."

"Nope. I want you to love this so I can get Jake to come with you." She grinned at me as she took the mat nearest to mine. "I think it would be great for him."

"Just saying, then you'd lose the built-in babysitter," I pointed out.

"The man speaks wisdom," Kate said. She glanced back in my direction. "So Drew, is this your first yoga class, or are you familiar with the practice?"

I felt the familiar tingle of anxiety, knowing that I was out of my depth here. "No, not familiar."

I noted that Kate was looking me over. Unfortunately, it seemed more like an evaluative glance and not one of interest. *Focus*, I told myself.

"Okay, well, take it easy today. Listen to your body. If something isn't working, try a modification. We want you to like the class and not injure yourself."

Kate's gaze was locked on mine as I worked to hold back the comments asking how I'd ever hurt myself in yoga. I mean, this was stretching, right? But that would likely be rude, so I stayed silent on that front. My sister, Steph, would be so proud. Instead, I attempted to reassure Kate I'd be fine. "I should be good. I run regularly, so I'm in shape."

I knew that had been the wrong thing to say when Ivy laughed out loud.

Kate, however, didn't laugh. She just gave me a look that made my entire body heat up, like she was preparing to school my ass. "Okay, Drew. We'll see what you have to say at the end of class."

With that, she turned and headed back to the front of the room. I looked toward Ivy and asked, "What does she mean by that?"

Ivy shook her head at me. "Sweet, sweet, Drew. I can't wait to see what you think of yoga in an hour." She plopped down onto her mat nearby and began stretching.

I followed her lead, lowering to my mat in confusion. I mean, true, I'd never been in a yoga class before. But I knew about yoga, who didn't? It was low impact. I supposed it wasn't easy, but it couldn't be harder than running a half marathon. And hell, after my time with the Hotshots in Colorado for the past seven years, this would be a piece of cake. Right?

If only I'd known how wrong I was.

Chapter 2

Second Guesses

Kate

I called out goodbye to another student who was headed out the door into the frigid January morning. Leaning to the right, I let my side muscles stretch as I contemplated the prone man lying on the floor in the back of the studio in a puddle of sweat as he groaned. Drew. I wondered what god—or goddess, as Ivy would say—I had to thank for the gorgeous man in front of me. Ivy mentioned he worked in the brewery. I'd been there several times since moving to Highland Falls a few months ago but hadn't run into him before. That, or I hadn't been looking. To say I'd been preoccupied since moving here would be an understatement.

Drew let out a labored breath. I had a feeling power yoga had changed his tune about what yoga class could be. I felt a twinge of guilt. I certainly hadn't taken it easy on him.

I'd seen guys like Drew before. They thought yoga was something for women and older people, not for athletes such as themselves. That's why it was such a validating feeling when the class they chose to come to was power yoga. Don't be mistaken. Even a typical yoga class can teach people a thing or two. I was of the firm belief that everyone would do better with a little yoga in their lives. Besides keeping your body limber, allowing you to avoid injury, yoga helped people deal with symptoms of arthritis, bad backs, and could decrease stress and relieve anxiety. But for many people, they just saw yoga as stretching and a precursor to the *real exercise* they did in their lives. I was a fan of all forms of fitness, but I was a big believer in the benefits of yoga.

My eyes skated over Drew's body. I was pretty sure he was just resting, no real injury. His joggers probably hadn't helped matters, overheating him as we flowed. His shirt was plastered to a wide chest, though his build was one of a runner, not a power lifter. His dark hair was longer on top than it was at the sides, and it was damp with perspiration. And his beard made me want to do improper things. Interesting. I couldn't remember the last time I'd been attracted to someone, though there was no danger of me acting on it.

Ivy chose that moment to appear by my side. We'd spent a lot of time together since I came to town and moved into an apartment over her bookstore. I was actually staying in the space that had been her grandma's place when she owned these buildings. I knew I was the first tenant since her grandma had passed, and I was honored she trusted me with it.

It had been a stroke of luck that my business partner, Kristine, had known Ivy and mentioned in passing that I was moving to town and needed somewhere to rent. Small towns like Highland Falls don't tend to have a lot of rental properties. Ivy had even let me keep a lot of the furniture that had been her grandma's. It was funky, vintage, and worked out perfectly for me.

"So... think he'll live?" I asked, nodding over at Drew, who still hadn't moved.

Ivy shrugged. "Not sure he'll be the best hype person for your power yoga class, but he should make it." She raised up her phone, zoomed in on Drew's sweating body, and took a photo.

"I can hear you, you know," Drew said with a groan from his spot on the mat.

"Shush, you," Ivy said. "I'm getting the best photo for our group chat."

"Bookstore..." Drew's voice was more of a whine than anything else. "I thought we were friends."

"We are, Drew, but Jake and Steph would never forgive me if I didn't immortalize this moment for them."

"I think I'm missing something here," I said. "Want to fill me in?"

Ivy looked down at Drew as he raised an eyebrow up in response.

"Not sure I have the energy left to explain my siblings," he said, wiping sweat from his brow. He pushed himself up to a seated position, leaving a wet outline on the mat.

Ivy laughed. "Not sure there is any easy way to really share the bond you three have."

Drew reached a hand up to Ivy, and she quickly took it, helping him up off the ground.

Upright, Drew looked my way with a rueful grin. "Want me to hose down the mat? Burn it?"

I laughed. "You're good. We've got some spray."

Drew shook his head. "Your class kicked my ass, Kate. I run daily and had to be in pretty great shape at my old job. This is next level."

"Oh? What was your job?"

I watched a shadow cross Drew's face before he blinked it away.

"Oh, he was in the Hotshots out in Colorado for years," Ivy said.

"Yeah?" I looked back at him.

"So my siblings," Drew said, changing the subject. "Ivy knows that our group text thread is a thing of beauty, and I cannot believe that she betrayed me by posting a photo on there."

Ivy laughed as she held up her phone. "Oh yeah. Posted and the messages are already rolling in." She'd clearly missed that Drew had skillfully avoided a conversation about himself. Interesting.

Drew shook his head. "Do I even want to know what they're saying?"

Ivy looked back to his mat. "Where's your phone?"

He shrugged. "Back at my place."

That caught my attention. Someone in their—and I was just guessing here—late twenties, early thirties, and they didn't have their phone with them? Interesting. This guy was not what I had assumed.

Then my stomach clenched. I remembered had another unanswered text from Alex last night. It wasn't fair to him; I needed to reply. I owed him that.

Oblivious to my inner turmoil, Ivy continued taunting Drew. "Want me to read any messages to you?"

Drew laughed. "Nah, I'll enjoy it later. Remember this, Bookstore. Paybacks are hell."

"Promises, promises, Drew. Do anything too horrible and I'll have you babysit Addie and tell her that art projects with glitter will be the activity of the night."

"Addie loves me. I owe her a spa day soon," Drew said with a shrug as he grabbed his sweatshirt to tug on.

"Spa day?" I interrupted their conversation. Really, there was no choice but to lean in to whatever this was. "I thought Addie was like four or five?" Ivy's daughter was a trip. I'd worked with kindergarteners over the years and loved that age group. Brutally honest, full of life, just like Addie.

"Oh, she is," Ivy said. "Drew and Jake often babysit her, and she loves to paint their fingernails."

Drew waved his bare nails at us. "Yep, need to get them done again," he said with a chuckle.

Yeah, I was going to have to fix up my thinking on this guy. He wasn't who he'd appeared to be, but I should've known better than to judge him; that wasn't cool. I worked to dismiss the irritation at myself. I mean, he was a potential new student for our studio, nothing more. And Goddess knows, we needed all the business we could find.

* * *

Almost an hour later, Kristine found me lying flat on my back, legs up the brick wall in the back of the studio. I had a lavender-scented towel lying over my face, which she gently lifted.

My eyes met hers, and I noted the look of concern.

"Bad morning?"

I looked into the cool blue eyes of my business partner and longtime friend.

"Not bad, not great."

"How about some tea?"

"Please."

I swung my legs down and rolled to my side, rising to my feet as I moved to follow Kristine to the counter at the front of the studio. There we kept an electric kettle, a few mugs, honey, and some tea. I plopped down on a stool we had up there as Kristine grabbed the kettle and headed toward the sink in the back. When she returned, she put it down and flipped the switch before turning her attention to me.

"Spill."

I sighed, dropping my head to my arms folded onto the counter. "I don't even know where to start." Some days just felt like too much. For whatever reason, this was seeming like it was on track to be one of those days.

"Let's think backward. You had power yoga this morning. Issues?"

"No. We had a new student. I misjudged him. He's the brother of Ivy's fiancé, but he's fine."

"Ah, Drew Spencer, I know him. Cute. Young. I'm surprised this is the first time you two have met, but I suppose I'll let you slide with *fine* as an accurate description."

"Well, he was fine. And he's not that young, just a few years younger than us." I realized I was still speaking to the counter, and I lifted my head to rest it on a hand with a long sigh, trying to stop the memories of Drew's warm eyes sparkling with humor when he mentioned Addie painting his nails. I didn't have it in me for an attraction right now. I needed to be focused on our new business.

Glancing to Kristine, I motioned to the counter. "Hey, I'm making up some spray bottles of facial mist. They're essential oils of rose hips, frankincense, and lavender. Ivy mentioned that there are a lot of people interested in items like that, and she doesn't have the time to make it, so that could be an extra income."

"Hmm, let's note that you're feeling somewhat defensive and changing the subject. Interesting. So one, love the facial mist idea. We can start that anytime. Back to the topic of Drew Spencer, *fine*, emphasis absolutely intended, I'll give you. The man is gorgeous, and he's also kind. At least that's what I've noted in my few encounters with him at the brewery. So no issues with the class. What's all this about?" She waved in my general direction of Eeyore-ness.

How did I explain a general feeling of despair that I couldn't pinpoint? "I don't know. I guess I was pissed at myself for judging someone so quickly. That's not okay. And then, I don't know, I was thinking about Alex."

"Oh, babe. Why now?"

I looked out the window to the snowy downtown of Highland, my emotions swirling much like the snowflakes that were starting to fall fast. I needed to snap out of my mood, but honestly, I could've said that for much of the past four months.

"He messaged me last night."

"He did? What did he have to say?"

"Just that he hoped I was doing well, and he wished me the best."

"Rat bastard." Kristine took the kettle off the heating element and filled up some mugs, plopping the tea bags in them, and then turned her attention back to me.

I shook my head at her. "No, no, no. No demonizing Alex. You remember this was my call, right? This is all my fault. He wanted me to move with him to England. I'm the one who decided that we were done." I blinked back tears, which only served to piss me off more. Jesus. At some point I needed to get my emotions in check; thus the need to sit with my legs up the wall earlier. Unfortunately, it hadn't done the work to release the tension I'd been fighting.

"Kate, talk to me. This isn't like you." Kristine reached across the counter to grab my hand, squeezing it as she continued in her gentle way. "What has it been, twelve years since we met in that class?"

I smiled at the memory. "Thirteen." It'd been the start of sophomore year at the University of Kentucky, which was like a different world than growing up on the south side of Chicago. I'd walked into a yoga class offered at the rec center and found a lot of girls far more concerned with some social a fraternity was throwing that night than on any actual health benefits of yoga. Kristine had been the instructor. She was a year ahead of me in school, and while she was all for being friendly, she took her class seriously. Once she realized I did too, we became fast friends. Friends weren't a commodity I traded in often. I could count the close friends I'd had since middle school until I moved to Highland on one hand with three fingers left over. First, in my freshman year of college, there was Alex. Then, sophomore year, Kristine. It had been enough—until it wasn't.

Kristine had been there through it all: changing majors, horrible roommates, failures, disappointments, insecurities, and—relevant to today's conversation—my first love in Alex.

I felt like I had some cheesy movie montage running through my mind. I could see Alex when I first met him jogging across the grass near the library. He'd had shaggy brown hair and had been talking to a friend over his shoulder, not watching where he was going, and collided right into me. My books had shot all over as I hit the ground, and Alex had apologized profusely.

A feeling of such overwhelming loss flowed over me as I had flashes of our first year as we moved from friends, to dating, to the other half of my soul, or so I'd thought.

Through watery eyes, I gave Kristine a shrug. "I'm just in such a funk. I mean, I know it was the right decision. *I know it* deep, deep down. And still I hate it. I hate thinking

I hurt him. I hate that I wasted all this time thinking we were *it* for each other, only to realize that I'd settled. Alex doesn't deserve it. I love him too much for that." I thought about what I was really struggling with and fessed up. "And honestly, I just miss him."

"Of course you do. Alex had the honored role that he shared with me of your best friend." She moved in front of me, spinning me so she could wrap her arms around my waist. "I know you say you struggle with finding friends, but do you still feel that way here? I mean, I know it hasn't been long, but I feel like you've met some contenders here, right? Not that Alex is going anywhere, even in England. I think he'd tell you that."

I nodded. "Yeah, I've met some wonderful people here. It's just making friends is *hard*. I mean, I thought it was as a kid, but as an adult? I feel like a dork, wondering if they like me, if I'm intruding, if, if, if."

I dropped my head to her shoulder, tears escaping my eyes.

Kristine squeezed my waist. "My dear Kate, why the waterworks? You know you made the right call. Is this regret?"

I let out a cleansing breath in a bid to center myself. "I talked to my parents last night."

"Ahhhh." She didn't need to say more, she knew.

I didn't lift my head to meet her eyes. This was easier with mine closed. "My mom mentioned that I seem to run away a lot when I get scared."

A growl emanated from Kristine that made me grin in spite of myself. She was only a year older, but she sure could go into mama-bear mode when needed. "I'd love to have a word with your mom. Hell, your dad too. They wouldn't know what a supportive parent looked like if it bit them in the ass."

I sighed. My parents meant well, but we weren't close. They were old school, children should be seen and not heard. I never left a conversation with them without feeling like I'd disappointed them. "She's not exactly wrong..." I began.

Kristine leaned back, necessitating me to lift my head off her shoulder. "Kate, none of that. We're ignoring your *super supportive* mom and moving on for now before I say something I'll regret. Back to Alex. You know I'm joking when I call him a rat bastard, right? He'd hate that you're this torn up." She smoothed my hair back at the sides where it had escaped my bun. "He told you that you were the brave one to admit it. That he'd felt the same but hadn't spoken up."

I met her eyes; it was easier now. "I wonder sometimes if I made a mistake. If we should have stayed together. I mean, we love each other, but not..." I loved Alex, but I wasn't in love with him. But selfishly, I wondered if that would have been better than nothing. There were no guarantees that everyone got what Ivy had been lucky enough to latch onto recently.

Kristine tipped my chin up to meet her eyes. "No. There is someone out there for you, someone out there for Alex. One day you will both find that person. I swear it, Kate. And you'll be so damn glad that you were brave now."

My chest rose and fell as I worked to calm myself. "I'm thirty-two, Kristine. I want kids, I want a family. Sometimes I wonder if I should look into adoption, into sperm donation, something. And then I wonder if I'm just weak."

Kristine wiped the tears off my cheeks. "Listen, lady. None of this right now. It's been four months. Only four months. After over thirteen years together, it's absolutely okay to grieve. But I have to tell you, I think you're looking at it wrong. You and Alex had a beautiful relationship. You *still* have a strong friendship. Who's to say that the relationship failed because you aren't together forever, married, with a kid, or some bullshit?"

"Um, society?"

"Well, our society is fucked up, but we all knew that. Your relationship was great for what it was. Maybe it was what you needed at the time, what Alex needed. And now you're both ready for more. You just outgrew each other. I think that's okay and to be celebrated."

I swallowed past the lump in my throat. "So why do I feel embarrassed? Like I failed?"

"Because our world is seriously screwed up. I have to say I think this isn't just about the breakup but more."

"Like..."

Kristine laughed and stepped back to grab the tea, tossing the bags and squirting some honey in for me, just the way I liked it. We had some kick-ass mugs made at our local pottery studio that we used in our studio, kind of like advertising for them. She handed me a mustard-yellow one and took a navy one for herself.

"I don't know. Take your pick: the breakup, the close friend moving to another country, moving to another state, starting a business in a new line of work. Any of those sound like they might be part of this?" She leaned against the counter and blew on her mug before taking a drink as she gave me an appraising look.

I took a drink of my tea as I thought about what she said. I glanced her way again as I conceded. "Yeah, I guess this fall and winter has been a little much."

Kristine snorted. "You think? Just saying, you might feel

a hell of a lot better if you scheduled some time to actually talk to him. You're still friends. Act like it. And just an FYI, you might want to do something about that." She gestured at my face.

"Oh God, I can't even imagine." I reached for some Kleenex we had on the counter, certain the little mascara I liked to wear was black streaks down my cheeks by now as the door opened to the winter wonderland beyond.

"Hi, I was here earlier. Did you find any keys…"

A male voice had me turning toward the door where I saw Drew standing there.

"Oh my, um, Kate? Are you okay?" He started moving in my direction but then froze as if he was unsure what to do.

Snapping out of it, I grabbed the Kleenex and stood. "Um, yes, I… Kristine… I think there's a set of keys on the counter… I mean, I'll just be a minute." And I fled to the bathroom in the back.

A few minutes later, I came back to the studio, mascara cleared off my face and cool water splashed on to try to eliminate any evidence of crying. Kristine was sitting at the counter, watching my return as she sipped her tea, a knowing expression on her face. There was no sign of Drew.

I moved over to pick up my tea again. As I did, I glanced out the windows that overlooked the town square. As casually as possible, I asked, "So were the keys Drew's?"

"Yep." She took another drink.

"Oh good. And then he's all set." My palms were sweating. Good Lord. Thanks, hormones, ignoring you.

"Yep."

"Okay." I watched the snow fall, noting that my heart

rate had increased. My body clearly wasn't listening. "That's good."

"Mm-hmm."

Was it wrong to watch to shove your friend off their stool?

We sat in silence, the snow globe outside the window enveloping us in peace and quiet as I stewed without reason for several minutes. Finally, Kristine spoke.

"So did you want me to share anything else?"

"Like what?"

"Not sure. I could start with what Drew asked about you."

I squeaked. "He asked about me?" What in the ever-loving hell? Was I thirteen? Reminder to myself: I was working on me right now. We were not here for this.

The devil on my shoulder reminded me that working on me didn't prevent romance happening along the way, so a little crush wasn't hurting anyone.

"He asked if you were okay."

Of course he did. He was a decent human being and walked in to see me looking like a member of that band KISS.

"And he said your class kicked his ass."

A warm feeling flooded me at that comment.

"And that he'd be back for class tomorrow."

My head spun to look at her. "What? He will? Which one, my class or yours?"

Looking like the cat who swallowed the canary, Kristine regarded me over the brim of her mug. "Wouldn't you like to know."

"Kristine!"

"So are we ready to admit that maybe, *just maybe*, you

might have made the right call with Alex and there is a life after a long-term relationship comes to an end?"

Cold water to the face.

"Kristine, I'm willing to admit that Drew is *fine*, to return to our earlier conversation. I'll even own the fact that I'm reacting to him like a middle school girl. But do not get your hopes up. I am not looking for a relationship. I am not ready for that, not for some time." I gave myself a mental pat on the back.

Kristine watched me for a moment, then took a drink. Looking back my way, she said, "So still want to know which class?"

Refusing to look at her, I whispered, "Yep."

Chapter 3

Goals and Dreams

Drew

I jogged down the snowy street toward the Homestead Brewery. It was a beautiful January day, which was lucky because I'd worn light layers to yoga. There were snowflakes swirling, but the temperature was right at thirty degrees, so it was cooling me down but not freezing.

I'd been at the bookstore, talking to Ivy after class, helping her move some new stock around, when I'd realized I didn't have my keys and headed back to Nomad Yoga. Kate's tearstained face was one I couldn't erase from my mind. No idea why, but I fought the urge to pull her to my chest, wrap my arms around her in a hug, and whisper that everything was going to be okay. What in the hell was that about?

I guess yoga hadn't done the job in clearing out my mental space, though I did feel more at ease.

Turning on the street where the brewery was located, I noted the lights from within. It was before eleven, so they'd be preparing for the lunch crowd about now. Reaching the door, I stomped the light snow off my shoes and headed inside.

Jake was just inside the front door. It looked like he and the hostess, Laurie, were looking over the reservations for the day. I slid up beside them as Jake looked over and raised a brow.

"Recovered from yoga class, did you?" he said.

I needed to use my middle finger to rub the bridge of my nose.

"Get Ads to school already?" I asked, switching the topic.

"Yep. She said to tell you she missed you."

It was hard to describe what Ivy's kid did to me. She was so good for my heart. Somehow, she was able to help me be present, to forget my screw-ups. It had been a few days, and I was ready to see my girl.

"I'll give you and Bookstore a night off this week, if that works." I said, mentally going through my schedule at the brewery.

Jake nodded, then turned back to Laurie. "Looks good. Let me know if the servers think they'll need extra help with the large group at noon."

"You bet," Laurie said. She picked up a tablet and headed over to the table of servers in the dining area, likely waiting for the rundown of the day. Also, Pete, their head cook, had come out to share the specials they'd have for lunch and let them sample them before the crowd started coming in. My stomach let out a rumble at the thought, which Jake, of course, picked up on.

"So want to tell me about your morning before or after we get something to eat?" Jake asked.

"Ass," I said. "I'm sure Bookstore already filled you in

on yoga." I sniffed, trying to guess at the smells coming from the kitchen. "What's the lunch special today?"

"Buffalo Chicken Toasted Ravioli. It's an appetizer but could be a meal. And hell yes, Ivy shared. She also let Steph and me know that your phone was at home. You have so many excellent messages waiting for you."

I shook my head. These people. I loved them, and they also pushed every single button I had. Then again, they were the ones who installed them, so that made sense.

Jake headed toward the bar and I followed. After a couple of months, this place was beginning to feel like home. Jake and his partner, Cole Sullivan, had approached me at the end of this past summer, looking for investors in the canning startup for the brewery. I'd signed on. It just so happened that I was looking for something new for me too.

Leaving the Hotshots had been difficult but necessary. I'd always be grateful to Jake and Sully even if they didn't know the entire reason why. Today, however, I didn't have to work. A whole day stretching ahead of me as empty as a blank notebook, which wasn't great, so I figured the very least I could do was to hang out for a while and grab a bite to eat.

Jake motioned toward the taps, inquiring if I was going to be drinking beer with this lunch.

"Nah." I shook my head. "I'll just take some water and that special. Throw in a side Caesar, and I'm good to go."

Jake poured a water for me, some coffee for himself, and sent in our lunch order. Interesting choice of beverage, though it seemed fitting when I looked at the shadows below his eyes. Bookstore and/or her daughter, Addie, must be keeping the old man up later than normal. My money was on Ivy.

"Tired?" I said with a nod toward the coffee mug.

"A lot on my mind," Jake said as he looked at the mug in front of him. Bringing his eyes up to meet mine, he took a breath. "So at what point are you going to share why you're here?"

My gut clenched. I'd told my family in November that I was moving to Highland Falls, leaving Colorado and my job behind. They'd been supportive and worried. I knew they were. But they'd given me space when I'd asked, and I appreciated that more than they'd ever know. Apparently, that time was running out. I had a pang of guilt at the notion that I'd been contributing to whatever was on Jake's mind.

I wasn't sure how to talk about something I didn't understand myself.

Tell him that. My damn conscience spoke up. Well, I guess it would be a starting point.

I let out the breath that I hadn't realized I was holding and looked across the wooden bar at Jake. He seemed to be holding his breath too, like he wasn't entirely sure where this conversation would go. That made two of us.

"First, thanks for giving me some time to get my head around everything," I said, figuring why not acknowledge the elephant in the room.

"We just want to be here for you. It's hard to do that when we don't know what we're here for." Jake was back to staring at his coffee cup like it held the secrets I wasn't able to share.

Fuck. Process this, get it out, I knew Jake would be understanding. "Being part of the Hotshots was everything to me—until it wasn't." Sweat beaded up on my brow. I felt a trickle of it down my back. "We had a call that didn't go well—"

Jake's eyes met mine in alarm.

"I know, I'm not ready to go there yet. Clearly I'm fine."

"Not fine if you had to leave," he pointed out.

"Yeah, well, let's say that experience left me with some anxiety that I'm still working through. I found myself as more of a liability than someone who was helpful on our team. Add that to some other personal shit I had going on, and I felt like I couldn't trust myself anymore. Or, at any rate, it made me reevaluate my plan, what I wanted out of life, only to realize I had no clue. None." Just this conversation, which was the tip of the iceberg, made my heart beat harder. Kate's hard work in yoga class this morning was getting wiped away.

Jake studied me, waiting. When he realized I wasn't going on, he spoke up. "Okay, there's a lot I want to say here, and I'm not sure where to start."

I nodded.

Jake looked from me to his mug, out to the brewery, then back to me. "First, I'm worried. I want to know more about what happened with the Hotshots—"

I start to interrupt him, but he raised his hand to ward off my protest.

"—but I know you are still dealing with that. Suffice to say, if you're struggling, and the anxiety you mentioned indicates you are, you need to talk to someone. I think you know Steph or I would be here for you, but if that isn't what you want, there's lots of help out there and no reason not to get it if you need it."

"I plan on checking into talking to someone," I said quietly, mainly to let Jake know I was working toward improvement.

Jake watched me and seemed to settle. "Good. Now for the rest of your statement, you know Sully and I are happy to have you working here, right?" Jake raised an eyebrow as he waited for my reply.

"Yes." I met his eyes even though part of me wanted to look away. I was feeling every bit of my younger-brother self right now.

"So are you not sure if it's for you?" Jake appeared puzzled. I wanted to tell him to join the club.

"Honestly, I have no idea." I cleared my throat, wondering how to make my feelings clear when they weren't even clear to me. "In college I joined the local volunteer firefighters because it seemed like a good thing to do."

Jake watched, clearly waiting for me to continue.

"I know you didn't go the college route, and honestly, I almost didn't."

Jake's expression morphed into one of surprise.

"I know, I know, I never mentioned it. The end of high school was hard. Everyone seemed to know where they were headed and what they were going to do. I had no fucking idea beyond wanting to get out of our town." I looked down at my hands, thinking back to high school. It was lucky I didn't know back then that ten years into the future, my career path would be no clearer.

"So why did you go?" Jake asked the logical question.

I shrugged. "Honestly? Not sure. Mom and Dad seemed to believe it was a forgone conclusion. I didn't want to disappoint them. And I figured maybe I'd figure it out along the way."

"So the major in environmental studies was just a whim?"

"Yeah, I mean, I had some classes in high school that made me want to learn more about our part in the climate crisis. That led to me taking some related classes in college. Funnily enough, one of my professors was the first one to suggest I look into firefighting with the Hotshots. He thought my knowledge of firefighting from my part-time work in Boulder combined with my study of our environment and the land might be a good combination. He happened to have a family member who worked for the group out of Fort Collins, so he made a call. They posted an opening in January of my senior year. By that time, I'd already met the guys, done a few workouts with them, and they'd talked to my chief. It felt like it was meant to be, so I didn't question it or if it was something I saw for myself long-term."

Jake cleared his throat. "But it's not."

Emotion flowed through me. "It's not." I paused and considered those words. "Well, it might have been at one point. It's not now."

Silence filled the space between us.

Jake broke it. "So is being a part owner in a brewery's canning business and working at said brewery not working out for you?" His voice was gentle, which was not how we typically talked with each other. I hated it that he felt the need to treat me with kid gloves while also understanding why he did.

I looked back to the bar, struggling to put words to the internal mess I was dealing with. Finally, I just decided to lay it out. "I'm not sure. I feel like I want more, but I don't know what more looks like." I met his eyes and continued. "And when I say that, I worry I come off like a jackass. This brewery, this space you and Sully have created, it's amazing. I feel lucky to be part of it in my way and also think I'm somewhat of an asshole for not wanting to be here full-time."

Jake was already shaking his head at me when I paused, and he butted in. "Nope, no guilt. This place? This is what I want for me. Without a doubt, I know I'm happy to work here, to be in business with Sully, to now be settling down with Ivy and Addie. Don't feel bad that you aren't sure if it's for you. You're a partner with us in the canning side, so you get a percentage of the profits whether you're working here or not. I'm assuming you also still have some money from being a Hotshot since you like to hoard your money like you did vacation days."

"Just saying, those hording tendencies worked out well for you when you were looking for a canning partner."

"Truth."

"And yeah, I saved the majority of my salary every paycheck. Dad's mandate paid off."

"Well, that's what happens when you're a banker."

"Also, I did a lot of overtime on the Hotshots. That and training the new recruits in the off-season allowed me to invest with you and still have a cushion left over."

Laurie came over at that moment, raising our plates up to us. "You want to eat at the bar or a table?"

Jake looked to me, and I jerked my head toward one of the high-tops and we headed over.

Laurie left our plates, and we dug in after giving her our thanks. My mouth watered around the first bite of toasted ravioli. I wouldn't have thought to pair it with buffalo chicken, but damn was it good. Jake had homemade tomato soup and a grilled cheese that looked all kinds of upscale but also like the absolute perfect food on this snowy day.

After a few bites, Jake put down his spoon and wiped his mouth with the napkin. I waited, knowing he'd be accepting but wondering how much of the older-brother-listen-up advice I might get.

He didn't leave me wondering for long. "So you have a cushion and you've landed here. How do you plan on exploring your options? Do you want to stay around here, or is that up in the air too?"

My heart skipped a beat. I think my location was the only thing I was sure of, or as sure as I could be. "I want to stay here. Highland Falls feels right to me."

Jake's smile was wide. "Good to hear."

"Think you and Ivy could keep an ear open to any rentals in the area? My Airbnb is feeling a little tight."

Jake grinned. "Ivy will be all over it." He sat back on the barstool, giving me a harder look. "I have to tell you; my sibling radar is going off with the comment about anxiety. Want to share anything with me? Does this have anything to do with your new interest in yoga? Anything?"

I looked away from Jake as I shook my head, but then turned back to him as a thought crossed my mind. "Not diving into the anxiety discussion yet, but what do you know about the yoga instructor named Kate?"

If anything, Jake's smile grew even larger as he let out a chuckle and shook his head at me.

Chapter 4

Hey, Neighbor

Kate

The sultry voice of Adele poured out of my speakers as I moved through a yoga flow. Briefly, I wondered if I should send the lyrics to Alex and tell him to go easy on me. I shook my head in frustration; that wasn't fair, he'd been great. Maybe a better person to send this to would be my parents. I felt a twinge of guilt as I thought of the countless phone calls and messages I'd ignored. There are only so many times you can have someone tell you that you've disappointed them, again, and not get a complex.

Moving on.

Working my way through the warrior series, I let Adele's voice bring me back to myself. She'd had life handed to her a time or two and was still rocking it out. I just needed to suck it up and stop my pity party of one. The rest of my morning practice helped me work back to my zen space, and when I finally felt centered, I left my mat for the siren call of a cup of coffee. After morning yoga, it was how I began most days.

Part of me wasn't crazy about having an addiction to

caffeine, but I told myself it was better for my body than my college days where I'd guzzle diet pop by the caseload.

Coming into my small galley kitchen, I moved as if on autopilot. Grinding the beans, the smell hit my nose and gave me an immediate kick of joy. Automatically, I got the pot started and then glanced around my small slice of heaven.

I'd been in this space for almost three months now, and it was just beginning to feel like mine. Ivy's grandma's furnishings helped it feel like home as soon as I'd moved in, which helped since I'd had a whole lot of nothing.

When Alex and I broke up, it had been easier just to make a truly clean break. I walked away with my laptop, my clothes, some personal items, and a few framed pictures. I didn't want anything else. Honestly, either did Alex. He'd sold all the furniture before moving to England, sending me half the profits. That hadn't been necessary, but was a nice gesture, nonetheless.

My new place was small but perfect. The front door opened in to the eating area which had a large pass through to the galley kitchen. The living area was off of that with large almost floor-to-ceiling windows overlooking the town square and the courthouse. A short hallway took you back to the bedroom and bathroom. The walls of the space were a bright white that made the tapestry and baskets that lined them stand out all the more. The sofa was vintage, a tufted gold velvet that I loved to curl up on with my chunky white throw. And my plant addiction was thriving here. I had only brought a few with me, but I'd propagated them as they grew and purchased a few more. Well, more than a few, if I was being completely honest.

Looking around at this space that felt so much like an extension of me, I found a peace that had been lacking for some time. Whether that had been since Alex and I parted or it was something missing before I likely needed to examine when I had the mental capacity to do so.

Which was after at least one cup of coffee. And maybe a few thoughts as to whether my new student would be in today's class. He'd been in several of them in the past week, and I saw improvement. More than that, I'd enjoyed getting to know Drew Spencer. He was a good guy, as long as I ignored my physical reaction to him. *Friends, friends, friends*, I chanted to myself.

Sure.

As I waited for the coffee to finish brewing, a thump came from the hall. I froze. A glance at the clock on the microwave told me it was only just before eight in the morning. My first class today was at nine, but my commute was down the stairs and right next door, so I wasn't too worried about being on time. Even so, Nic lived up here, but she shouldn't be up and moving around yet. The other space had been rented by Elle, but she moved out a few days ago to shack up with her boyfriend Nate, as I liked to tease her.

It had been nice to move to town and have my neighbors be two amazing women who were also relatively new to the area. We'd done a weekly dinner since I moved in, rotating between our apartments. Elle swore we were going to keep up the tradition, just adding in her and Nate's place that wasn't too far from downtown. I honestly hoped so. The time I spent with Nic and Elle had really helped me settle in and feel like I wasn't just tagging along after Kristine but truly making my own way. And the person in me that struggled to have friends was secretly just glad to finally be finding people that I clicked with.

Another thump pulled me back to the present. What in the ever-loving hell was going on out there? I put down the mug and headed to the door. I double- and triple-checked that the door was unlocked so I could get back in. Being separated from the caffeine would not be even remotely funny at this point. Right now my brain had a two-bullet point list: find out what the noise was and get coffee in my body. Stat.

I opened the door and looked across the hall at apartment two, Elle's former place. The door was standing wide open. Hmm, Ivy hadn't said anything about renting the space out yet.

I glanced down at my bare feet and my pajamas, then I shrugged. They were comfy for my quick yoga session on my own, but not superconservative in terms of coverage. Oh well, I was dressed, more or less. It would have to do.

Sticking my head in the place, I called out. "Hello?"

Another thump from the hall in the back. Well, someone was here. Hopefully they weren't murderers.

"Hello?" I called again.

A grunt came from the back, then a voice. "Hey, just a second, I'll be right out."

Goose bumps popped out on my arms. That was weird. It was actually pretty toasty up here. I leaned against the doorframe to wait. Elle's place was a mirror image of mine, as was Nic's. Elle had rented her place furnished, like I had, so the place was only missing her personal touches. Still, I felt a pang of loss for the friend who was no longer across the hall from me.

"Hey, sorry to keep you."

I looked to the hall just in time to see my hot guy from yoga class, otherwise known as Drew, come walking out.

Well, that was unexpected.

"Kate?" His voice indicated his surprise to see me standing in the doorway. Then his gaze tracked down my body and back up to look in my eyes with an unreadable expression.

Whoa. Well, now I felt undressed. To be fair, that wouldn't take a lot at this point.

"What the fuck are you wearing?" His voice had turned raspy, and I felt it. Yep, sure did. Ignoring that. Moving on.

"My pajamas." I gestured at him. "I hadn't expected company. What are you doing here?"

Drew held up a palm. "I'll come back to that. These"— his hand waved up and down in my general direction—"are your pajamas?"

I barely controlled an eye roll. Men. "They're multi-functional—you can sleep in them and do yoga in the morning. Nothing special, just a jumpsuit and bralette, and it's from a company called Anthropologie that makes gorgeous clothing. Point?"

Drew shook his head, running a hand over his jaw and into his hair in a way that shouldn't be as attractive as it was. "Hmm. Anthropologie, you say? I think I should email them my appreciation for their designs."

He smirked at me in a way that managed to be not at all creepy but like we were sharing a secret. The tingles in my gut increased as I had a strong desire to run my fingers through his beard. I worked to suppress my irritation at myself.

I crossed my arms then uncrossed them when I realized it pushed my boobs up. Considering the jumpsuit that Drew was giving me a commentary about was unbuttoned in the front, giving him a perfect view of that bralette, I figured we didn't need any more cleavage. Drew's smile told me he was aware of my dilemma.

"Okay, we discussed my pajamas—"

"Or lack thereof," he said.

"Moving on. What are you doing here?"

Drew shrugged and pointed to some boxes in the living area. "Moving in."

My heart definitely skipped a beat. Well, this was a new direction for our upstairs crew, our all-girls group was getting an injection of testosterone.

"Wow, okay. Sorry, I didn't know." I stammered out my reply, which wasn't like me. Let's see, one of the first impressions this guy had was me judging him. Then he took my class and was on the floor in a puddle of sweat. After that, he returned to the studio to find me with raccoon eyes. We'd recovered over the past week in class to a neutral friendship where I ignored my ever-increasing attraction. And now I was setting our progress back wearing pajamas with bare feet in his space, and I can't even sound intelligent. Jeez.

I really needed that coffee.

Drew didn't seem fazed by my rudeness. "Yeah, it was kind of last minute. I've been renting a studio Airbnb from some guys in town. Great space, but half the size of this." He gestured to the space behind him. "Maybe less. Had dinner the other night with Jake and Ivy, and Ivy had a brainstorm."

I couldn't help myself; I laughed. Ivy had lots of great ideas, and when she got them, she was rather animated. I could absolutely picture her jumping up to share her sudden and brilliant idea for Drew to move up here. Add that to her need to take care of those she loved, and I was pretty sure she was thrilled to help Drew out.

"Ivy does tend to get excited when she thinks she can be of service."

"Yep, Bookstore has a heart of gold."

I glanced at him and saw that he was completely

sincere, not at all being sarcastic. Anyone who truly looked for the good in others was someone I wanted to know better. "So you're a fan of your brother's fiancée?"

Drew laughed. "You could say that. Jake started talking about Ivy months before they got together when we'd talk in text messages or on the phone. Honestly, I gave him some grief for the amount of times he brought her up. Then there was a bizarre thing with her car and a snowstorm, and the caveman actually had her at his place for the night. By the next week, he was babysitting Addie after she got out of school. My sister Steph and I came to town to for a party at the brewery but also to check out this woman who had finally captured my big brother's heart."

"So was it unusual for Jake to have a girlfriend?" I was fascinated by Drew. Even though part of me felt something when I was near him, a large part of me just felt relaxed. Like we'd been confiding in each other for years. I wanted to curl up on his couch and have him tell me everything.

Drew looked away from me to the windows of the apartment. I could see the town's grain elevators just outside. He seemed lost in thought for a moment, but then he looked back to me and shrugged. "Not really my story to tell, but let's just say that Jake had been burned in the past."

"Enough said. I get that." Alex's face popped in my mind. A pang of loss hit me, but also a wave of relief. Getting past the end of our relationship seemed like it was going to take more time than I had anticipated.

Drew tilted his head as he scanned my expression. "Sounds like you have some experience there."

"Sure, I mean, who doesn't?"

"Well, me," he said, raising his hands in a gesture of *what can you do?*

"No relationships for you? Are you anti-relationship?"

My heartbeat sped up, like his answer was truly important. But it wasn't, which might have been a lie I decided to tell myself.

Drew rubbed his bearded chin and looked unsure, or hesitant, which wasn't a look I was familiar with on him. He stammered, working to find his words. "Well, I mean, I thought I was on that path recently, but I was mistaken…"

I raised my hands up to stop him. "I'm sorry, that wasn't my place to ask. You don't need to share."

He let out a frustrated breath. "No, it's fine, I honestly don't know why I'm struggling to speak. It's just I don't talk about this stuff a lot. But no, no real relationships. I'm not anti-relationship, if that's even a thing. Beyond that, let's just say it was a little messy. Not a lot of free time when I was on the Hotshots, and then when I did try for something, it went to shit."

Hotshots. I'd heard about them, of course, and Ivy had said something before, but Drew had avoided the conversation. With the climate in danger as it was, the fires out west had been out of control for the past few years. Maybe that was why he didn't want to talk about them? My heart thudded with the thought of Drew in danger like I was certain he'd faced. I wanted to wrap him with protective Bubble Wrap and ask him to stay home. Not sure where that came from. And I had to admit my curiosity was piqued at his mention of the messy relationship, but I didn't want to pressure him to talk about it.

Instead, since he brought up his former job, I decided to start there. Maybe that was the easier conversation? "So Hotshots? What made you make the switch to Highland Falls?"

Instantly, Drew's eyes shuttered. Hmm, interesting. Not the easier conversation. Well, hell.

After a long pause, he spoke. "Needed a change and figured I could use some time around my brother."

Clearly, he was holding back something, but that wasn't mine to ask for. Moving on. Again.

"So you're moving in here?"

Drew's face quickly relaxed. "I am."

Tingles raced through me. This man was going to be next door? "We're going to be neighbors?"

He gave me another quick scan. "We sure are."

Heart rate speeding up, I gave him an awkward wave with a breathy, "Hey, neighbor."

Drew's smile kicked up in the corner, making his beard twitch. "Hey, neighbor."

Aw, damn. I had a feeling this was going to be trouble. A beep sounded from my apartment indicating that the coffee was done. "Coffee?" I asked. Where did I go from here?

Chapter 5

Small Steps

Drew
I glanced down at my phone again. Five minutes. I took a deep breath. Then another one. It had been over two weeks since my first yoga class with Kate, and I had to admit the breathing exercises helped.

But I knew I needed more.

I thought back to my second class. I had to laugh. Kate had come straight up to me to apologize, saying she hadn't pulled any punches in the power-flow class the day before and that maybe that hadn't been fair. I'd told her to keep at it.

Because what I'd realized that night was that Jake—hell, my whole family—had been handling me with kid gloves. I knew that was my fault. The lack of information I'd given them had let their imaginations fill in the gaps on what was going on with me, allowing them to assume the worst. Yet I still hadn't been able to open up. Hence the call to my former chief.

I was taking back my life. Today was a big step, but I'd started two weeks ago with that yoga class. Next, I'd pushed away all the voices in my head telling me I was weak and should be ashamed and called the chief of my Hotshot crew. He'd been welcoming, as I knew he would, and given me the number to the therapist he knew. I'd contacted the office and set up today's appointment. That had been step one.

At the brewery I'd asked for some more shifts, helping ease the burden on Jake. His business partner, Sully, had reduced his hours for the past month after the birth of his new baby and Jake had helped to pick up some of the slack. In my own spiral, I hadn't realized how run-down he was getting. Taking on some extra hours did a lot of good—giving Jake a break as well as filling some of my downtime. While my anxiety had lessened, it was still ever present. Today, if anything, it was heightened.

Not that I was surprised in this situation. I was hopeful, which felt dangerous. I knew this wouldn't be easy and I wouldn't get over my fears in a session, but the notion that I could take charge of my life again felt good. Yet I was worried I'd somehow screw this up or not know what to say.

I fought the urge to pace around my apartment and fired up my laptop, clicking over to my email to pull up the link they'd sent. I wiped my palms on my joggers and glanced out the windows at the grain elevators. The January morning was crystal clear and, fortunately, sunny. Some winter days in Illinois were dreary and gray, but today the sun was bright and the sky was blue. It looked deceptively welcoming, but I knew it was likely freezing outside.

A glance at my phone told me I still had three minutes to wait.

My stomach felt like a swarm of butterflies had taken up residence. Like I was preparing to walk onto stage or step up to the starting line of a race. I was uneasy, nervous, which was ridiculous.

Another deep breath. I closed my eyes, feet flat on the floor, trying to remember what Kate had said about grounding yourself in our last class. I curled and uncurled my toes, concentrating on the feeling of the floor beneath my feet. Deep breaths. Placing my hands together, I rubbed my palms quickly, letting the sound wash over me. Then I placed one warm hand on my heart, one on my belly. I focused on inhaling all the way into my belly, I began to relax.

Another glance at my phone told me that it was time. I clicked on the link to begin the call. The butterflies began their song again, but I stomped my feet to remind myself that I was here, I was present, and I was taking back control.

The call connected, and I clicked to allow the camera and microphone access as I returned the smile of the older lady with tight gray curls and large glasses framing warm eyes on the screen in front of me.

"Good morning, Drew. Are you ready to begin?" she said.

Inhaling through my nose, I nodded. Here we go. Some of the anxiety melted away, and we got started.

Two hours later, I headed down the street to the brewery, my mind pinging from one thought to the next. Jess, the therapist I met with today, had been the right step, of that I was certain. I felt like I was finally taking control of something that seemed out of control for so long.

I was grateful that Jess did sessions through video conferencing. Not that I was opposed to going into an office, but as nervous as I'd been, it had been comforting to talk to her from the privacy of my home. Add that to the fact that she was familiar with some of the stresses of my job, and I felt like we were a good fit.

Jess had given me some homework to try before we

met next. She said yoga and practicing mindfulness were great first steps. I hadn't realized that was what Kate was teaching us in class, but apparently that's what it was called. I was also to work on journaling this week, paying attention to my thoughts and feelings, when they occurred, and be ready to share any observations at our next session.

I felt a little skeptical that this talking and journaling would beat back the worry that pervaded my nights, but I was willing to try.

Shivering, I came back to the present and picked up the pace, breaking into a light jog. I likely should have layered up more to head down the street to the Homestead. It had to be in the teens. The sun was still shining down, reflecting off the snow-covered streets and sidewalks. Some trees even had it clinging to their branches. The crunch underfoot surrounded me as I ran up the sidewalk and into the brewery.

Warmth hit me like a wall as I stepped through the door. Finn McHale, the manager, glanced up from the hostess stand where he was looking at something on the tablet. He looked me over and shook his head.

"Colorado toughen you up so much you don't need an actual coat like the rest of us?" he asked, nodding to my fleece.

I snorted. "I mean, I do have a stocking hat."

Finn raised an eyebrow.

"But yeah, it was colder than I anticipated when I headed over. Too lazy to go back upstairs for a jacket. Figured since it was only a few blocks, I'd be fine." I wondered when I'd be able to feel my fingers again.

"So what you're saying is mistakes were made." Finn looked at me as if he had many years of age and wisdom on me, when in fact I'd bet he was in his late twenties just like me. However, he was correct in this case.

"Yup, mistakes were made. I'm grabbing lunch before working a few hours this afternoon. Bar okay?"

Finn nodded with a swipe at the tablet. "We have a big group in the center at noon, Rotary Club. Then tonight it looks like we'll be slammed. Get some fuel in you; you're going to need it. There's a local brewery pub crawl coming in at happy hour toward the end of your shift. They have a bus rented to drive them from place to place."

"Sounds good." I nodded to Finn, then headed past him toward the bar.

A few tables here and there were filled up for lunch, but the pace didn't really pick up until noon. Then there'd be a steady stream for an hour or so, another lull until about four, and then all hands on deck until closing. I was only scheduled from two until six but already volunteered to stay on if needed tonight. Frankly, what else was I doing?

Reaching the bar area, I saw the back of one Maxwell Harp sitting at a stool, talking to Sully across the counter.

"How's the baby doing today?" I asked as I got closer. "She taking after your ugly mug?"

"Nope, she's gorgeous like her mama," Sully said with a proud smile. "Finally sleeping a few hours more too." He gestured to the taps. "What will it be, Drew?"

Max turned on the stool to nod a greeting as he kicked the stool out next to him. I slid in, damn grateful that I'd felt so welcomed by Jake's friends since moving to Highland this fall. Leaving my crew behind had been tough, but these guys made it easier.

"Just water, I'm on in a few hours."

Sully nodded as he filled up a glass and sent it my way.

"Keg's blown. Back in a minute to take your order," he said as he headed off to change one out.

Max grunted his greeting while he inhaled his lunch. Looking over, I couldn't say that I blamed him. My stomach growled in response to the aromas surrounding me. Pete had been experimenting with the smash burgers that had been so popular in this area lately, and it looked like he'd finally perfected it. I knew some people preferred the more traditional thicker patties, but these burgers with the crispy edges and multiple patties were all right by me. Add to that some sweet potato fries, and I figured I knew what my lunch would be. Maybe I'd live on the edge and add a side salad.

"How's the woods?" I asked Max. He'd moved back to Highland Falls about nine months ago and took a job out at Highland Woods, the state park outside town. From what Jake had shared, it was essentially his dream job after growing up here.

Max grabbed a napkin before turning to me. "Good. You get out there much?"

"Yeah, I hit the trails with Jake from time to time."

"Must be different from Colorado for you. You thinking of joining up with the volunteer firefighters here?"

I worked to school my expression and kept my breathing even. "Nope, leaving that behind me."

Max either didn't notice or didn't pry on that front. "What's your degree in?"

"Environmental studies."

"You were in college in Colorado before the Hotshots, right?"

"Yep. University of Colorado at Boulder, or CU." I felt a tug thinking of life back then, when shit had seemed a lot simpler.

Max grunted around another bite. Where the hell was

Sully? I didn't think I was that hungry until I had to sit by someone else eating. Might be time to hit up the grocery store and actually have food in my place instead of bumming all my meals here or filling up on protein shakes. Especially since I actually had a place for the foreseeable future.

Max brought me back from my dreams of shelves filled with food. "You planning on working here at the brewery full-time or did you want to do something with your degree?"

Twenty-million-dollar question right there.

"Not sure." Jess, and more likely Kate, would be proud of me for the concentration on my breath here. My heart rate remained steady. Considering it, this situation seemed to call for some honesty.

I glanced Max's way before answering and found him watching me. "Feeling adrift would be the no-bullshit answer here. Thought I was planned out, now it seems like I need a new plan."

Max nodded like he got what I was saying. "And working here"—he nodded at the bar—"is it the new plan?"

I glanced around the Homestead. "I mean, yeah? High-land Falls feels right. This place feels right. It's just..." I was at a loss as to how to describe what was missing.

Or was there something missing? I mean, maybe it was just that I wasn't where I'd thought I'd be. Maybe it was that I wasn't part of the Hotshots anymore, that my identity had changed, but my mind hadn't caught up with that. I made a mental note to write this down to discuss with Jess.

"It's just not what you had thought?" Max guessed. I nodded. He took a swing of his drink and tossed his napkin on the bar. "If you ever want to use that degree, hit my boss up, Logan Traub. Logan works out at Highland Woods in coordination with the university on some sustainability shit. He might have some ideas of what's out there for someone with your background."

A sliver of excitement rushed through me at the thought of even talking to someone about the topics that used to dominate my daily life at CU. Hell, even in the Hotshots, we pored over environmental impact articles often not to mention dealt with the effects of climate change as part of our job. Moving here, I'd left so many of those conversations behind, but it wasn't like that interest was gone.

"I'll do that, Max. Thanks."

"Tell Sully I'm off. Have to get back to the park." He nodded at me, tossed some money on the bar, and headed for the door.

Vibrations from my phone had me tugging it out of my back pocket. I noted another text from James that I'd missed sometime this morning. Guilt flooded me. I needed to talk to him, but hell if I knew where to start.

Murph: *This is ridiculous. We need to talk. Call me.*

My heart rate kicked it up another notch. I owed him a call. Hell, I'd needed to call him for months. James and I'd been close, like brothers, since I'd joined him in the Hotshots. But I had no fucking idea as to where to begin. Pencil in another topic for Jess. Fortunately, looking at the other messages rolling in, my siblings did what they did best, which was to take my mind off things.

Steph: *Remind me why we're all living in Illinois. Winter can bite it. I'm cold. I'm grumpy. I need some light in my life.*

Jake: *Aw, Steph, you messaged us because we are your light, didn't you? Not your husband, not your kids, your baby brothers.*

Steph: *Picture of both of Steph's hands flipping off the camera.*

Jake: *Double unicorns, I knew you loved us.*

I shook my head. Sometimes I was astounded that I was related to these two. On the other hand, I was grateful for them every single day.

Me: *Now, now, baby brother is here. Make this chat PG.*

Steph: *I just snorted my pop. You are the least PG one of any of us. Seriously, you two. I need something to look forward to. Look at your calendars—maybe not this weekend, but the next. Anything on the schedule? I need something. Anything. Hell, I might even be able to swing this weekend. Desperate woman here.*

Jake: *With kids or without?*

Steph: *I was thinking Theo and I could come down to you all. Mom and Dad would take my girls, but I know Ivy would have Addie, so maybe I'll bring them. They'd love to hang out with her more.*

I felt a burst of jealousy. Steph and Jake would have their families. I'd be flying solo, as per usual. For a moment, I let myself think about what might have been, then promptly pushed that aside.

My nieces, though, I'd love to see them all.

Me: *I can watch the girls if you all want to go away for a couples thing.*

Steph: *Don't make promises you don't want to keep.*

Me: *Wouldn't do that, you know I love them all. Need to see Ads again anyway. My nails are looking dull.*

Jake: *You serious? Steph, we could keep it local. Highland Woods does weekend specials for people who want to stay at the mansion on weekends they don't have anything scheduled.*

Steph: *If they're open, book it. I'm having a whole "fuck my life" moment. Work is bonkers. Both of the girls just finished up dance recitals. Theo has been putting in so many hours. Jennie just told us she wants to join soccer this spring. AHHHHH.*

I laughed. Steph was dramatic at times, but not to this level. If she said she needed help, she really did.

Jake: *Looked at their website. They have two rooms available Saturday night. That work? Drew and I can swing it at the brewery if he's really up to uncle duty. Come down early Saturday, stay till late Sunday?*

Three dots appeared as Steph apparently composed her text. I mentally jumped ahead a few days, thinking of the weekend. No surprise, not much on there. Work Friday night, Sunday afternoon. Otherwise, my schedule was yawningly empty.

Steph: *Shit, I love you two. I can't tell you how much I need this. I love my life, I love my girls and, clearly, Theo. I just need a moment.*

I chuckled before thumbing out a reply.

Me: *Sounds like a real FML moment. I've got you, big sis. Bring those girls down. We'll play beauty shop. They can camp out in my new place, and we'll make a fort. I'll order pizza or McDonald's, and we'll eat crap all weekend. Sounds perfect.*

Jake signed off to go make the reservations, and I thought back to my empty shelves. Looked like it was time to hit the grocery store for real.

Chapter 6

Dinner Date

K*ate*

The smell of the pork in the Crock-Pot greeted me the minute I opened the door. I enjoyed cooking—there was a meditative quality that really appealed to me—but I wouldn't say I was talented at it. Instead, I could follow a recipe and get something decent on the other side. This was one of my favorites because who didn't enjoy the concept of tossing ingredients into a bowl in the morning to come home to a cooked meal? It was some type of magic.

Tonight's meal was a favorite, pulled pork. I mean, I knew Maggie and Emma sang the praises of Sully's pulled pork that he made thanks to his smoker, but there was no such fancy equipment when you lived in an apartment. Instead, a packet of McCormick's seasoning and the recipe on the back did it for me. Still, it was nothing to dismiss. I loved it for the flavor and the simplicity.

It was my turn to host dinner for Elle, Nic, and myself. I'd debated inviting Drew since he was now one of our neighbors, but wanted to run it by Elle and Nic at dinner before injecting a dose of testosterone into our monthly date.

My phone chimed with an incoming text as I moved to the kitchen to check out the pork and see if it was ready for shredding. As I dropped my keys on the counter, I took a glance at the screen. It was my group message with Elle and Nic. Leaning against the counter, I opened it and felt disappointment wash over me.

Nic: *Don't hate me you two, but I told Ivy I'd work another shift and stay after to help with inventory. She and Jake are trying to get out of town on Saturday, and I know she's got a late night ahead.*

Nic was the kind of friend everyone wanted, kind and full of empathy. I couldn't fault her. I knew everyone that worked at Pages looked out for each other on a regular basis.

Elle's reply appeared before I could type out my own.

Elle: *Shoot. I'm so sorry, Kate, but I have to bail too. Nate's parents just messaged that they are popping by for dinner. Apparently, the weather is truly embracing winter next week and they want to get in a visit before hunkering down. Sorry! Rain check?*

I fought the internal voice that told me Nic and Elle were bailing because I thought of them as friends and they didn't see me the same. I knew that was old insecurities talking. Right? Right. With a glance at the Crock-Pot, I debated my options. Maybe I'd be eating pulled pork for the next week? Nachos? Tacos? Salads? Not sure how else I could use up the meat.

Selfishly, I hated to miss out on time with these two. *They were true friends,* I told myself. They'd made me feel so at home after moving to Highland. In the past few months, I'd confided some of my heartache and confusion over my breakup with Alex, and they had been great listeners. It took a lot for me to feel like I could open up to someone. For sure, who I'd hoped would be friends in my past had proven that they shouldn't have been labeled as such. But Elle and Nic had been great so far, and I needed to remind myself that they weren't like others I'd known. I was grateful for them, for so many of the people I'd met since moving here.

Me: *Nothing to apologize for you two. Nic, shout if you want me to run some food down or leave it in your place. I'll have leftovers, but I bet I can freeze it or something. Love you both.*

Nic: *You should invite our new neighbor. He's super nice, and I don't know if he knows a ton of people in Highland yet.*

Elle: *Wait a minute, are we talking about Drew Spencer? If so, KATE!!!! I agree with Nic. Invite him to dinner and have him stay until breakfast, if you get what I mean...*

I laughed out loud. That sounded like something her sister Ava would say. I'd only met the high school English teacher once, but it was on point.

Me: *I'm sorry, is your sister rubbing off on you? Elle, that's a rather bold comment.*

Nic: *And truth. The woman speaks the truth.*

Elle: *I'm sorry, you're right, Ava is absolutely rubbing off on me. And possibly Maggie, though she's been home more with the baby. I shouldn't objectify Drew, that's a double standard.*

Me: *Though he is cute... and nice...*

I shook my head. What on earth was getting into me? I was nowhere near ready to get back into anything approaching a relationship. Nope. No way, no how. And

Elle was right, Drew didn't deserve us drooling over him. He had been nothing but nice since I met him. Though I'd be lying to myself if I didn't acknowledge that I was attracted to him and wondered if the feeling might be mutual. Nope, it didn't matter, I wasn't acting on it. Friends. That's what we were. And neighbors.

Nic: *Okay, Elle's right. No objectifying, but the man does need to eat, and everyone can use a friend. That's all I'm saying. Kind of.*

Before I lost my nerve, I placed my phone on the counter and headed through my apartment, out the door, until I found myself staring at Drew's door.

I took a deep breath. I could do this. It was neighborly, right? Friends... just friends... just looking out for him... and God knows I had enough food. As I raised my hand to knock, the door swung open and I jumped back in surprise.

"Whoa, sorry!" Drew jumped back himself.

I laughed at the two of us. "Where were you headed?"

His cheeks heated up like he was blushing, which made me want to know more. He looked... embarrassed?

"Well, I told myself yesterday that I was going to hit the grocery store and finally get some food in here, but I stayed late at the brewery and didn't get that done. I also didn't go today, so..." He shrugged.

I felt my smile widen at his predicament.

"I think I can help you with that," I said. With a nod back toward my apartment, I turned back to Drew. "I made some pulled pork and was supposed to have friends over. However, they canceled, so..."

Drew's eyes lit up. "So you're taking mercy on your neighbor who is too lazy to get off his ass and go to the grocery store?"

I laughed. "Something like that."

"What can I bring?" Drew asked. "Answer that with the knowledge that I have ketchup, a bottle of ranch, some Cliff Bars, oatmeal, and—quite likely—almond butter."

Shaking my head, I took a step back to my apartment. "Bring yourself. I've got you covered."

"Be right there," he said.

I headed back into my place, leaving the door cracked for him.

In the kitchen I grabbed some forks and opened the lid on the Crock-Pot to begin shredding. As I did that, I heard Drew step into the apartment.

"Damn, what is that amazing smell?" he said, closing the door behind him.

"Pulled pork, but it's from a Crock-Pot and not a smoker." The pork was super tender, shredding quickly. I gave the mixture a stir to get the liquid distributed, then replaced the lid to let it cook for another twenty minutes.

Drew came to the half wall that separated the kitchen from the dining area. "One, I don't give a damn what the source is of the pulled pork. I'm much happier that there is pulled pork in my future."

I grinned at him. "Excellent. We're all set then. And two?"

He laughed. "Two"—he slid a four-pack of beers in my direction—"I forgot that my brother had dropped off some beer for me from the brewery." He nodded toward the cans. "I guess I actually have something to contribute."

I leaned against the counter in front of me. "So what you're telling me is that you have a variety of condiments, some energy bars, oats, and beer?"

Drew cracked open a beer before giving me a solemn nod. "That about describes it."

I pulled the four-, now three-pack toward me. Barn Owl

Stout. Sounds perfect. Opening mine, I poured it into a glass and took a drink.

"What do you think?"

I slid a glass toward Drew for his beer.

"I'm a fan of stouts, most beers actually, so this is good." Putting the beer down, I opened the freezer and considered our options. "Thoughts on sweet potato fries?"

"All good thoughts. Love them at the brewery."

I tugged out the bag and grabbed a cookie sheet. "Well, these can't rival the ones at the Homestead, but they're pretty awesome. I was going to have this, some salad, and the pork."

"What can I do?" he asked, putting his beer down.

I gave a nod to the fridge. "It will be tight in here, but you can start on the salad."

Drew immediately moved around to the fridge and began scanning the contents.

"You might be confused after living in your barren wasteland for the past week, but that is what a refrigerator should look like," I said, needing to tease him just to see how he'd take it.

He took it well. Snorting, he pulled out the lettuce and some various vegetables I'd cooked for dinner earlier this week. "Yeah, yeah, I deserve that. I actually like cooking, just haven't felt like the work of making a list, meal planning, all for one."

I glanced over, but he was looking down at the cutting board where he had brussels sprouts spread out with some leftover cooked bacon.

Clearing my throat, I found myself grateful when he met my eyes. "I know that cooking for one kind of sucks. We can trade off a few times a week cooking for each other if you'd like."

I wanted to kick myself. Maybe that wasn't what he meant, and I was an ass for presuming. I began second-guessing myself, wondering how to rescind the invitation when Drew nodded.

"Yeah, I think I'd like that a whole lot."

My heart stuttered at the vulnerability on his face. I had a sudden desire to grab him by the beard and pull him in for a kiss. Oh boy. I thought I might be in some trouble.

A voice in my head whispered, *you think?*

After a surprisingly enjoyable meal together, there were no awkward pauses in conversation with Drew, I'd found. I learned that he was a *Schitt's Creek* virgin. That simply couldn't stand; everyone should be well versed in the world of David and Alexis. Drew consented to watch one episode, and we'd each taken corners of the couch, he on one end with another Barn Owl Stout, me curled in the corner with some hot tea and a throw.

"Stop," he said with a smirk.

"What?"

"You're watching me watch the episode."

"No I'm not." I looked back to the screen because I absolutely had been.

"Kate," Drew paused the show and looked at me. "You watched me right before David walked in on his parents so I knew something was going to happen."

I laughed, remembering the scene. "I couldn't help it, it was a good one." I stretched my legs out under the blanket and looked back toward the television.

Drew hit Play again and rested a hand on my ankle, squeezing it lightly. "It's fine. I have to admit the show is growing on me."

I worked to school my reaction because his hand on my leg was making my heart race. "Told you. The Roses are hilarious." I concentrated on the end of the episode and not the cardiac emergency happening in my chest.

An hour later the credits rolled on another episode. I looked over at Drew whose long jogger-clad legs stretched out to my coffee table. He shook his head at me.

"We have to stop," he said with a grin. "I think that's the eighth one tonight, and I should head back to my place and get to bed."

I was choosing to ignore the happy feelings that flooded my body at the use of the word *bed* from this man's mouth.

"Agreed. I have class at nine tomorrow. You coming?" I didn't want to own how much I wanted him to say yes, but there it was.

Drew stood, stretching for a moment. The tiny sliver of skin above his waistband drew my eyes immediately, like there was some type of magnetic pull. Shaking my head, I refocused as Drew took on a more subdued expression than he'd had just moments before. I briefly wondered where his mind had just gone. It felt like he was erecting walls after a night where the vibe had been relaxed. Heck if I knew why.

"Yeah, I'll be there. Hitting the grocery store after that in preparation for the weekend." He picked up his glass and the plates we'd brought with us to the coffee table and headed toward the kitchen.

I had an unexplainable urge to wrap him up in my arms and hold him, as if he needed comfort. Hmm. That was new. Shelving that to deal with later.

"So you stocking up before the storm?" I bumped him out of the way with my hip so that I could begin loading the dishwasher.

"Storm?" He had a crease between his eyebrows. I wanted to smooth it down with my finger.

I shrugged, my focus on rinsing the dishes so I didn't do or say anything ridiculous.

"Elle canceled tonight because her boyfriend's parents came into town ahead of some storm, but I haven't checked the weather to see what that's about."

Drew tugged his phone out from his pocket and tapped a few times. His brow furrowed more. I'd only known the man for a little more than two weeks, but part of me wanted to know so much more about him. And no, not the part that Elle's sister, Ava, would say was calling for him. He was still so vague about leaving his former profession. He could be light, filled with humor one moment, then lost in thought and serious the next.

That was likely true for all of us, but with Drew I sensed something more. Ivy said Jake and Drew were close, that he was friends with the guys Jake knew. But there was something there, and I just couldn't put my finger on it. Loneliness? Possibly. Whatever it was, I knew that Nic had been right. He could use a friend. So what if he was ridiculously gorgeous? Ignoring that, reaching out as a fellow human being instead. Yep. Sure.

Drew was still sliding his finger across the screen of his phone.

"You not a fan of winter?" I asked. "I mean, you did live in Colorado before here, right? Snow has to be part of your DNA at this point."

He shook his head and looked up at me from his spot where he was leaning against the counter like he'd forgotten where he was. "What? I mean, yeah, sorry. I was just looking at the timing. My sister, Steph, is in major need of some stress relief. I promised the other day to watch her kids and Ivy's daughter this weekend so my siblings and their partners could spend the night at the mansion out at Highland Woods. I was just checking to see if the snow would cancel their plans." He stood, returning the phone to his pocket. "Looks like their plans are safe. It shouldn't really ramp up until Sunday night. However, once it hits? Elle's right. Batten down the hatches and all."

So many things I wanted to say. One, my heart did skip a beat that this guy seemed to have no issue watching several of his siblings' kids for a night? And that he cared that his sister was stressed? All that was amazing. But then I couldn't help but wonder if he minded being left out of the time with his siblings.

"Thanks for dinner, Kate. I'll see you in yoga tomorrow." He started for the door, but then turned back. "Hey—"

I turned from my spot at the sink to face him.

He continued. "I don't think I've said anything, but I really enjoy your class."

Yep. I was a sucker for this guy. Wave the flag, sound the horns, done.

"Wow, that's, um, awesome," I said like the fool that I was. "I mean, I'm glad you like the classes. And if you need any help with your nieces, or is there a nephew in there too?"

"Three nieces since I'm claiming Addie, though Jake and Ivy aren't married yet. Emily is six, Jennie is five, and Ads is four." Drew ran a hand through his hair. "I'm sure it will be interesting, but we'll be okay."

I nodded. "Well, I'm sure it will too, but I worked with that age group for several years, so if you need anything, say the word."

Drew stood, watching me for a moment, then came back in, holding up his arms ahead of time with a tilt of his head, a universal signal for a hug.

My heart skipped a beat as I nodded with a small squeak when he tugged me to him.

Drew huffed out a laugh as he folded me into his arms. I melted, feeling like I finally found where I belonged and wanted to burrow in and never leave.

Drew's lips brushed my ear, the roughness of his beard brushing the side of my face. "Thanks for dinner, Kate. I really needed this."

And just like that, he backed up and was out the door before I could even stammer a reply.

What in the sweet hell was that and how could I get more of it in my life?

Chapter 7

Cookies and Unicorns

Drew

My eyes took in the time on my phone's display, and I groaned. How in the world had it been only seventy minutes since Steph and Jake dropped their hellions—kidding, kidding—children at my place?

I mean, I knew the four of us crammed into this tiny space would be tricky. I could have gone to Jake and Ivy's house and stayed with the girls there, but I figured it might be fun for them to stay at my place. Since Jake and Bookstore were taking their dog, Chief, with them to the woods, there was no reason we had to be at their place. However, at this point, I was questioning the wisdom of this decision. I mean, the girls would likely have been more independent there. Here, I was on duty and hadn't been allowed to slack off in my responsibilities *at all*.

"Drew, oh *Dreeewwww!*" Addie's voice sang out from my bedroom. "Is our fort ready yet?"

Jake had no reason to worry about this kid when she got older. She knew her mind and went about getting what she wanted. Heck, in the past hour we'd had manis for all, to the delight of my nieces. Personally, I hadn't thought anything of it the first time Jake and I let Ads paint our nails. Like, it was just nail polish; who gives a fuck?

Then we'd helped Bookstore out with some kid's event at Pages the week between Christmas and New Year's. She'd had the idea to have a craft time for parents where they could drop their kids off in the space she used for book clubs while they shopped in the store. It brought business in and gave parents that had kids home from school and daycare a moment of peace.

After the hour was up, when all I'd wanted to do was flee the glitter-strewn room, Ivy shared with me that a mom had talked to her about my nails. That day I was rocking alternating colors of purple and pink. Sometimes I left the polish on for days, sometimes I took it off. Since I'd watched Addie the night before, it was still on.

Seems this mom's five-year-old son liked painting his nails, but some kids at school had teased him about it. Her son had pointed my nails out to his mom and asked if they could go home and do his again. The mom hadn't wanted to make me feel uncomfortable, but Ivy said she was choked up as she expressed her thanks for empowering her kid.

It blew my mind that something as simple as having nail polish on could make a kid I didn't know feel more okay with himself. If I could, I'd take out a damn billboard telling him—hell, all kids—that they should feel free to be themselves; fuck the haters.

Not in that language of course.

Well, maybe. I mean, really. Fuck them.

At any rate, nails were done, butter and eggs for cookies were sitting on the counter to come to room temperature, and only seventy minutes had passed. My house was stocked with groceries after my trip to the store yesterday after yoga, which was just in time for this crew to descended upon me this morning. We had Wi-Fi, a deck of cards, and every streaming service known to man. Some show called *Bluey* was currently playing on my television, and I was in charge of creating a blanket fort.

And I had zero ideas as to what we'd do next.

"*Dreeewwww,*" called my tiny captors.

"Working on it, ladies," I sang back. A trio of giggles was the only response I got. As I moved to drag a chair from the table to my small gray sectional, there was a knock at the door. Before I could do anything about it, the sound of a stampede thundered through the apartment, preceding my nieces.

"We have a visitor!" Jennie shouted, her brown hair flowing behind her.

Emily's legs were just a smidge longer than Addie and Jennie's, so she reached the door first. Showing her wisdom as the oldest of this crew, she turned to me before throwing the door open. It had to be one of my neighbors up here, so I nodded that she could open it, saying a quick prayer that Kate was on the other side.

The door was swung opened to answered prayers.

When Kate smiled, she transformed from the sweet girl next door to breathtakingly beautiful. From where I stood, I could see the freckles that were scattered across her nose and on her cheeks. I loved that she never seemed to wear makeup. Today her long brown hair was woven into two braids. She was in leggings and a fitted long-sleeve that I noticed she tended to pull on over the sleeveless tanks she typically wore to teach yoga.

I thanked whatever god—or goddess, as Bookstore would remind me—gave the inspiration to some designer somewhere for leggings.

"Well, hello, girls." Kate looked over the girls with a welcoming smile, like she wasn't at all put off by their pulsating energy levels. Brave woman.

"Kate!" Addie bounced up from behind her cousins. "Jennie, Emily, this is Momma's friend, Kate. She teaches me yoga."

Kate laughed as she watched Addie begin to spin around in a circle. Ads wasn't in a dress today, which was unusual. Though she still had her flair for fashion happening with rainbow leggings paired with a long-sleeved T-shirt with the earth on it. Jennie and Emily were in leggings and T-shirts that clearly showed their love for dogs. I'd purchased those for them for Christmas in response to their request to persuade their parents that they needed a pup. It hadn't worked yet, but I had faith in them.

"How you holding up?"

I looked up at Kate's question. Her expression was kind, watchful. I wondered if she thought I couldn't handle the girls. I mean, they were a lot, and it felt like hours had passed rather than just a little over one, but I still loved the time with them.

I gave her a reassuring smile, I hoped. "It's been an eventful hour."

She glanced down at my hands, then back up with a raised brow. "Didn't invite me over for the manicures?"

"I can give you a manicure!" Addie's voice rang out.

"Me too," Jennie and Emily said in unison.

Kate laughed, holding up her hands. "Okay, okay, maybe later. I over to see if you guys would want to do our very own yoga class downstairs."

Three sets of eyes spun my way, hands flew together in pleading gestures, eyes widened. Good God, these three had joined forces. We were all screwed.

"Please, Uncle Drew," they cried out as one.

I looked from them to Kate. "You sure you're up to this?"

Kate shook her head at me. "Kristine and I have a preschool class once a week. These three will be a breeze."

"Three?"

She tilted her head to the side. "Well, I mean, you're welcome to join us. I just figured I'd give you a quick break if you wanted one."

"Oh no, neighbor. This is practically a private session. I'm not missing it for anything."

"I can give you a private session anytime."

My dick pulsed with that comment even as Kate quickly slapped her hand over her mouth, clearly realizing how that might have sounded.

I laughed out loud, watching the flush spread up her neck and onto her cheeks as I worked to regain control over my own thoughts. "I just might take you up on that, Kate."

We quickly rallied the troops and headed downstairs.

In the studio Kate transformed. She was clearly in charge in the classes I'd attended, but this felt like she was in her element in a way I hadn't seen her. She'd mentioned working with this age group before. I wondered if it was just with yoga or something more. I'd have to ask.

Kate sent the girls to tiptoe to get their mats as a line of quiet mice. I watched in awe as my three rambunctious nieces transformed to do what she asked. Before I knew it, we had the five of us in a circle instead of lined up like a normal class and were ready to begin.

"Okay, my beauties"—she gave me a quick glance—"and Drew..."

"Insulted," I said with a smirk.

"You know you're gorgeous," Kate muttered.

"Heard that." As always when I was around this woman, my body vibrated with interest. I worked to breathe deep and focus.

"At any rate, what animal do we want to start with today?" Kate looked to Addie who clearly knew the assignment.

"A lion!" Addie shouted.

Kate glowed as she guided us through a series that ended with a lion roar. I watched as she gave directions, both modeling poses and gently adjusting my nieces to help them find their own flow. She whispered quiet words of encouragement as they bent this way and that. The class as a whole was far from the normal yoga class I was used to. There were simpler poses with more chances for imagination. I also noticed how Kate added in imagery to capture their attention as we moved from mountain pose to one she called flying bird. The girls hung on to her every word. She moved on to a game that she called *mirror, mirror* where we all took turns being the leader and making everyone else imitate our poses. I think the girls created their own, which were interesting. Before I knew it, Kate was calling for a cooldown as she walked us through a body scan.

"Our bodies are magical," she was saying.

"I'm magic," Addie said in a reverent whisper.

"You sure are," Kate said. I could tell she was walking around our circle as she walked us through the relaxation exercise. "Remember, you are the one in charge of your body. Take in a deep breath, feeling it fill you up from your chest to the tips of your toes. Hold it. Then breath out any negative thoughts. You are perfect exactly the way you are. Hold on to that."

As I listened to Kate, I thought about how all kids could benefit from a class like this. Heck, in the past forty-five minutes, she'd worked on flexibility, talked about the importance of nutrition in a way that made these three ask me for carrots, and walked us through some mindfulness exercises. I wondered if all their preschool classes were like this.

As we trooped back up the stairs, I noted that the girls were more mellow than I'd ever seen them before. Well, at least not when in each other's company.

"You're a magician," I whispered to Kate as we opened the door to my place and trooped on in.

Her smile was warm. "Glad I could help." She hesitated outside my door, as if she wasn't sure what was next.

What was next? I knew I sure as hell didn't want her to leave us. Not yet.

Jerking a thumb over my shoulder, I took a chance. "Want to come hang out with us?"

She beamed. "Absolutely."

I shook my head at her.

"What?"

I glanced over at my sectional, counting six small feet waving back and forth. The girls were flipped upside down, heads hanging over the cushions, their legs straight up in the air.

I nodded toward them. "Your apartment is probably peaceful, and you're choosing mayhem."

Kate looked in their direction and shrugged. "I miss being with kids this age sometimes. They are filled with wonder and possibility. Their imaginative world is a hairbreadth away from reality, and they dip between both. I wish I were more like them."

"Well, you sure are good with them. I know you said you've worked with kids before. Was it in yoga?"

"Not originally. During college I worked at a daycare in the preschool and kindergarten classrooms." She looked sad for a moment, but then continued. "I loved it. When I left college, I got into yoga instruction. I've had classes for kids before but not regularly until moving here." And she left it at that.

There was more there, but I figured I should let it go for now. From the direction of the sectional, I considered the girls, who I could hear weaving stories together. "My mom always says that kids are the best of us."

"She's right," Kate whispered. Then, seeming to shake herself to the present, she glanced at me, a little hesitation obvious. "Am I intruding? Maybe you want time by yourself with your nieces?"

I laughed out loud, then raised my hands up in protest when Kate appeared alarmed. "Oh, I love these stinkers—"

"We're not stinkers, Uncle Drew!" Jennie called.

I glanced back to them, their feet still all that was visible over the back of the sofa. "Sure you are, ladies. That's why those feet are waving in the air, right? Airing them out?"

Addie scrambled to face us, her little face surrounded by a mess of curls, her hair far from the neat ponytail she arrived here with.

"Uncle Drew, be serious." She rose up, hands on her little hips, visible over the back of the couch. "Now." She glanced at her cousins, then back to me.

I waited. *This should be good.* God, I loved this kid.

"Raise your hand if you like cookies." Voice serious, Ads raised an eyebrow in my direction, like she was daring me to say no.

Emily and Jennie shot their hands in the air. Addie looked at them, nodding, then looked back to Kate and me, arching her little eyebrow again in our direction.

Kate laughed, then looked at me and slowly raised her hand with a shrug. "Everything in moderation."

I was no fool. I said the only thing I could when faced with the clear alpha in our small group. "Chocolate chip?"

My question was met with a chorus of cheers.

I ushered Kate farther in the apartment, closing the door behind us, and headed to the kitchen. She trailed behind me. As I stepped into the room, I noted that she'd shed her shoes by the door. Part of me loved that she seemed comfortable in my space. However, I remembered that she'd been in here on more than one occasion when Elle had rented it out.

I glanced back to the couch where three sets of eyes were locked on me. "You girls want to help make the cookies or do you want to do something else while I make them?"

Their heads immediately came together as they debated this very important question.

Kate glanced from the girls to me. "Mind if I offer up an option?"

"Sure. What is it?"

"My students at the daycare used to love to create their own books. I'd staple together several sheets of printer paper, and they'd create stories for hours."

I thought about that. Addie would love it for sure. Jennie and Emily probably would too. "Sounds good, but I'm not sure I have the supplies."

Kate's smile lit up the room. "Give me a minute."

Kate went over to the sofa and whispered to the girls. There was a chorus of excitement, and I watched as she raised up a finger in a *wait a minute* gesture before heading out of my place and across the hall to hers.

While she was gathering what I assumed the girls would need, I checked the butter and eggs that I'd set out earlier on the counter to make sure they'd lost the chill from the fridge. This wasn't my first rodeo, Addie *always* wanted to make cookies. Steph had taught Jake and me the merits of homemade cookies when we were in our teens. She said she'd nailed the secret and that was chilling the dough along with starting with room temperature ingredients. Not sure I'd have time for chilling in the fridge today—the patience of my three guests was not especially long.

Pulling the ingredients together from memory, I thought of all the times I'd made cookie dough to have in the fridge at our station when I was with the Hotshots. If we had a fire, we could be gone for hours, possibly days, at a time. When we were back, however, for whomever was around, it was an indulgence. You had to be in great shape, of course, to do the job we did, but everyone needed a reward once in a while. And cookie dough could keep for months in the freezer, so I made some often.

Too bad I didn't have any already on hand here. I just hadn't gotten into the routine. Hell, until I knew the girls were coming, I hadn't even really gotten any groceries, choosing to eat out instead. I needed to get my shit together and work on taking care of myself again. Running and yoga were only going to get me so far.

Kate came back in with supplies in hand, and the girls met her with more cheers.

"Okay, ladies. Who has a story in them today?"

"Me, me, me!" Addie raced around the couch to get to the table, immediately pulling out a chair and climbing up into it. "My story is about a princess and her best friend, Kevin the Unicorn."

I nodded. *Kevin the Unicorn* was also the name of one of Addie's favorite picture books. I'd read it as part of her bedtime routine more than once in the past few months.

Emily and Jennie made their way to the table too.

Jennie was walking on her toes, her arms floating around her like she was a dancer.

"Mine will be about a girl name Emily who got a puppy for Christmas," Emily said as she sat down at the table.

"Mine too!" Jennie sang out.

"Oh, I've always wanted a dog," Kate said to Emily and Jennie.

"We do too!" the girls chorused.

"Why don't you have a dog?" Addie asked Kate, resting her arms on the table and focusing all her attention on her. "Chief is my best friend."

Kate smiled at the girls and glanced my way with a twinkle in her eye like she was in her element. Turning her attention back to the supplies on the table, she whipped together three books as she talked.

"Well, my parents never wanted a dog, and I haven't lived in a space as an adult that I felt like would be big enough for one."

"What kind of dog do you want?" Addie asked, head tilted like she was debating what would be best for Kate.

"Oh, I'm happy with any. I always thought maybe a golden retriever or a goldendoodle..." Her voice trailed off as she got lost in thought for a moment before looking to her audience. "And you girls want one too?"

"Our parents said maybe soon!" Jennie answered with excitement.

"Lucky!" Kate tapped Jennie's nose.

While my heart tugged for the wistful note in Kate's voice, I bit my lip to keep from laughing. Subtle, girls, subtle. I bet they were going to hand these books to their parents the moment they walked in the door. Maybe I'd see if Kate had some ribbon that we could tie around them, diploma like.

"You all sound like you have excellent stories in mind." Kate handed out the books to each girl, leaving another stack of paper and a stapler in the middle of the table. She also pulled out a zipped pouch that she upended on the table. Colored pencils, thin markers, pens, and pencils tumbled out. "Here are some supplies. Now once you make your first book, you're welcome to make another one, just let me know."

With that, she headed in my direction. I watched as each of the girls selected something to write with and got to work. Addie's tongue poked out of her mouth as she drew.

Glancing at Kate, who had reappeared by my side, I whispered, "I'm not sure Addie, and possibly Jennie, know how to spell too many words."

Kate glanced back at them. "Doesn't matter. If they feel like it, they can use invented spelling. Or their books can be wordless, or they can dictate to us. I used to have my preschoolers create stories anytime I needed a second of time to catch my breath. They'd work on them for a surprisingly long time. Then, when they 'read' their stories back to me, I was always floored by details they'd layer in that I would have missed."

"You're a savior," I said.

"So we're going to make cookies?" she asked, glancing at the items gathered on my counter.

"Yep."

"I think you forgot the chocolate chips," she said, looking over the counter.

"What if we want sugar cookies?"

Kate gave me a look.

"Or oatmeal?"

Another look.

"Chocolate chip it is." Without thinking, I leaned past her to open the cabinet behind her shoulder.

Kate let out a little gasp, and I realized that I'd inadvertently put us just inches apart. I glanced down to see Kate looking up at me as she leaned back against the counter.

"Shit, sorry." I started to take a step back to get out of her space.

"No, it's okay." Kate sounded breathless, and I froze as her hands came up to my sides.

Her eyes stayed locked on mine as her lips parted. What did *it's okay* mean? My body seemed to act independently of my mind—or was quite possibly listening to a lower brain as I stepped back into her space and brought my face to hers.

Kate's grip on my waist tightened as she pulled us even closer together.

My lips hovered over hers for a second. "This is okay?" I asked.

"More than."

Permission granted, I brushed my lips against hers. Holy God, it felt like a current of energy shot from Kate to me. My hands slid to her hips, pulling her to me and then...

"Uncle Drew, stop kissing Kate and come look at my book!" Addie sang out and then broke out with a giggle. Emily and Jennie joined in.

I dropped my forehead to Kate's. Shit. Yep, I was babysitting.

Kate joined in their laughter.

"This is a laughing matter, neighbor?" I asked.

"Well, I mean, that was unexpected—"

"Bad unexpected?" I immediately worried. I thought we were on the same page. I mean, I hadn't planned it, but wanted to make sure we were good here.

"Heck, no. Good unexpected."

"So then why the laughter?"

Kate looked up at me; her expression was mischievous. Pulling my hips flush against hers, she gave me some wide eyes. "Just wondering, *Uncle Drew*, when you're going to be able to go out there and see Addie's unicorn book."

Yeah, there was no masking the raging erection that had joined the party as soon as that little breath of air left Kate's lips. Not analyzing that right now. Nope. Ignoring it. Absolutely.

"I'll give you a unicorn horn to talk about," I said instead.

Sometimes the middle school boy never leaves us.

Another burst of laughter burst from Kate, and this time I joined in.

Chapter 8

Surprise Confessions

K*ate*

I worked to distract myself from the heat and tingles coursing through my body. Yeah, kissing Drew had not been on the day's agenda. Holy God, it had been over a decade since I'd had a *first kiss.* Surely that could explain the electricity that seemed to arc between us.

What else could it be?

I was grateful for Addie's interruption, or that was the story I was going with for now.

Drew and I had gotten started with the cookie dough, but before I could help him scoop the dough for chilling, I'd been paged by the ladies for a nail session. So now I was sitting across from Emily who was armed with a bottle of bright pink nail polish and doing an astonishingly good job of painting my nails.

All while the girls grilled me on my life so far.

I mean, I hadn't met anyone in the police department in this town yet, but these girls had a future ahead of them if they so desired.

"So you went to college, and that's where you met Kristine?" Emily asked.

We'd already covered siblings, none; parents, lived in Ashville; and early college life, including my introduction to yoga.

"Yep. We met in college in yoga class, and a friendship began immediately. Have you met people like that? That you're friends with as soon as you meet?" I asked the girls. Jennie was focused on my nails, but Emily and Addie were still working on their books while participating in the conversation.

Emily nodded, focused on my thumb.

"Yep, my friend Avery," Jennie said.

"Ohhh, I know." Addie looked at me with wide eyes. "That's like when I met my big boys."

I felt my eyebrows draw together in confusion. What four-year-old could be considered a big boy? "Who's that?"

She laughed and pointed to the kitchen where Drew was washing dishes. "Daddy Two and Drew, silly."

Wow. My eyes misted as I turned my head to meet Drew's gaze. For a man who looked like he could walk off the pages of a *Nordic Gods* wall calendar, he was a big softie.

I cleared my throat, looking back to the girls and ignoring the heated look Drew had just given me. Mmmm.

"So yeah, college was good," I stammered.

I heard Drew chuckle but ignored that.

"And did you have any boy-friends?" Jennie sang the last word.

I looked down at my nails for a moment. There was no reason I had to tell the girls about Alex, but part of me felt compelled to.

"Sorry, you don't have to answer that," Drew said from his spot at the sink.

"But—" Jennie began.

"No, Peanut. People are allowed to keep their private life private." Drew's voice didn't allow for argument.

I met his gaze. "It's all right." Looking back at the girls, I nodded. "Yes, I did have a boyfriend. He's a great guy, and his name is Alex."

Addie's face was pinched in confusion. "Does he live here? I don't think I know an Alex. Well, there's an Alex in my class, but that wouldn't be your boyfriend, right?"

I laughed. "No, Alex doesn't live here. He lives in England."

Addie gasped, dropping her colored pencil and placing her hands over her heart. In a voice filled with awe, she whispered, "Does he know the queen?"

This time my laughter was combined with tears. This kid. "No, sweetie, he doesn't know the queen. But he only moved there four months ago. Maybe in time."

She nodded like that made all the sense in the world. "Well, if he meets her, can he introduce me?" She picked the purple-colored pencil up and started working again.

Emily began working on my last finger. "So is Alex still your boyfriend?"

My eyes watered. Dammit. "Nope."

Jennie looked over my way. "How long did you date him?"

"A long time. Around thirteen years." My heart tugged. "And we were friends before that."

Jennie's eyes were filled with the love of a child who didn't realize the empathy she was sending out. Again, another reason they were the best. "Did that make you sad?"

I nodded.

Jennie patted my hand. "Did you break up with him, or did he break up with you?"

I squeezed her hand. "I broke up with him."

"Because he was in England? That would be far away for a boyfriend to live."

"Well, he only moved there four months ago, but yes, that was partly it."

Emily looked up from her spot at my nails. She blew on them, then met my eyes. "What else was it?"

"Why we broke up? Well," I paused, wondering if kids their ages would get it. "I just realized that while Alex was a good friend, I didn't like him like you should like a boyfriend anymore." I paused as I thought of Alex. We'd texted yesterday after he'd had his first social hour for his new job. He'd been overwhelmed with work since moving but had finally caught up and gone out with some people in his office. It was the first time he felt like he was really clicking there, and I was happy for him. Looking back to Emily, I finished my thought. "We're still friends, just not boyfriend and girlfriend."

Three little heads nodded at me with all the wisdom of their ages.

"My friend Lizzie broke up with her boyfriend Tommy for the same reason," Jennie said. "I mean, he didn't move to England, but she didn't love him anymore. They're friends now too."

Ahh, kindergarten relationships. They were the best.

"So you're starting over, just like Uncle Drew," Addie said, turning the page in her book to color on the back.

I looked to Drew who I found had his eyes locked on me.

"Starting over..." I thought about that. "Yes, I guess I am."

Drew's eyes flashed with something I couldn't name.

My heart thudded in my chest and my cheeks heated up, but I couldn't look away.

Several hours of heated glances, lots of cookies, and more episodes of *Bluey* than I wanted to watch again, I collapsed onto the sectional, ready to wave the white flag. So far today I'd led these pint-sized warriors in yoga, we'd created multiple books, I'd helped Drew make cookies, had my nails painted while being grilled about my life choices, and then we'd made homemade pizza for lunch.

To say nothing of the inappropriate thoughts I was having on repeat.

Now it was the late hour of three in the afternoon. I knew I could head home, leave Drew and the girls to their weekend. And while I was tired, I was also having the best day that I'd had in ages.

Dilemmas.

The girls were pulling over the chairs from Drew's table to finally make the blanket fort they'd started before yoga this morning. Drew came from the bedroom with several blankets in his arms and dropped onto the couch next to me.

He knocked his leg into mine. "Hey."

I knocked my leg back into his. "Hey."

He tossed the blankets onto the couch near him so they could begin construction on their fort. Addie pulled them toward her, adding to the pile she'd just grabbed from my place across the hall a minute ago. They were all stocked up.

Drew turned, sliding one leg onto the couch as he faced me, and stretched his arm out across the back. "You okay?" His gaze was searching, scanning my face.

I shivered under the weight of his stare, but damn if it felt awkward. It felt heated, full of promise and care. I needed to process all this, but that was for later.

"I'm assuming you are referring to my earlier interrogation by these three innocent girls who will one day grow up and run this country?"

"Clearly." Humor was sketched onto his face.

I turned to him and met his gaze. "I'm fine. We haven't really talked about our pasts yet, but now you know more about mine."

Drew was silent for a moment as he sat with that, but then he nodded. "You feel like you made the right choice?"

Not what I thought he was going to ask. Interesting.

"Yes. I miss Alex, but more like I miss a good friend who was my constant companion for over a decade. We still talk, but he's far away."

"So it didn't screw you up that"—he nodded toward the kitchen—"you know, moment in there earlier?"

I bit my lip to keep from laughing. "You mean that kiss? Nope, not screwed up about that. Thanks for checking."

"Are you teasing me now?" He raised an eyebrow at me, his eyes twinkling.

I realized that this was the little brother in a family of three strong-willed siblings if Ivy's stories were to be believed. I'd likely do well to remember that.

But I also liked to live dangerously.

Well, kind of.

I looked off to the side and raised my hands up in a *what are you going to do about it* gesture.

"I mean, I'd never tease you, Drew." I let my voice singsong just to mess with him.

Only child over here. Check.

Drew grinned, and for a moment I could imagine

what he looked like with his siblings when he was younger, right before he went after one of them. "Ads?" His voice rose to get her attention, though his eyes stayed locked on me.

"Yeah?" she called from over by the chairs that they were setting up.

"What do we do when someone needs to be reminded to behave and I'm babysitting?"

I could see Addie begin to bounce with glee.

"We have a tickle fight!"

My eyes went from Addie back to Drew.

Oh boy.

Drew's voice lowered. "We only have one rule."

"What's that?" Damn. My voice sounded breathy. Drew's smirk told me he noted that little tidbit.

"If you say stop, I'm stopping. We always listen to each other, so just a heads-up on that."

Yep. This guy. Maybe I should just throw myself at his mercy. I didn't think there was a point in resisting.

"So I have to stop if you say it too?"

Remember, only child reporting for duty. I didn't back down. Even though I wanted to march to the bedroom and volunteer as tribute.

"I won't say stop," Drew said.

"Neither will I." I was tensed, ready to pounce.

"When does the tickle fight start?" Emily called.

I looked over at the girls, and that was my error.

Drew reached out, grabbed me, and flipped me to my back on the couch. He stretched out on top of me, his fingers digging into my side, as the laughter began. I mean, I couldn't tell you the last time I was tickled.

I felt younger. Like a weight I hadn't been aware of had been lifted.

"Drew..." I gasped, wiggling my own fingers into his side, relishing the feeling of him on top of me.

"Mercy?" he asked.

"Never," I said, tears of laughter now streaming down my face.

And then a voice I didn't recognize interrupted us. "Well, well, well. Isn't this cozy. Sam, did you see that Drew has a new friend that I somehow knew nothing about? Aren't you so glad we decided to come down?" The entire question was laced with humor.

A low chuckle was the only reply.

Drew stilled on top of me, his head rising just as I opened my eyes to see a gorgeous woman who had to be in her late fifties, maybe older, staring down at us.

"Look, Uncle Drew. Nana and Pop-Pop are here!" Addie squealed with glee.

"Your parents?" I whispered to him, well aware that I could be heard, but better to be certain.

He nodded, his eyes tightening like he was preparing to brace. "I'm thinking Ads didn't lock the door when she came back with the blankets."

Drew's parents? Super.

"Hi?" I called from under Drew. Yep, sure did. Best. Impression. Ever.

Drew's mom seemed to clap her hands together in what looked like glee. While Drew dropped his head to mine.

Well, this should be interesting.

Chapter 9

Those Types of Friends

Drew

Fuck my life.

I mean, that likely sounded dramatic to someone who didn't know the situation here, but if Jake or Steph was here right now, they'd back me.

Margot Spencer did not have a subtle bone in her body. Not one. Not even in her little toe. And now that her middle child was settled, engaged, and had given her another grandchild in the form of Addie to adore, she was eager to turn her sights on me.

This scene she just walked in on wasn't helping my case, that I wasn't on that path right now.

More to the point, why was my mother here? Or my dad, for that matter.

Looking down at Kate, whose wide-open eyes were shooting between me and my mom, I could only apologize.

"Sorry."

Kate's eyes crinkled. I had a feeling that while she was surprised my parents had burst in, she was also more than a little amused. I could only hope she held on to that feeling.

85

I slid off the couch, and Kate, to face my mom. My dad was conferring with Emily, Jennie, and Addie, likely preparing to help them construct the best fort ever built.

They really were fabulous grandparents, even if my mom was a busybody.

"So Mom and Dad, just happen to be in the neighborhood?"

My dad had the decency to glance over with a remorseful look and a sheepish shrug. Mom, though, didn't back down. Not that I'd ever dream she would.

"Absolutely. We thought we'd check in on our granddaughters, and of course you." She gave me a look that dared me to challenge her.

Mom, Mom, Mom... she should know me better by now.

"*Really.*" My eyebrow was absolutely raised in disbelief. "Your house is at least two and a half hours away."

"So?" My mom raised the same eyebrow.

Genetics.

"So how does that fit the definition of being in the neighborhood?" I bantered back.

She gave a dramatic sigh, Oscar worthy really. "Drew, one day you will be blessed with children, I pray. At that point you will realize that there are no limits to what you will do for said children. Two and a half hours is but a blip; you might as well be down the street. And what else could I do, really, since you swooped in to agree to babysit when I had already told Steph that we'd be happy to?"

Cue the violins. "Mom, really, guilt trips are beneath you." The words flew out of my mouth before my brain analyzed what I'd said.

Danger, danger. Alarm bells were ringing.

When Margot's hands landed on her hips, the hair on

the back of my neck stood up. I needed to play this carefully.

However, Mom surprised me. A look of calm came over her face as she dropped her hands, like she hadn't realized what she'd done. Smoothing down her jacket, she looked from me to turn her attention on Kate.

Oh hell.

"Forgive my rudeness, dear. I'm Margot Spencer, and this"—she looked over her shoulder to my dad to give him what I was certain was a get-over-here-now glance—"is Sam. We raised Drew, but clearly, some of our lessons on manners didn't stick. I do so hope you'll forgive us."

Kate rose up, straightening her shirt. As she turned to my parents, I couldn't help but appreciate her leggings and the way they highlighted her toned legs. Pulling my eyes up to catch my dad's gaze, I saw that he was fighting back laughter as he watched me.

Guess I hadn't been as subtle as I'd hoped. Noted.

Kate grasped my mom's hand, then my dad's, introducing herself. Then, as if on command, all three of them turned to look at me.

"Yes?"

"Well, I'm just wondering," my mom began, "why you hadn't said anything about Kate in all the times we've talked recently?"

"Oh, we're not dating." Kate blushed, apparently deciding not to gang up on me anymore.

"Really." My mom looked skeptical.

"No, Mom. Kate's my neighbor."

Her expression grew more hopeful, not less.

"Yeah, Nana," Emily piped up. "Kate just broke up with Alex, and they'd dated forever."

"Over ten years," Jennie helpfully added.

"But Drew and Kate did kiss earlier in the kitchen," Addie ever so kindly contributed to the conversation. "So maybe they do like each other?"

Shit.

Kate's eyes flew to mine and they widened. "Um, maybe I'll let you all spend some time together. I need to get back to my apartment."

"You do?" I asked, giving her a look to say *you're leaving me to this?*

Her glance back said *you bet your ass I am.*

Kate hurried around the sectional, sliding her shoes on before bending to hug each of the girls. "I had so much fun making books with you, my lovelies. Thanks for my manicure."

"But Kate, we haven't had popcorn and watched a movie. And Uncle Drew is going to play the guitar!" Addie's arms were wrapped around Kate's waist.

Kate looked at me and mouthed *you play the guitar?*

I nodded, a smile spreading as I watched the girls dance around her. Every moment in her presence, even when torpedoed by my parents, I knew I wanted to be around her more.

As friends, right? Yeah, friends. Sure.

"Sorry, girls. I really do need to get to my place." She walked over to my parents. "Mr. and Mrs. Spencer, it was lovely to meet you."

"Margot and Sam, dear. And you simply must join us for brunch tomorrow." She held a hand up as Kate started to try and interrupt. "No, I won't hear anything against it. Plan on it. I do throw a good brunch, even when I'm not in my"— she turned to me—"*neighborhood.*"

Point to Mom.

Addie tugged on Kate's sweatshirt until Kate lowered

her head so Addie could whisper in her ear, though Addie's whispers were never very quiet. "There will be donuts."

Kate smoothed down Addie's hair. "Well, then I have to go, don't I?"

With a final goodbye, Kate ducked out to her place. As the door closed, five sets of eyes turned my way.

"So who's up for a movie?" I said.

My dad burst into laughter as my mom headed my way.

Hours later, the girls were finally asleep, three angelic faces sacked out on my bed, all in a row. I'd said all along that I'd take my couch. I mean, it was ridiculously comfortable, so no hardship there. The girls had brought sleeping bags anyway, my brother and sister insisting I should sleep in my own bed.

Nope, nothing doing. The girls got my room, end of story.

I sank into my couch and kicked my feet up to my coffee table, considering the day. The morning with Kate had been like something out of a dream. I was trying to remind myself not to jump ahead. We'd only met just over two weeks ago. Sure, there was a foundation being built of friendship.

Was I attracted to her?

I'd be lying if I said I wasn't.

Was I really going to pursue anything?

Honestly, I wasn't sure. I didn't know if I could trust myself.

With that, my phone seemed to call out to me. I picked it up, heart rate increasing as I opened up the text messages and scrolled back.

I knew what I was looking for.

And there was James's message from four days ago, unanswered, just like so many had been since I'd moved back. Hell, since before that too.

Murph: *This is ridiculous. We need to talk. Call me. Yesterday was too late.*

My thumb hovered; uncertainty washed over me. I thought back to my session with Jess. I worked to concentrate on what I could control, taking a few breaths to clear my mind and work on pulling my thoughts together.

Finally, I decided on action.

Me: *Sorry for the radio silence. Working through some shit. I'll call when I've done that.*

Phone tossed to the couch, I picked up the remote. Maybe I just needed to binge watch some mindless television to distract me from shit memories or the desire for a woman right across the hall.

Before I could even select something to watch, my phone vibrated with incoming texts. I told myself to ignore it, but that lasted all of a few seconds before I had to look to see what James had sent back.

It wasn't James, it was Jake. And Steph.

Jake: *Report in. You've been taken hostage and the kids have taken over, correct? It was all Emily's doings, wasn't it? She's got leadership running through her veins.*

Steph: *Surely you jest. Addie is the powerhouse. My girls will be leaders one day, but right now I'd put money on your pint-sized dynamo being in charge.*

Bookstore: *That's my girl.*

I rubbed a hand over my face. It was a debate over who was more exhausting, the girls or these three.

Me: *One, the girls are asleep. More to the point, is Theo even there? Did you all lose him in the woods? Call*

Mountain Man Max. I feel certain he has some SAR training.

Me: *I mean, did they even do search and rescue in the northern part of the state when he was up there? Maybe not, but he seems like the type.*

Steph: *Oh, don't you worry about Theo, he's here. He's sitting in this long room with us, no idea what the purpose of this space would have been originally, but it has giant leather sofas and a fire going. He's in heaven and just keeps muttering, "It's so quiet. I've missed the quiet."*

Me: *Poor Theo.*

Steph: *Okay, please note that I gave you several moments to share, but you're a fool, so I'm diving in. MOM FOUND YOU ON TOP OF SOME WOMAN?*

Bookstore: *Steph, this was not easing in like we talked about.*

Me: *Are the three of you in the same room? Like middle school kids, sitting around and staring at your phones instead of conversing with each other? For shame.*

Jake: *Avoidance.*

Me: *One, we're getting back to the whole "Mom and Dad are here" moment in a second. But really, it was nothing. Kate and I were having a tickle fight.*

Steph: *So much to unpack here, I don't even know where to start.*

Jake: *I mean, that's your method of foreplay? No wonder you're single.*

Steph: *But is he?*

Bookstore: *I, for one, want to note that I'm ecstatic that this was Kate in your apartment. I love this for you!*

Steph: *But a tickle fight?*

Me: *Shut it. All of you.*

Bookstore: *Hey!*

Me: *Okay, maybe not you, Ivy.*

Bookstore: *Whoa, you first-named me. You doing okay?*

Me: *I've had better days. Return to the above message about my parents walking in on me stretched out over Kate.*

Me: *And did any of you know they were coming down?*

Steph: *Nope. Promise. First I heard about it was when Mom texted about what they walked in on.*

Me: *Jesus, you make it sound like they walked in on a porno. I'll repeat, it was a tickle fight. We were messing around.*

Jake: *Sure sounds like it.*

Me: *You're all dead to me.*

Steph: *But we'll see you for brunch tomorrow? With Kate?*

I groaned.

Me: *Yep. Now go be social together. That's my quota of text messages for the night.*

I looked up from my phone at a light knock on the door. Dropping it to the couch, I headed to answer it, having an internal war the whole way over whether I wanted Kate to be on the other side or not. It was her, right?

Opening the door, I found Kate standing with an uncertain look on her face.

"Hey," I said, keeping my voice low. "Did you want to come in?"

"No, I just wanted to make sure everything was okay," she whispered.

"They're out, asleep in my bedroom, and won't hear us as long as we don't throw a crazy party. You don't have to whisper." I nodded toward the couch.

Kate hesitated, then passed me to find a seat on my sofa. She curled up in the corner and pulled a throw over her lap. She glanced around, a timid look I didn't love evident on her face.

"Um, are your parents still here?"

Margot could be a lot. Maybe that was giving Kate some anxiety?

I sank down in the corner of the sectional across from Kate, giving her some space. "Nah. They went to Jake and Ivy's place a while ago. The girls sacked out shortly after that. I'm sorry we got the surprise visit earlier, but I promise, they're mostly harmless."

Before Steph could somehow teleport into my place and chastise me for being a bad host, I spoke up. "Did you want anything to drink?"

"No, I'm good." Kate glanced at my phone between us. The vibrations weren't subtle. "Do you need to get that?"

I groaned, letting my head drop back to examine the ceiling. "No."

Kate looked at my phone as it vibrated again. "Can I ask why?"

"Well, it's my sister Steph. And Jake. And Bookstore." I lifted my head to look at her and shrugged.

Kate's smile kicked up at the corner. "But not Steph's husband?"

I snorted at that. "That would be Theo, and no. He only lasted in our group texting thread for a short time before asking to be removed."

"You all are too much for him?"

I raised my hands up, the picture of innocence. "Oh, not me. It's all Jake and Steph."

"But Ivy can handle it?"

"Bookstore gives as good as she gets."

"So." She glanced at my phone, which vibrated again. "Why the multiple texts?" She was quiet for a second, but then her eyes widened and she looked at me. "Did your mom..."

"Tell them that she found me lying on top of you while babysitting? Why yes, she did." I bit my lower lip to keep from laughing at the horror of Kate's expression.

"Oh no!" Her cheeks immediately began to flush. She waved at the phone. "You need to text them back. They're going to get the wrong idea and—"

I slid across the couch to get closer to Kate. Space be dammed. Laying a hand on one of her flailing arms, I tried to calm her. "Easy, Kate. They'll be fine. They find this all hilarious. And let's be honest. While what my mom saw was innocent, we did kiss in the kitchen earlier."

Her eyes widened as she looked up at me, her tongue darting out to lick her lips.

I took a deep breath, praying for strength.

"Yeah, we did."

"You regretting that?" I felt my stomach clench, hoping the answer was no, but also not sure if I was ready for it to be yes.

Kate shook her head to indicate the negative but did so slowly, like she was really thinking about the question.

I waited.

Finally she looked at me. "I hope this doesn't make me sound like a flake, but no, I don't regret the kiss at all."

"Glad to hear that."

"But..."

I groaned. "Doesn't sound promising."

She leaned forward, putting a finger on my lips. "But... I'm not sure I'm ready for more."

I noted that her eyes welled up. Shit.

"I'd be lying if I said I wasn't attracted to you."

"Feeling is mutual," I mumbled from behind her finger.

"Hush. I'm just saying I like you, Drew, but I'm also sorting through some shit, and I don't want to rush into this and then mess up something good because I'm not ready."

My heart skipped a beat. Sounded a lot like Kate and I were coming from similar spots. And, I noted, I knew a lot more about what she was dealing with than she did for me. At some point, I needed to share with her.

Soon.

Lifting her finger off my mouth, I asked, "Can I talk now?"

She laughed. "Yes."

"I get you, Kate. More than I'm ready to talk about. And as I mentioned, I'm attracted to you too. So where does that leave us for now. Friends? Friends who cook for each other multiple times a week? Neighbors?"

"Neighbors who occasionally kiss just to see if the electricity is still there?" she asked.

I tilted my head to give her a look. "So you felt that too."

"Hard to miss."

"So neighbors who eat together, sometimes kiss, but are working on becoming friends while sorting some shit out? Those type of friends?" I rubbed my jaw and gave her a look.

She pursed her lips as she thought, then looked my way. "Works for me." She stood up, stretching, apparently deciding to torture me in her leggings and tee. "Bye, neighbor," she whispered, leaning over to brush her lips against mine.

I groaned, which earned me a smirk. Just for that, I let her get all the way to the door, before I called, "Remember,

Kate, brunch tomorrow with the fam. We can walk over together."

She glanced back over her shoulder, a look of trepidation written on her face. "You seriously want me to come to that with you?"

"Sweetheart, if you don't come, Margot will be at your door to bring you there."

"And you don't think it says something that I'm coming to family brunch?"

"No more than me lying on top of you said."

Kate closed her eyes, appearing to breathe herself into a state of calm. Opening her eyes back up, she looked my way. "What time?"

I gave her a victorious smile. "Ten."

She shook her head at me before heading out the door and calling back, "See you then, neighbor."

Aw, yeah, I think I would like being this type of friends just fine. Now I just needed to sort my shit out and see how we could add to this friendship.

Chapter 10

Gives Good Brunch

Kate

My reflection was not helping here, not at all. No exaggeration, I'd tried on six outfits this morning. Six! For a person who typically lived in yoga clothes, this was borderline ridiculous. I'd messaged Drew to ask how dressy his family got. The man was no help. He said I could wear whatever I wanted and we'd meet on the landing in an hour and we could all head over together.

Men.

So I did what I should have done from the beginning. I texted Ivy.

Me: *What does one wear to a brunch?*

While I waited for a reply, I looked at the mess that was my bedroom. Leggings, jeans, sundresses, and sweaters were strewn all over the bed. My mental state could be summed up with a nod to one item in that list, *sundresses*. I mean, it was January in Illinois and weather was moving in this evening, but sure, sundresses made sense.

My phone vibrated.

Ivy: *I love this so much. I was in your shoes only three* *months ago and had to go to a family brunch after my first night with Jake. Soooooo, how closely are you following my lead?*

Me: *Slow your roll, Bookstore. I do not know Drew in that way. He's a friend.*

Ivy: *Sure. I have always had guys like Drew stretched out on top of me during a tickle fight. Sounds completely logical.*

Ivy: *And did you just call me Bookstore? Drew is rubbing off on you. If you were texting Jake or Steph, they'd have a comment about rubbing off to insert here.*

Me: *And a comment on what could be inserted. But focus woman. What do I wear? Drew just said anything was fine.*

Ivy: *Yeah, they don't understand the need for more guidance. But he's accurate. Jeans, leggings, anything goes. Margot and Sam will be dressed up because I don't think they know how not to be. I've already seen Steph today. She and I are both in leggings and long-sleeved T-shirts. Does that help?*

I breathed out a sigh of relief. I wasn't a person with anxiety, luckily, with the exception of going somewhere for the first time or meeting new people. I don't know if I'd call it anxiety or just uncertainty. Kristine often mentioned that anxiety and excitement were closely related and it was a matter of perspective.

I worked to adjust my mindset. But if I was excited, did I need to examine why that was? Drew and I had discussed this last night. We were friends who were attracted to each other, but certainly not more than that. At least right now.

Because God knows I was not ready for more right now. Was I?

Me: *Yeah, helps a ton. See you there.*

Ivy sent me a smiley face emoji, and I dove back into my closet.

Ten minutes later I had on leggings, a gray light-weight long-sleeved T-shirt, and black booties. A glance at my phone told me that January was doing its thing and the temperature had dropped to just below freezing.

I tugged on a red stocking cap and grabbed my coat as my phone vibrated with an incoming text.

I pulled on my down coat as I looked to my phone, expecting something from Ivy or Drew.

Nope.

Alex: *Saw the sunrise this morning and thought you'd love it. Let's talk soon.*

The picture he'd attached was gorgeous, but my stomach was off. I didn't feel anything romantically for Alex anymore. Honestly, that was one of the reasons I'd broken it off, because as shitty as it was to admit, I wasn't certain when I last had. So why did I feel like this? Like I had gotten caught doing something, and if he knew I was going to brunch with Drew, that I was cheating? Nope, not cool on my part.

As I zipped up my coat, I debated Alex's text. Flipping my hair out from under the collar of my coat, I took in a deep breath and tapped to open my phone and thumb out a reply.

Me: *Love the pic.*

Alex: *How goes it? Winter in Illinois as crappy as always?*

Me: *You know it. Heading to brunch with my neighbor.*

Alex: *Elle or Nic?*

Me: *Nope, Drew. Moved into Elle's place.*

I couldn't help but notice the three dots, but not a rapid text. My stomach clenched again. Finally, it came through.

Alex: *Not sure if I should ask if this is as friends or not. Is it weird that this is a little weird?*

I exhaled in relief. It wasn't just me.

Me: *No, a little weird for me too. Drew is a friend, but possibly more. Should I apologize?*

Alex: *Heck no. We talked about this, and we're friends now. I love you and want you to be happy. And in the spirit of total honesty, I went out on a date last night. That was one of the reasons I wanted to text. I felt like you should know.*

I checked myself. Yep, no sadness at that reveal. Interesting.

Me: *I'm happy for you. Need to run so I'm not late, but wanted you to know.*

Alex: *I'm happy for me too. And for you, whatever this is. Before you run, you talked to your parents lately?*

I groaned. Damn it, Alex. He knew me too well.

Me: *Yeah, a couple of weeks ago.*

Alex: *And?*

Me: *It went as well as you can imagine.*

Alex: *You know I'm on your side here. Need to run anything by me before you talk to them again?*

Me: *No, just not in the mood to have every life choice questioned. Again.*

Alex: *Don't put it off. I'm here to bounce ideas off of anytime. Love you, Kate.*

Me: *Love you, Alex. Talk soon.*

There, that wasn't so hard. Well, other than thinking about my parents. Pushing that aside like I'd done time and time again, I felt lighter as I heard Drew's door open and he and the girls, or a herd of elephants, stepped out into the hall outside my door.

"Kaaaaaate!" It sounded liked Addie, but I wasn't certain.

I opened the door to see their three beautiful faces staring up at me. Drew stood behind them, gorgeous, naturally. The girls had on their puffy jackets and stocking hats. Drew looked, as always, like some dark-haired Thor, white T-shirt under a black winter coat, joggers. He had on a dark stocking hat that made his eyes stand out. They looked gray, but was that even a thing? Maybe blue, but there were hints of green and brown. I wanted to rub my face on his beard because that was totally normal.

And now I was staring.

And he was grinning.

"Ready?" he asked, looking at the girls, who were beginning to dance in the hall, their joy unable to be contained.

"Yeah, let me just grab something," I said. Turning back into my place, I tossed my phone in my purse, sliding it across my body, and grabbed the container I'd packed up after getting dressed.

"Ready," I said to our assembled crew after rejoining them in the hall and locking my door.

Addie raised her eyebrow at me and gave me an innocent look. "What's in the Tupperware, Kate?"

I gave her a knowing look; I knew where this was going. "Chocolate Chip Scones."

She threw her little arms up and twirled.

"You like scones?" I asked.

"I love chocolate chips," she said.

This I knew. Ivy often bemoaned that Addie could happily exist on a diet centered around sweets. This was contrary to the way Ivy ate. She didn't believe any food was off-limits but absolutely tried to nourish her body through healthy eating. I'd been around when Jake reassured her that the modeling she was doing for Addie would matter more in the end, but I knew it was something she thought about, wanting her to love nutritious food too.

"I bet you do. I'm thinking there will be all sorts of yummy food today." I thought about mentioning fruit, but in all honesty, it wasn't like I had any insider information on what was being served.

Addie's hands clasped under her chin, and she looked at me with barely contained excitement. "Yeah, like donuts."

Good Lord, this kid.

The girls preceded us down the stairs as Drew fell by my side. "You sleep good?"

"Yeah, you? Did your pint-sized guests wake you early?"

Drew looked from me to the girls, who had just reached the door to the street. "Emily, hang a left. Jennie and Addie, stay together and not far ahead."

As he reached the door, he put an arm out to hold it open, gesturing for me to proceed. "I don't tend to sleep great, haven't for a while, but the couch was just fine."

We followed the girls onto the street. I noted that Addie had pulled up her hood, which looked to be a unicorn's head, complete with horn.

Glancing back at Drew, I tried to look him over without being obvious. He didn't look well rested, and now I was wondering if he ever had since we'd met.

"How long have you had an issue with sleep?" I asked, hoping it came across in a caring way and not like I was nosy.

"Here, let me take that," he said with a gesture toward my scones.

I handed them over, wondering if this was his way of

moving the subject off of him. If so, I'd take the hint. I didn't want to pry.

"Girls, wait to cross," he called.

We caught up, got our crew to the other side, and were moving away from the business district to the quiet neighborhoods now. Turning on the tree-lined street that Jake lived down, I breathed in the peace and quiet of a Sunday morning. Some folks were driving around, but there was a serenity about it. Like even the birds and squirrels knew the snow was descending upon us tonight, so they were finding a way to get tucked away until it passed.

"Eight months, give or take," Drew said.

"What?" I looked over, only to see that he was looking straight ahead, not meeting my eyes.

He cleared his throat, discomfort written all over his expression. "My sleep. It's been fucked up for a while. Started at the end of May..." His voice trailed off.

I wracked my brain, trying to remember if Ivy had mentioned anything about this. Looking over at Drew, I felt my heart tug. Here was this giant—well, compared to me— and he was willing to be vulnerable, though he wouldn't look at me.

It was unbelievably attractive.

He had my scones in his right hand, and luckily, I was on his left side. I took a chance and reached out, entwining our fingers and squeezed. He responded in kind, looking at me quickly, then back to the girls.

I lowered my voice so it would only carry to him. "Is there something that caused you to begin to lose sleep? Or is it random?"

Drew looked down for a minute as we walked. He bit his lower lip and appeared to be debating what to say. Finally, he looked to me. "Yeah, had some shit go down on a fire call with the Hotshots. I can get asleep, but not always stay asleep because I dream about it."

"Want to talk about it?"

He squeezed my hand. "Later, okay?"

I nodded, my heart going out to this big beautiful man.

He gave me a soft smile and then let out a laugh as the three girls cheered upon seeing Jake and Ivy's house just a half block away. They picked up speed and began jogging before turning in the drive.

We continued at our leisurely pace.

When we reached the driveway, I tugged his hand before we got to the sidewalk that led to the backdoor.

He turned, looking down at me with a questioning expression.

"I just wanted to say I'm sorry you're struggling, but if there's anything I can do, say the word."

His wide smile made his teeth stand out against his dark beard. "You offering to wear me out before bed to make sure I get some rest?"

I laughed out loud. "Not sure that was on the list of the type of friends we were going to be."

He nodded, then stepped closer to me, likely noticing I'd begun shivering. In all honesty, I wasn't certain it was completely due to the cold. More likely, my body was reacting to the proximity of Drew.

"Can't say I'd be against it," he whispered, tucking a strand of hair that was flying in my face behind my ear.

My breath caught at the wave of rightness that washed over me. I reminded myself that we were just attracted to each other. That didn't equate to dating. We were friends and, as we'd decided last night, friends that occasionally kissed.

Right?

Right.

With that thought in mind, I stepped closer to Drew, which made him smile. His free hand came up, tilted my chin until it was at the angle he wanted, and lowered his head to mine.

When our lips were a breath apart, he whispered, "This okay?"

"More than," was the only thing I could think to reply. I'd analyze this one later.

With that, his lips met mine. As his tongue slid across, my mouth parted, granting him access. I slid my arms around his waist, pulling him closer to me so that there was no distance between us.

Which led me to realize how much he was enjoying this.

You and me both, Drew. You and me both.

I lost myself in the kiss. He nibbled on my lower lip as I slipped my hands under his jacket, sliding them up his back. I itched to take off my gloves, touch him skin to skin.

Too soon, far too soon, Drew pulled back and rested forehead on the top of mine.

I sucked in a shuddering breath.

"So was that okay?" he asked, not bothering to hide the emotion in his voice.

"Okay doesn't really cover it. The electricity is still there," I said, fighting a grin.

"You bet your ass it is," he whispered.

Yeah, we could be these kinds of friends, right? We'd figure this out on our own. We had time.

I squeezed my arms around him again, then let them drop as we turned to head into Jake and Ivy's.

Only to see Jake, Ivy, and a woman whom I could only

assume was Steph, standing there watching us with what my dad would call shit-eating grins on their faces.

I lifted my hand to give a half-ass wave. "Hi?"

Ivy hooted with laughter. "It's nice to be on the other side of this scene."

Jake wrapped an arm around her waist, "Now Ivy, we can't give Drew too much shit. Though I remember he looked me over for love bites when the tables were turned a few months back. Need any help with that, baby brother?"

Drew shook his head and glanced my way. "Ignore them. They're idiots," he said out of the corner of his mouth.

I shook my head. This crew. They were dangerous.

We hit the steps to the back porch, and Ivy immediately pulled me in for a hug. "Promise, this group is terrific, just can be overwhelming at first."

I nodded.

Steph was hugging Drew and sharing her thanks for watching the girls.

"Yeah, Peanut said she had a blast and even ate something green," Jake said with a grin.

"We had some trees for snack," Drew said with a shrug.

I laughed, remembering our broccoli and ranch conversation yesterday. Addie had wanted nothing to do with it until her cousins showed her that ranch was like snow on the treetops and told her that their mom said the more trees with snow you ate, the more snow would fall.

Addie was all in with that idea.

"Hey." Steph came to stand in front of me. "I'm Steph. If I need to have a chat with this one, you just let me know. I've been working to make them better humans for their entire lives."

I reached out and shook her hand. "In that case, I think you've done a good job."

"Oh, Kate, don't give this one an inflated ego," Jake cautioned.

"That's you," Drew said, looking at Jake and ducking to avoid a slap to the back of his head. "I'm a self-aware human, fully acknowledging that I'm a work in progress."

Steph gave him a look of surprise. "That was very evolved, baby bro. Where did that insight come from?"

Drew shrugged. "Jess, my therapist. Mom and Dad inside?" Looking at me, he said, "Let's head in. Mom gives good brunch. It's not to be missed." He tugged my hand, leading me toward the house, but I couldn't miss the surprised expressions that flew between Steph and Jake.

Hmm. This man. He kept me wanting to know more.

Work in progress indeed.

Chapter 11

Future Plans

Drew

We stepped into the kitchen and right into some serious déjà vu. Was it only three months ago that we had the first Spencer family brunch with Ivy and Addie? Then, as was still true now, Mom and Dad stood at the stove, debating pancakes.

"Plain is the way to go," Mom was saying to him. I noted her hands placed on her hips. Over twenty years of marriage and apparently Dad liked to play things a close to the flame.

"Now Margot, you know Addie will want chocolate chips. And Emily loves blueberry. Jennie needs whipped cream. I'm just looking out for my girls," Dad said with a sheepish expression, though he seemed committed to holding strong.

I thought about bringing up the fact that when we were kids, we were lucky if we got Bisquick pancakes, plain, and were damn glad for it. But a glance at the two of them kept my mouth closed.

I wanted pancakes too, after all.

As the youngest, I'd learned a hell of a lot just by watching. What I was observing right now was that Margot was not in a mood to be trifled with. She was in the I-will-make-this-perfect mode of her brunch preparations, and I would not be playing with her today. No way, no how.

"Morning, Mom, Dad," I called to get this train back on track.

Mom turned, and her eyes skipped over me to catch sight of the girls hovering near the donut platter, waiting for permission.

"Good morning, my beautiful girls! Could I get a kiss before you are sugary and sticky?"

All three of the little hellions cheered different versions of *Nana* and *Pop* or, in Addie's case, *Pop-Pop* as they rushed my parents and hugged each in turn before racing back to the donut platter, hands at the ready.

Dad laughed and called out, "One each. No more until after brunch."

Fingers flew as they all picked their favorites and then, donuts held high, raced to the den to watch cartoons.

Mom pulled an apron that I was one hundred percent certain was hers from home over her head and folded it as she moved toward Kate and me. Laying it on the counter, she leaned up to kiss my cheek.

"Hello, my youngest. Have any tickle fights today?"

I kissed her back and shook my head at her. "Behave, Margot."

She gave me a smirk I knew I'd inherited from her. "I always behave." Turning to Kate, her smile widened as she held her arms open for a hug. "Welcome, Kate. We're so glad you're here."

Kate dropped my hand and stepped into her arms, squeezing her back. I watched as she closed her eyes and leaned into it, which made me realize I didn't know anything about Kate's family. I wondered if she was close to them and mentally reminded myself to ask her later.

Moving back after their hug, Mom held on to Kate's shoulders and looked her over. "Well, aren't you adorable when you don't have this big lug on top of you? Now let's lose your coat and get you a drink. Mimosa? Tea? La Croix?"

Nice, Mom.

Kate shrugged out of her down jacket, which I quickly grabbed from her to hang on the hooks by the door with my own. However, I had to pause as I worked to hold back a groan at my first sight of today's figure-skimming leggings and tee. I mean, yay?

"La Croix would be great, thanks, Mrs. Spencer."

"Margot, dear."

Kate glanced my way, then quickly looked back to Mom. "Sorry, I mean Margot."

Mom hooked her arm through Kate's and guided her around the island and toward the fridge. I could hear her saying, "Now we didn't have a chance to get to know each other last night. Tell me about yourself. Drew says you teach yoga? I've always wanted to try it…"

As I dropped the coats off, Bookstore and Jake slid up on either side of me.

Ivy said, "Maybe you can take your mom to power yoga. Somehow I feel certain she would dominate."

"Without a doubt," Steph said, joining our group. "Margot is made to rule the world."

Couldn't deny that. "Yep," I said. "One brunch at a time."

I glanced over at Kate standing with my mom at the refrigerator and caught her glancing back to me. I watched to see if she'd have a "rescue me" look, but instead, she broke into a wide smile. Yeah, the rightness of her with our crew was something I felt deep in my soul.

"Uh-oh," Steph whispered. "Think little bro here has finally fallen."

I stepped away from the group, middle finger raised behind my back, and headed for Kate.

Jake's laughter followed me.

An hour later, we sat around the dining room table, and while I couldn't speak for my siblings and their significant others, I was grateful I'd stuck with joggers because I was Thanksgiving-level full.

"Dad, did we really needed pancakes, egg casserole, hash brown casserole, fruit, *and* biscuits and gravy?"

"Um, you're forgetting donuts, coffee cake, and the kick-ass scones Kate brought." Theo looked down the table at me with a smirk. "However, I'm surprised at you, Drew. Did you believe for one moment that a meal with the Spencers wouldn't include a ridiculous amount of food? Are you new here? I mean, I only joined this family a little over ten years ago, and I know the drill."

Well, he had a point.

"True story." I adjusted in my seat, seeking the comfort that would only be found through digestion.

Kate leaned over to whisper in my ear. "Holy God, Drew, I'm stuffed."

I gave her a side-eye. "So you're saying it's time for some intense core workout?"

She wrinkled her nose. "Be serious. That would make me gag right now."

I found her abso-fucking-lutely adorable and fought not to lean over and press a kiss to her nose, quickly reminding myself that we had an audience.

Theo cleared his throat to catch my attention, clearly deciding to help me out. "Drew, have any thoughts on your next steps now that you've moved to Highland?"

Scratch the thought that he wanted to help.

Turning from Kate, I saw that I had the attention of everyone at the table, which only included the adults because the girls along with Jake and Ivy's dog, Chief, had escaped the table at least thirty minutes ago.

I shifted in my seat, feeling put on the spot. Jake was watching me like he'd intervene if necessary.

Nope. Not necessary.

I ran a hand through my hair as I felt Kate slide her hand on my thigh and squeeze it under the table. While part of me was thrilled at her touch, I found greater comfort in that she was trying to reassure me when she didn't even know the whole story behind my struggle, though I'd told her some. Guess having a weekly session with Jess for the foreseeable future was a good call. I needed to figure out how to unpack all that I was carrying.

Looking at my family around this table, I knew there was no turning back. It was here that I dropped the bomb that I was leaving the Hotshots and moving to Highland. Might as well lay a few more cards down.

I dropped my hand to squeeze Kate's, and she linked her fingers with mine. Leaving our hands intertwined together on my thigh, I took strength from her.

"Honestly, I have no idea." Deep breath. "As you all know, once I joined the Hotshots, I thought that was my path. Loved it, loved my crew."

Kate squeezed again, her thumb rubbing back and forth over my joggers. Yeah, we'd need to chat more later.

"Some stuff happened late spring, early summer, that I'm not ready to go into yet. Nothing huge, but it led me to coming here. Jake and Sully have been amazing at letting me work at the Homestead, but I'm not certain that's where I see myself for good."

I took a deep cleansing breath like Kate had us work on in class, and it helped to slow my heartbeat back into a more normal rate.

I was shocked as shit that no one had interrupted yet. That likely spoke to how concerned they were for me.

Clearing my throat, I caught eyes with Jake. "I haven't said it enough, but thanks."

Emotion was clear in his voice. "No need."

With a nod to him, I continued. "So I'm thinking about what the future looks like next. I talked to Max the other day at the brewery. He mentioned I should talk to his boss, Logan Traub. I texted him this morning before heading over here, and we're going to talk next week."

My dad was on my left, and I watched as he slowly set his silverware down, laying his napkin on the table in almost a methodical way, and then slid his chair back to face me. "Drew, you know your mom and I are proud of you, whatever you do. I think I speak for your whole family in saying that we've been worried because you're not quite yourself, not because we feel like you need to measure up to some job or standard that you've created for yourself."

"Dad, I—"

"Hold on, son."

I watched as he closed his eyes and did a cleansing breath that Kate would be proud of.

"Selfishly, I'm glad to know that I don't have to have a pit of fear eating away at my insides anytime I hear of a fire out west anymore. Not that we weren't damn proud of you, and I also recognize that Steph would say I have the privilege of being allowed to let that fear go—"

"Look at you, maturing at your advanced age," Steph said with a grin.

Dad shook his head.

"At any rate, I hope you're open to what your future holds and not putting some kind of bullshit parameters on what you choose in an effort to please anyone but yourself."

Mom was sitting on his other side, and she gripped his hand on the table as she gave me one of her don't-fuck-with-me stares. "We are proud of you. We were in the past, we are now, and will be in the future. You just let us know if we can help, and we'll be there, no questions asked."

I forced myself to meet their eyes, then the rest of the crew's, finally landing on Kate. Well, this was certainly a heavier conversation than I imagined when agreeing that she should join us all from brunch today. Fortunately, or shockingly, she didn't look like she wanted to run. Instead, she leaned in.

"You good?"

What could I do, but nod?

"Daddy Twoooooooo." Addie's voice and the sound of her feet reached us before the four-year-old dynamo did.

"Yeah, Peanut?" Jake looked over from his spot at the end of the table.

"We were thinking it was time to play hide-and-seek." Addie batted her long lashes. The kid could be dangerous.

Future world leader; I was calling it now.

Ivy laughed. "You were, were you?"

"I'm betting Emily and Jennie decided to go with the youngest here to use her big eyes to their advantage," Steph said, sliding back from the table.

"No, no, your dad and I can join the girls if you all want to clean up the kitchen." Mom stood from her spot, looking around the table to take the six of us in.

I briefly thought of volunteering to play instead, but knowing that would go over like a lead balloon, I instead stood and began to stack our plates.

Addie sandwiched herself between my parents, skipping off to report in to Emily and Jennie as the dining room cleared with Jake and I left rounding up any remaining silverware.

"Drew..."

I looked over, noting the serious look on his face, which usually was far from serious.

"Yeah?"

"You know we're all here for you, right? Margot does a lot of things, but one thing she doesn't do is bullshit."

I laughed. "That's the fucking truth."

Coming to stand in front of me, Jake pulled me in for a hug.

"Mean it," he said. "So damn glad you're here. And when you're ready, I want to hear more about this therapist that you ever-so-casually mentioned."

I closed my eyes as I breathed in the rightness of where I was, the way my family had my back. Always. If only I could forgive myself for how I got here. Or hell, trust myself again. That would be a start.

Thus, Jess.

"Thanks," I whispered as I opened my eyes to see Kate in the hall, looking our way, concern etched on her face.

An hour later it was just the two of us headed back to our apartments, our walk much quieter on the way home than it had been on the way there. Snow was just beginning to fall, dusting over the ground in the early afternoon winter sunlight.

The quiet neighborhood streets resembled a snow globe come to life as our footsteps echoed the stillness. Even after being here for months, I couldn't get over the difference between it and Fort Collins or, hell, my years at Boulder.

My parents and Steph's family had all headed back to the Chicago area earlier than planned to get ahead of the forecasted storm. Jake, Bookstore, and Addie were ready to hunker down with Chief and wait it out.

"You think the forecasters will be right on the snowfall totals?"

Kate's voice pulled me out of my own thoughts as I watched her drop her head back to watch it all come down.

I cleared my throat. "That's anyone's guess, really."

She paused, closing her eyes and letting the flakes land on her upturned face.

She took my breath away.

As she opened her eyes, she caught me staring. "What?"

I moved closer to her, sliding my hand around her back to bring her body flush with mine.

"You're so beautiful, Kate."

She smiled up at me. "I bet you say that to all your neighbors."

Laughing, I pressed a kiss to her forehead. "No, only the ones that help me babysit my nieces."

"Small group, then," she whispered, her eyes searching my face for who the hell knew what.

"Small group," I whispered.

Leaning down, I brushed my mouth to hers. The rightness of the feeling was not something I could describe or thought I had felt before. Even when I'd told myself I had.

"So friends who kiss?" I whispered as I slid across her lips again.

"Absolutely." Her hands made their way to my hips and pulled me to her even tighter.

Yesssss.

I nibbled at her lower lip, which only served to make her moan. Damn, I wanted to hear that sound when I was buried in her, not blocks from our apartments standing in the middle of ever-increasing snowfall.

"You're killing me, Kate," I said against her mouth.

"Is it a good death?" She asked, cocking an eyebrow at me. "I think you just need to kiss me some more, Drew."

Never say I couldn't follow orders. Done and done.

I lowered my mouth once again, sliding my tongue along the seam of her lips, then inside. God. I felt like I could drown in her.

As I raked a hand up to run through her hair, we were rudely interrupted by the honk of a horn. My arms tightened around Kate, holding her where she was while I lifted my head to see which Highland Falls native I needed to kill.

I was met with the sight of Cole Sullivan's ugly mug leaning out of his window with a demonic grin. Naturally.

I noted that neither Maggie, nor their daughter Ellen, was in the car. Though Maggie wouldn't have been the voice of reason in this situation, so maybe that was for the best.

"Well, hello, Drew. Fancy seeing you here. Kate, do you need a ride home? Seems our young man here has detained you." Sully winked aggressively in a way that indicated I would be hearing about this for some time to come. I wouldn't be shocked if he texted Jake before we even make it the few blocks we had left.

Kate laughed at the two of us. "Thanks, Sully, but Drew is taking good care of me. We're headed back to our apartments now."

Sully nodded slowly, mulling over what she said. "Hmm. That's right. I forgot that Drew is renting one of the places from Ivy. Interesting... very interesting."

"You can go," I said, shooing him away like a gnat.

He shook his head at us, then his voice became more serious. "You kids have fun then. Stay safe. Snow should be picking up in the next half hour and continuing overnight and into the day tomorrow. We're closing the brewery to keep everyone safe, so you can't have dinner there tonight, Drew. Maybe Kate can take pity on her neighbor who doesn't cook."

"Screw off, Sullivan. I finally hit the grocery store."

"Aw, our boy is growing up. I'll alert the presses." With a wave, he took off, heading for home.

I glanced down at Kate and she tightened her grip around me as she gave me a mischievous look. "That little conversation doesn't seem to have helped matters here." She pushed her pelvis against my erection.

With a moan, I dropped my head to rest on hers. "It will go away if we ignore it for a minute."

"Maybe I don't want it to go away. I mean, it seems we're going to have the next twenty-four hours to hang out together. Nic left to get up to Chicago to visit friends this morning, so it's just you and me upstairs. We could make the best of it?"

Yep. Any chance of getting this hard-on to die down disappeared in a flash.

"Kate, I like the way you think," I whispered with a kiss on her head. Grabbing her hand, I began to speed walk toward home.

Chapter 12

Baby, Just Let Go

Kate

My brain was a traffic light that kept switching from red to green, only to go back to red. We walked up the steps to our apartments, and the devil told me to jump Drew's body the moment we walked in the door, only to have the angel admonish me that it hadn't been that long since Alex and I should take things slow.

What in the world was a girl to do?

Realistically, it had been plenty of time since Alex and I had broken up. I wasn't in romantic love with him any longer, though I was still somewhat shaken in my confidence in myself. Point to the side of the angel.

However, I was an adult, as was Drew. Sex was perfectly acceptable between consenting adults who were attracted to each other, which we clearly were.

Point for the devil.

And yet this was a small town. We were friends. Would it be awkward if we crossed that line but didn't advance to a romantic relationship?

Did I want a romantic relationship?

Did he?

Did I deserve one when I'd somehow failed at the last one without even realizing it?

Hell.

"Earth to Kate," Drew said.

I refocused to realize we were standing on the landing between our two apartments. I looked from him to my door to his back to him.

The angel and devil were still in a tie. Now what did I do?

He took a step toward me and brushed a stray hair behind my ear. I felt goose bumps break out down my arms at the gesture. What on earth was happening to me?

"Kate, I know it got a little heavy back there on the street. I'm not expecting anything, so don't feel pressured."

My eyes welled with tears because of course they did. I was a hormonal mess. Who knew I had a type, and that type was guys who actually gave a damn about what women thought? Score. Then again, Alex and I weren't together, so no score?

Scratch that. Friends, Drew and I were friends. And sometimes more. But you were honest with friends, right?

I hesitated and, looked up at him, decided to go for it.

"Drew, what if I told you I wasn't sure what I wanted right now?"

He gave me a small smile that, as much as it killed me, looked a little sad. Damn. He pressed a kiss to my temple and then put a finger under my chin and tipped it up to him. "I'd say that's our answer right there. Slow down."

"But not for good," I said. The feelings of alarm that went through my body were my answer on how I felt about that.

He chuckled. "Sounds good to me. Do you want to be alone tonight?"

I thought about that. Did I? Not really. After being surrounded by the Spencers all day, my quiet apartment sounded like its own type of hell. It would be a flashing sign in my face of how alone I was in the world right now. Nope. Pass.

"Um, no? I don't think so."

"Want to come to my place or want me to come to yours?"

I loved my place, but after the day before at Drew's with his nieces, his place felt more like a home, cozier in a way. "How about yours? Do you want me to bring anything?"

"Nah, I'm stocked up now unless there's anything special you want." He stepped back, pulling out his keys.

I wanted to tug him back to me. Instead, I worked to regain control of my racing heart. "Do you care if I change into something more comfortable?"

He looked over his shoulder and raised an eyebrow at me, glancing down at my outfit. "More comfortable than leggings and a T-shirt?"

My cheeks heated. "I mean, I was going to grab some pajamas. I know it's still early, but I love snow days. As a kid, I'd go outside to play in the snow, but then come home and put on my pj's for the rest of the day, be lazy on the couch, have hot chocolate, read a book. Lounge. Part of me still loves that idea."

Drew nodded. "Sounds pretty good. However, just a warning, if the pajamas you're breaking out is that pair you were in on the day I moved in, not sure I can keep us on the 'taking it slow' path."

I thought back to that day. Yeah, a jumpsuit unbuttoned with a bralette beneath. That might have been a bit much.

Tingles rushed over me as I remembered Drew's heated glance that day, which, to be honest, was not a whole lot different than the one he was giving me now.

Yum.

I shooed the devil down.

I held up my hands. "Promise they will cover more skin."

He shook his head with a wry grin. "That should be a good thing, right?"

I laughed.

He gave me a chin lift, nodding toward my place. "I'll leave the door open. Come over when you're ready."

Getting myself in my apartment was a mental game of willpower. I felt Drew waiting just behind me like the gentleman he was. I was tempted to turn around and say fuck it. Instead, I gave an awkward wave because I didn't even know what to do with myself anymore and then rushed to shut myself inside, leaning back against the door in a flash.

His laughter followed me.

"I can hear you," I said. Yep. I'd put money on my neck and face being flame red right now. Super.

"Stop being adorable then," he replied.

I heard him shut his door, so I worked to figure out my next steps. I mean, he said I didn't need to bring anything, but I felt weird going over empty-handed.

No, pajamas first, then figure out what I had on hand.

In a matter of twenty minutes, I was back at Drew's door. Before going in, I glanced down once more, reassuring myself that this worked. Not as revealing as the jumpsuit, but far from conservative. I had on wide-legged pajama pants with a heart design on them. My bralette was red to match, though Drew wouldn't be seeing that, or at least not all of it.

He won't, I told the devil on my shoulder.

I had a button-down pajama top on over that had a deep V-neck in the front that necessitated the bralette.

I'd also grabbed some goat cheese, honey, salami, and crackers. I figured we could snack for a while this afternoon. Maybe watch a movie?

The sound of a guitar pulled me out of my plans, reminding me that Addie had said Drew played. I stood, frozen. I loved music, but the amount of talent I had for playing any type of instrument was zilch, zero, nada. I was in awe of anyone who was able to.

Drew sure as hell could.

I stood, listening, trying to make out what song it could possibly be, and then, holy hell, the man began to sing.

And. I. Melted.

The song was one I recognized off Nathaniel Rateliff's solo album a few years back, *And It's Still Alright*. I loved his band, so I'd gotten it. I listened for a few lines. Drew's voice was filled with emotion.

I felt like I was intruding. He was clearly working through something. But he knew I was coming over and said he'd leave the door open, so would he be okay with me coming in?

As he sang about times being hard, a deep need to make him know that he wasn't alone came over me and I found myself entering his place without even realizing I'd done so.

Walking in, I saw his head over the back of his couch. He was facing the windows. Through them I could see the elevators for Highland Falls Grain Company awash in snowflakes that were continuing to fall, though at a faster pace than when we were walking home.

I dropped my appetizers on the kitchen table and noted Drew's cell phone lighting up with what looked like a string of texts. I picked it up and moved around the couch to find a spot in the corner and curled up there facing him.

Drew glanced over with a nod, but didn't stop playing. His joggers-clad legs were stretched out to his coffee table, guitar held against him, as he watched the snow fall. It seemed he was working on one line over and over, about praying for wings and the need to let go.

As I sat, surrounded by the sounds from the guitar and Drew's voice, the snow falling outside the large windows, I felt a deep sense of tranquility. That seemed odd. Drew's voice had betrayed his emotions, even from the hall. I'd felt that urge to come in, to be with him. I'd felt worried, anxious. But once I actually saw him? Nothing but peace.

I wasn't sure what to do with that. It was like he settled me, and that wasn't an experience I'd had before.

Even with Alex, the devil on my shoulder noted.

Hush.

His phone in my hand vibrated again, reminding me I still had it. I slid it onto the couch cushion in his direction. Seeing my movement, he stopped singing to tilt his head, asking a question without a word.

"Your phone was lighting up on your table. Wasn't sure if the texts were important."

Nodding, he moved his guitar to the unused part of the sectional and grabbed his phone, scrolling through texts, shaking his head.

"You're good," I said, stating the obvious as I nodded toward his guitar.

He spoke without looking up. "I just like to fuck around with it. Relaxes me. Haven't played much since moving here, just for Addie really." He then laughed out loud and looked up at me with a wide grin. "Sully doesn't waste any time."

He held out his phone, and I took it from him, looking down at a photo of the two of us locked in what even I could admit was a hot embrace.

"Well..." I cleared my throat, a touch of embarrassment welling up while another feeling I recognized as lust went to war with it. I told my devil to shut it as I asked what I felt was a pertinent question. "Who was this sent to?"

Drew moved to take his phone back. "I'm sorry; that's insensitive of me. I'll tell him to delete it and not share with anyone else." He gestured to the phone. "This is my siblings' thread. Well, plus Ivy. Sully must have sent it to Jake. I'll text him now."

"No, no." I grabbed his phone, bringing it back to me. "I mean, look at us. We're hot."

Drew's laugh was loud and strong. "Fuck yeah we are."

"I was just trying to think of anyone I needed to give a heads-up. I mean, if he posted it on the town's gossip boards or shared with Miss Lou..." My voice trailed off.

"Jesus, no. We don't need Lou to be in the know," he said in reference to the town matriarch and resident gossip. "As far as I know, he shared it with Jake. I'm sure Max will see it too, but only so they can all give me shit the next time we're together. But I'm happy to tell him to stand down."

"No need. I'm not embarrassed. Thought maybe we should discuss what we're telling people."

"Telling people? Like why our lips are locked together here?"

"Yeah." I nodded as I put the phone down and moved toward Drew, sliding one leg across his lap so I could straddle him. His hands quickly made their way to my hips.

"Well, we can tell people we are neighbors who are friendly."

I laughed, running a hand through his hair. "True, we are friendly."

"And we are neighbors."

"That we are."

He cleared his throat. "Well, we haven't talked about this, really, but do you think we might be neighbors who kiss *and* date?"

I smiled down at him and pressed a kiss to his nose. "Does that make our first date today's brunch with your family?"

He laughed. "Well, our first meal together was actually at your place."

I tilted my head, considering that. "That was just friends sharing dinner."

"I wanted to devour you, so my intentions were far more than friendly."

"If that's our barometer, then ditto." I smiled at his surprised expression.

Drew looked down at our cores pressed together, then looked me up and down. "Loving the pj's, though I still want to tear them off. This V-neck is killing me."

I gave what I hoped was an innocent look. "Be grateful that it's not summer. This is the most conservative pair of pajamas I own. The warmer it gets, the less material I wear to bed."

He groaned. "Don't tell me that, Kate."

I laughed and continued to run my fingers through his hair while my other hand settled on his chest. I couldn't help but note just how defined said chest was.

"Um, Kate, would this be a good time to mention that this doesn't seem to be taking things slow?"

I leaned forward and pressed a quick kiss to his lips, his beard rough on my cheeks, enjoying the fact that his voice was lighter and filled with laughter compared to what I heard when coming in here.

"Slow doesn't mean standing still, Drew. We've got lots of wiggle room here."

He laughed and tugged me closer. "We do, do we?"

I nodded.

"Good to know." His voice was rumbly as his lips met mine.

Chapter 13

Old Ghosts

Drew

Honestly, if this weekend was any indication of what it would be like to be with Kate, sign me the hell up. She was chill with my nieces, handled Margot like a rock star. Hell, the whole clan, really. She wasn't fazed by my siblings and their desire to throw bullshit around and even tossed some back in their direction. And she liked old movies.

Seriously. Dreamworthy material here.

We'd taken a breather after getting cozy on the couch and watched several eighties movies back-to-back. We had a similar taste in movies but were both open to checking out ones we hadn't seen. Seems we both had parents who'd educated us in our teens with movies they'd loved. Movie education nights, my dad called it. We'd made a deal—I'd pick a favorite, and then she would. She watched Schwarzenegger's *Commando* when it was my pick, putting up with my need to text Jake at certain scenes, sharing one line and having him reply back with his own commentary.

A classic. Well, according to the males in our house.

Steph vetoed it every time it was suggested, and Mom just shook her head.

Kate took a break before our next viewing pleasure and had whipped up a batch of protein balls drizzled with chocolate. I'd turned up my nose at them, thinking they'd taste like cardboard, but had changed my tune with one bite. They were unreal.

Her cheeks had flushed as she shared that she and Kristine were trying to increase visibility of their studio by joining the Main Street's chocolate event coming up. Her vulnerability and honesty was something I picked up on and liked, a whole damn lot.

Then she'd picked *The Sure Thing* with John Cusack. I hadn't seen that one before but was actually into it and wanted to fill all my days with Kate, my couch, and a movie or two.

Now the sun had set hours ago. We'd eaten our fill of chicken chili with cornbread plus the awesome shit she'd brought over. Cookies and protein balls had been decimated, and we'd debated playing a card game before deciding that was far too much effort and popped in a final movie, *Ferris Bueller's Day Off.*

Which was right when she'd fallen asleep. Out like a light.

I watched her, which sounded far creepier than it was, I hoped.

Her feet were at my hip as she stretched out on one piece of the sectional, I was on the other side. Her pajama top had dipped down, exposing that bra-like thing she wore with it, which threatened to drive me to madness. I could see the lace at the top, and a large part of me wanted to see the rest.

It was like I was a hormone-crazy teen.

My phone vibrated with a text. I glanced down, expecting to see more shit from my siblings or Max and Sully.

It wasn't them. James was apparently replying to my text from a few days ago.

Murph: *Hate to hear that. You know I'm here. Call anytime.*

My anxiety immediately kicked into gear, the familiar dance I'd gotten all too used to over the past seven months. I thought of Jess and our session we had last week. We'd talked a lot about mindfulness but also facing the things I was running from. James was certainly in that category.

Through no fault of his own, more a fear of learning what he and the crew really thought of me.

I glanced at the screen. Ferris was in the restaurant, posing as Abe Froman. I turned the TV off and picked up the phone.

Opening the text, I tapped on his contact info and called.

As the phone began to ring, I gently picked up Kate's feet, placing them on my lap. Mindlessly, I ran my thumb back and forth, letting the texture of her cozy socks soothe me as I waited.

"You've got to be shitting me."

Murph's voice came in loud and clear. I could close my eyes and envision him kicking back on this sectional with me instead of being separated by almost a thousand miles. James had been my closest friend out west. Hearing his voice put me on edge while bringing me comfort at the same time.

I continued to stroke Kate's foot. "Not shitting you at all, Murph. You telling me you missed me?" I worked to make my tone light, like we could just pick back up and ignore the awkwardness of my ghosting him for months.

"Like I could miss your sorry ass. Especially after you just up and leave, going radio silent on us all. What the fuck, man? She wasn't worth that."

My hand spasmed around Kate's foot. I looked her way, worried I would have woken her, but luckily, she was still out.

So we were going there. I could do this. I really could.

Fuck.

I wondered if Jess ever did extra sessions to help you talk through hard things? A quick FaceTime? I mean, that would be a great service. Maybe I'd suggest it to her. She could join Murph and me, helping me wade through the crap I'd built up around us.

Fucking walls.

Instead, I continued a conversation I didn't want to have the only way I could. Avoidance. "Don't want to talk about her, Murph. And you know that isn't the only reason I left."

I could sense him shaking his head at me, even though I couldn't see it.

His voice held a tinge of annoyance. "Don't bullshit a bullshitter. She was part of it. And you need to forgive yourself for her, for all of it, Spencer. No one here holds any bad feelings toward you. Well, except you, you dumbass."

I focused on a long exhale. Before yoga with Kate, or my session with Jess, I hadn't realized that paying attention to your breath was a way to tame anxiety. Well, Kate didn't know that was what it was doing for me, but Jess had given me some tips. And hell if it wasn't helping right now.

As was the weight of Kate's foot in my lap. How weird. But not to question what worked and what didn't, I continued to rub my thumb back and forth on her foot.

"You there, man?" James's voice pulled me back from my thoughts.

I cleared my throat. "Yeah. Not sure what to say."

"That's why you should have stuck around so we could have this out back at the start of summer. A whole lot easier to do in person."

"Easier to leave than take a fist to the face."

He laughed. "Wasn't going to come to that and you damn well know it. Too much history between us. Add that as another reason you shouldn't have run."

I shook my head. "Didn't run, man. Gave my notice and everything."

James was quiet for several beats. I glanced at the phone to see if the call was still connected.

Just as I was ready to say something, he replied. "Felt like it."

My gut clenched. No matter what James said, I hadn't run. But I sure as hell hadn't faced the consequences of my actions, which made me feel like a coward.

I ignored the way my gut was clenching. "Does it help to tell you I'm sorry?" Kate's foot twitched in my lap, but a glance in her direction found her still sleeping away.

"I don't want to hear any more apologies from you." Murph's voice was deeper, which told me his emotions were high and he was likely at least a beer or two into the night.

"Well, they're coming your way, so you'll need to suck it up."

He laughed. "Same old Spence." He paused, then continued, "The guys are coming back in a minute; we're playing cards tonight, and they went out to get some food. Talk more soon?"

The relief of not having to delve too deeply in shit was extreme.

"Yeah, soon."

"We all fucking miss you. Hope your family is treating you right."

"My siblings are a pain in my ass."

"Excellent. All is right with the world then. Drew, I'm not kidding. Let's talk again soon, not five months from now."

"On it."

The silence hit me as soon as he hung up.

A vibration from my phone had me wondering if James was back.

Nope. It was the ever annoying, ever supportive, Spencer siblings group message.

And Bookstore, can't forget her. She might be my favorite of the bunch.

Jake: *So did Kate decide we were all too much? I mean, I'm awesome, but you all...*

Steph: *Jesus. We got home okay, in case you all were concerned.*

Jake: *I had Theo text us when you all got home. Jump to conclusions much?*

Steph: *Ivy, do something about him.*

Jake: *She can't help you now, she's doing bath time with Addie.*

Me: *You're missing out on bath time? I thought that was your thing?*

Steph: *Ha! You haven't told him?*

Jake: *...*

Oh, this should be good. I waited. Three dots, then nothing, then three dots, then nothing. Knowing Jake, he was writing, erasing, et cetera.

Jake: *Ivy decided I needed a break from bath time.*

Steph was ready for his bullshit.

Steph: *Because you got so much water over the bathroom that it dripped through the ceiling into the dining room below. You are a grown-ass child, I hope you know.*

Jake: *Hey, it's not my fault that it's so cool when you get waves rolling back and forth in the tub. Addie was a submarine, it had to be acted out.*

My stomach ached from trying to repress my laughter so I didn't wake Kate. My big brother really hadn't grown up. I could recall sitting in the tub with him when we were little. The two of us would rock back and forth in unison to see how high we could get our waves without having them spill over. We also got relegated to showers for a month as a result. Clearly, some lessons didn't take.

Jake: *Back to my original reason for texting. Was Kate cool with the crew?*

Me: *You asking me if we scared her off?*

Steph: *I mean, you two might have, but Ivy and I are an excellent addition to any friend group. I think we're the selling points for you, really.*

I shook my head at these two fools. While they were maddening, they were also my foundation. I'd never tell them, but the fact that I knew they were there, that I could count on them, was everything to me.

Moisture swelled in my eyes that I was damn glad they weren't here to see.

Me: *I love you two idiots. And no, you haven't scared Kate off. She's currently crashed on my couch after a three-movie marathon.*

Jake: *Were you watching* Commando *with her when you were messaging earlier? If so, whoa... it's like she just passed a test.*

Jake: *And I love you too, but you're the idiot if your woman is at your place and you're texting us.*

Me: *What am I supposed to do? She's asleep. Maybe I should take her back to her place.*

Steph: *Jesus. No. See if she wants to spend the night. I talked to Kate today. She seems like she's a little lonely, and being at her place alone after a day with a loud family might be hard. Besides, a guy carrying you to his bed is hot ten out of ten times.*

Steph: *And I love you too.*

Jake: *With that, I'm off to see if I can carry Ivy to bed. Thanks for the ideas, Steph. I'll let you know how that turns out. *Winking Emoji**

Steph: **Barfing Emoji**

I laughed and went to set my phone down when I saw I had another text notification. This one was from James. He must have sent it shortly after we hung up.

Murph: *The guys all say hello and they want to see your ugly face sooner, not later. Seriously, man. I know we're not in the same town or, hell, on the same crew anymore but want to plan something. See you soon.*

God, I felt that in my gut. How do you tell the guy that treated you like a brother that you were sorry you fucked his girlfriend or that you almost got your crew killed? Yeah, there wasn't really a card that laid old ghosts to bed.

I mentally penciled in a message to Jess. Maybe we could role-play this shit.

As I put my phone down, Kate moved on the couch as her eyelids fluttered open.

"Well hey, there, Sleeping Beauty."

She looked from me to the dark TV screen.

"I turned it off so we could watch it later." I explained.

"Now?" Her voice was thick with sleep.

"It's late." I realized I was still rubbing her feet and stilled my hand as I decided to go for it. "Feel like having a sleepover?"

Kate's eyes widened as she licked her lips. And yeah, my cock woke up at that; however, I worked to be cool, remembering what Steph said about Kate being lonely.

"Nothing needs to happen. I just thought it might be nice not to be alone tonight."

Kate blinked and then blinked again. I noted that it looked like her eyes were watery. Damn, Steph was likely right and I hadn't noticed.

Well, I knew now.

Kate slowly nodded.

"Words, princess. Do you want to stay with me tonight?" I gave her foot a squeeze.

Her tongue darted out as she began to nod, then shook her head instead. I started to worry, but then she finally found her voice.

"Sorry, I mean, yeah, I think I'd like that."

That was all I needed to hear. With that, I stood and scooped her up, remembering Steph's note.

"Drew, I can walk," she said with a gasp.

"I know you can, Sleeping Beauty, but this works too." I pressed a kiss to her forehead and moved to my bedroom.

My bed, one of the few pieces of furniture I owned, was a California King because I was not a small man. Anything beyond that and my feet would hang off the end, which sucked. However, tonight I wished it was smaller because I wouldn't mind Kate right up against me all night long.

Moving next to the bed, I lowered her to it, tossing back the green comforter as I did.

"Need anything?" I asked as she settled into what I usually thought of as my spot.

She looked up at me with wide eyes, like she might have thought she was still dreaming. Quite frankly, seeing her reclined on my pillow, I felt the same way.

"Water?"

"You got it. You know where the bathroom is if you need it." I hesitated, then decided fuck it. I leaned down and lightly pressed my lips to hers. She let out a puff of air as she relaxed back into the pillow.

Pulling back, I watched her eyes flutter, like she might go straight to sleep again. I turned to go get her the water as requested and adjusted myself as I did.

Damn, this night of sleep might not be relaxing, at least for me.

Chapter 14

Restless Nights

Kate
I blinked up at a dark room that felt like my own but didn't at the same time. A weight across my stomach reminded me that I wasn't alone, and I sure wasn't home.

Drew.

Thinking back through my sluggish memories, I vaguely recalled him carrying me in here from his couch, heading out to get me water, and then nothing. I was out. My sleep had been off for the past few weeks. No real reason other than the normal stresses of starting a newish business, just a brain that struggled to be quiet, to let me rest. That hadn't been an issue tonight. Sitting on the couch with Drew, I had felt relaxed, at home. It was a dangerous feeling.

Somewhere early in our third movie, I gave up the fight against eyelids that didn't want to stay open only to wake to Drew asking if I wanted to have a sleepover. That darn devil on my shoulder wanted me to shout yes from the rooftops, but fortunately it took me a while to click my mouth into gear. Likely because I was dreaming of his body next to mine, or fantasizing. I mean, who wouldn't?

And then he carried me to bed like something out of a romance book. White flag, I was done. When he laid me on his bed, part of me wanted to stay awake, see where that took us. A larger part of me got nervous. That, combined with my low levels of alertness and his ridiculously comfortable bedding, made the call that sleep was the way to go. I could figure out what was next for us in the morning.

Which brought me to now. I had no idea what time it was, but it was clearly still dark outside, and I felt like I hadn't been asleep that long. I wasn't the type of person who woke up wide awake in the middle of the night, so I had no idea what caused this tonight. Maybe sleeping in an unfamiliar place?

The arm slung around my waist tightened, and I snuggled back into Drew. It felt like it had been so long since I'd been with Alex, though it was only months.

I missed sleeping next to someone. I mean, I missed sex, sure, but more than that, I missed the feeling of being with someone, being part of something. My bed felt so vast, so empty, so cold on my own. Drew felt like a wall of warmth that I was cocooned in. He felt safe.

His arm twitched again. I'd begun to wonder if he was an active sleeper when I heard him murmuring. I turned slowly in his arms to look at him in the low light from the moon.

Good Lord, the man was gorgeous. Let's be honest here. It's not like I hadn't noticed his looks when he walked into the yoga studio almost three weeks ago. However, in that time, I'd gotten to know him as a person. It only made him more attractive.

His brown hair looked like it would lighten in the

summer when he was outside. Longer on top, he often had it styled so that it spiked up a little. His beard had me itching to run my fingers through it. Alex had facial scruff, a closely cut beard. Drew looked like he could have hung out with a Viking. I wondered if this was a typical length for him. It wasn't mountain man long, just a little past his chin.

It drove me crazy when we kissed earlier. I wanted more, but I also wanted to be smart and protect my heart. It seemed like a guy who was kind, had a great family, was liked by his friends, and could play the guitar while singing some of my favorite songs just might be a recipe for heart-break down the road.

I wasn't sure if I was ready for that. At the same time, I really wanted to roll on top of him and wake him from his dream just to see where that would lead. Watching him sleep, I revamped that idea. Drew's face was tense, and his arm twitched around me again.

Was he having a bad dream? He'd mentioned on the way to brunch that he occasionally struggled with sleep. I'd just thought he was talking about insomnia; this seemed bigger.

I placed a hand on the side of his face, stroking down to his neck, then to his shoulder. "Drew, Drew." Leaning forward, I placed a light kiss on his cheek.

He began mumbling, nothing that I could make out, but it sounded like moans—and not the happy kind I'd like to hear coming from him. His arm tightened around me again while his body jerked.

"Drew." My voice was louder. "Drew. Wake up."

"Wha—?" He was moving around, but his eyes popped open, scanning the room and landing on me. "Kate?"

His heart felt like it was hammering in his chest, his breathing shallow. I let my hand land above his heart and started doing some deep ujjayi breaths in and out like we'd done in class, hoping he'd join me.

Slowly, he did, matching my inhalations and exhalations. I noted that his heart rate was still elevated, though slowly lowering, and his shirt was damp, as if he'd been exercising. What was going on?

We sat there for several minutes in the moonlight, staring into each other's eyes, the sound of our breath swirling around, as I wondered how on earth to begin this conversation.

Drew broke the silence with a voice much raspier than I was used to from him. "I've been struggling with anxiety for a while." He looked away like he couldn't meet my eyes. "Sorry." His voice wasn't more than a whisper.

My hand came up to his bearded chin, turning his face so I could meet his eyes. "Why in the world would you apologize for that?"

His eyes looked into mine with such emotion I caught my breath. Then he closed his, as if it was too hard, too open.

"It isn't something I've talked much about."

I kept the pressure of my hand to his chest while leaning forward to brush my lips against his. I wasn't sure why, I just felt deep down that he needed reassurance, but I kept it light.

As I pulled back, I scanned his face. Eyes still closed, he was clearly tense.

"Define a while."

He glanced at me. "What?"

"You've been struggling with this for a while, and you mentioned it yesterday. Want to tell me more?"

I noted that his heart rate had slowed down some, so I moved my hand to his arm, stroking it gently. Whenever I was stressed, my mom used to use a light touch, stroking my hair, my back, as I tried to wind down and go to sleep. It was one of my few good memories of childhood. I thought that might help Drew some.

"It's been going on for months. Since June."

His voice was stronger, his breathing deeper, like he was coming back to himself.

Good.

I began gently. "You said that you knew what started this, right?" We'd been hanging out for weeks, but I was under no delusion that Drew owed me anything and wasn't sure what I was asking of him.

His eyes shot to mine. Pain was evident in his expression, and I worried that I'd overstepped.

"Sorry, you don't have to answer that. I don't mean to pry," I whispered, letting my hand trail over his arm.

His tongue ran over his lower lip in a way that I wanted to meet it, but also I wanted to sit back and let him lead.

I took a deep breath, hoping he'd do the same. He did, mirroring me as I held it for a few beats, then slowly let it go.

"Yes." His voice was raspy. "I know why it started."

I put a finger to his lips. "You don't need to tell me. I truly wasn't trying to be nosy."

He captured my finger in his hand. I could feel the calluses, which—ridiculously—set off tingles through my lower region.

Hush, devil.

"You talk a lot for"—he glanced at the watch he still wore—"three in the morning."

I grinned at him in the soft light from the window.

"I know why it started, but—and I mean no disrespect at all

when I say this—but I'm not completely ready to talk about it yet. I'm sorry." He looked toward the window, seemingly lost in thought. "Tonight, though, I talked to a friend from Colorado while you were snoring on the couch. I guess that brought some stuff to the surface?" His voice was filled with questions.

I lightly slugged his arm. "One, I don't snore. Two, we already covered this. No apologies." I thought back to yesterday as we were walking into Jake and Ivy's for brunch. He'd said something about a therapist, and I dismissed it at the time as just a fact, but now I was recalling the expression on his siblings' faces of surprise.

"You said something yesterday at brunch about your therapist. Is that new?"

"Yeah." He cleared his throat. "My chief back at the Hotshots had recommended someone. Fortunately, she does telehealth since we're just a few states apart. I saw her for the first time last week."

I ran my hand through his hair and over his cheek again, noting he leaned into the touch.

"Do you mind if I ask how it was?"

"No. Her name is Jess, and she is older than my parents. It was great."

I smiled. "Even in the little light we've got going on here, I can tell you're surprised by that."

He laughed, and the reverberation lit me up inside.

"Yeah, I wasn't sure what to expect. To me, therapy might be lying on a couch and talking about your childhood. However, we just talked about how I was feeling and what I was doing so far that felt like it was working. We're going to meet weekly for a while, see if I can get a handle on this." His hand snaked out to squeeze my side, then he rested it there.

I felt enveloped in him and never wanted to leave this bed.

Instead of declaring my new residence, I snuggled up so we were touching, our legs tangling. It could be sexual, but it was more. Something I'd felt with Alex after years of being together.

And I'd only known Drew for less than twenty days. Interesting.

"Did she give you any tools for now?" I asked, wrapping my arm around him.

I felt him kiss the top of my head, and he cleared his throat. "Yep. We worked on breathing."

My smile was wide, though I buried it in his chest, inhaling his scent. "I'm a fan of breathing."

His arms squeezed around me, pulling me closer and erasing any breath that had been between us. I could feel his cock hardening but ignored that for now. Though part of me really wanted to address that.

"Yeah, I told her that I'd been attending a yoga class and the instructor was a stickler for breath work."

"It's the most important part of yoga, where all the power comes from." I replied without a lot of thought but more from a core belief.

Drew was quiet for a moment, and I wondered if he was drifting off despite a part of him that seemed very much awake.

"I am still working on the breath thing." He hesitated, then continued. "In class I can get it. When I'm just going about life and decide to practice, it's fine. But when my anxiety perks up and decides to overwhelm me, I forget."

My heart broke. He sounded, well, defeated. Nope. Not allowed. He had this; he just had to see how strong he was.

No matter what it was that he'd faced, I was certain he could get to the other side.

I peppered kisses down his neck, across the top of his chest, and into the crook of his neck on the other side. Resting there, I spoke into that kissable spot. "Drew, I've been doing this—yoga, breath work, mindfulness—for close to fifteen years. And I've been blessed not to ever have to battle anxiety while doing it. I absolutely believe that it can help you, but I also think it will take practice."

I paused as I waited to see if he'd say anything. It seemed he was just soaking it in, so I continued. "I want to reiterate I don't need to know what happened, though if you ever want to share, I'm here. But I'm glad to help you practice any of this, anytime." I thought for a minute about his dream earlier. "Can I ask, do you often wake up like you did tonight?"

He rested his chin on my head and one of his hands played with the end of my hair. "Yeah."

My chest squeezed. Yep, this was what was keeping him up at night. "What happens then?"

I felt him press another kiss to the top of my head as he took in a deep breath. "I eventually wake up. Sometimes I remember the dream, sometimes I just come awake without any idea what happened. My heart is racing, my shirt is sweaty. It's like my body is humming."

"So how do you get past it?"

Silence.

I let him tell me on his own time.

After a minute that felt like twenty, he whispered, "I don't, really."

I felt moisture seep out under my eyelids. He sounded broken, alone, not at all like the fun-loving Drew I'd come to know. I wondered if Jake and Steph knew about this, but I had a feeling they didn't, or at least not to this extent. If they did, I was pretty sure he would have been invited to stay at their places for a while. Not that they would think him incapable of dealing with his issues; they just wouldn't have wanted him to do it alone.

"I actually found your studio because of a night like this."

I worked to fight back the emotion I knew would be clouding my voice. "Really?"

Drew cleared his throat. "Yeah. When I was staying at the Airbnb, it was a great place, but small. I couldn't move like I needed to in the middle of the night, so I went running and went by the studio. A few hours later, I was in your class."

My mind went back to that first session, my misconception of the kind of guy he was, and the puddle of sweat he ended up in by the culmination of class. I wish I'd known then what he was struggling with. "Did it help?"

I felt him nod above me.

"And you've kept coming back."

I felt his laughter building in his body before he let it out. "Well, to be fair, I wasn't coming back just because it helped my anxiety."

He was trying to lighten the moment, and hell if I didn't want to give him that. "Oh really, do tell."

He tugged so that I loosened my grip and slid me up until we were at the same level, my head resting on a pillow facing him. "See, there was this girl."

"There always is."

He leaned forward, his mouth meeting mine, before sliding back. "I should note, she was the last thing I was looking for."

I thought back to that day a few weeks back, hell, even now. "Ditto."

"I guess sometimes you have to take a leap and hope for the best."

I tilted my head, looking at him. "Is that what we're doing here?"

He watched me carefully, then tipped my chin as his face came closer. With his lips just grazing mine, he whispered, "I fucking hope so."

I met his mouth and began to drown with no hope of surfacing anytime soon.

Chapter 15

Monsters

D*rew*

I sat on my sectional, strumming my guitar as lightly as possible, hoping I wouldn't wake Kate. It was early, just before seven, and the scene outside my window still resembled a snow globe. The grain elevators were barely visible. A text from Jake informed me that Addie had already been out with a ruler to measure the snowfall in their backyard with Chief, their dog. She reported eight inches thus far. Jake had made some crack about eight inches, which Steph had rightly given him hell for. However, that amount already on the ground with at least five more today and high winds meant the town was pretty much closed down.

No brewery, no yoga studio, no bookstore, no grocery store. Nothing. The street outside my place was often quiet when compared with Fort Collins or Boulder, but right now? It was a ghost town.

Kate and I were in a bubble, and I didn't hate it. Not one bit.

Still, I hadn't been able to sleep in. I woke around six

and kept thinking back to the middle of the night, to our conversation about my battle with anxiety, and how it seemed to be winning.

I wished I could say I didn't regret opening up, but part of me did. Not that I thought Kate would judge me, no. But deep down I felt less of a man, which Steph would have a damn field day with. So would Bookstore.

Fuck.

Kate and I were just exploring whatever this was. I wasn't ready for anything serious, but would she even want something temporary with someone who couldn't sleep through the damn night? I felt like damaged goods and no idea what to do with that bullshit.

I was lost in thought as I continued to play as the snow fell when I realized I wasn't alone. Looking to the hall, I saw Kate leaning against the wall, listening to me.

"Sorry." My voice was husky from the morning. "Didn't mean to wake you."

She shook her head and came fully into the room, nodding to the corner opposite me. "Mind if I sit?"

I shook my head and fought back a groan as she sank down into the couch. She'd changed out of her pajamas into greenish leggings and a long-sleeved white top that had a wide neck. As she got comfortable, it slid down her shoulder, leaving it bare.

Sure. That was going to be easy to ignore. I went back to the beginning of the song, trying to refocus on the chords, hoping they could distract me from wanting to pounce on her like some mountain lion.

"What song is that?"

Her question required me to actually consider what I'd been strumming. Sometimes I just got lost in thought and certain songs I'd worked on over the years bubbled to the surface, as had been the case numerous times this morning.

"'Monster' by Mumford & Sons." Appropriate for my mood, I guessed. Honestly, that album had been on constant repeat after this summer; it was no wonder I was drawn to it now. I looked to Kate. "Do you know it?"

She nodded as she leaned over to grab a throw from the basket below my coffee table. "Go ahead," she said as she settled back.

I played and, as often happened, memories flooded me. I played and played and played, long past the point that my fingers registered that they were done. My mountains in Colorado, the station for the Hotshots, some of our calls, the guys, James, Tiffany.

Fuck.

I felt the tears on my cheeks but hadn't been cognizant of them even starting. They pulled me out of the spiral, and I stopped playing to glance at Kate.

She breathed deeply, reminding me to do so.

We sat for a few minutes, staring at each other as I fought the urge to flee. If I was watching anyone else do this, I'd make some crack about romance. However, right now, as much as it was making me uncomfortable, Kate was my lifeline.

I took another breath, concentrating on the noise. While I hadn't wanted to get into all this with her—hell, I hadn't even got through it all with Jess—I wondered if I could share part of what was currently fucking me up. Either it would make her realize she needed to get the hell away from me, or maybe sharing would alleviate some of this weight on my chest.

I knew I had to do something.

I lowered the guitar and turned to face Kate. "Would it be okay if I held you for a moment?"

She tilted her head and looked at me, considering. Eventually, she pulled back the throw and stretched out her legs in a V. "How about I hold you?"

I paused, uncertain.

She scooted down and patted her chest. "Rest your head here. No offense, but I think you could use someone taking care of you. At least for the moment."

That sounded beyond good, and I didn't give a damn what that said about me. I slid onto Kate, my cheek to her belly, her arms and legs wrapped around me, the blanket over us both.

It was heaven.

After a few moments, I became aware of the fact that she was doing deep breathing again and I'd unconsciously matched her breath for breath, which was helping. I repeated the phrase Jess had told me to practice when I needed to get back into myself, *I am safe, I am safe, I am safe.* Slowly, I felt myself relax.

Opening my eyes, I looked out the windows in front of me. It was easier to do this without looking at Kate.

"I'm not sure if you remember, but when I first moved in you asked me if I'd been in a relationship."

Kate murmured in agreement, her hand trailing up and down my arm like she'd done last night. I decided to keep going.

"I told you I thought I was on the path to something serious once, but I'd been wrong and it had been messy."

Her hand kept moving and helped me ignore the tightness in my gut.

I am safe.

"I'd dated in high school and college but was never

really serious about anyone. While my parents' relationship is traditional, and possibly a smidge patriarchal at times, I have no doubt of their love for each other. Ditto for Steph and Theo. I've wanted that, I've always wanted that, and last year, I thought I found it. Briefly."

Her hand stopped for a moment, but then continued its up-and-down trek.

"In Fort Collins I filled in at a local brewery when they needed shifts covered if we weren't on a call. One night this blonde came and sat at the bar. We talked and talked, long after her friends had left, until the bar was closing down around us, and we weren't done. Not even close." I closed my eyes, feeling ill remembering back.

I guess I'd stopped talking for a while because Kate eventually spoke.

"You don't have to share, Drew. If you're not ready, that's fine."

I followed her with another deep breath and opened my eyes to watch the snow again. "Her name was Tiffany. I started seeing her then. My schedule was shit, it was off-season for the Hotshots, but I did trainings for them and all the off-season work to get us ready for the spring, which was just a few weeks away. Between that and the brewery, I didn't have a ton of free time, but any I did have, I found a way to see her."

The background faded as my memories brought me back. Our hikes, dinners at her place, plans I had begun to make for the future, our future. "In retrospect, the fact that we only hung out with each other or a few of her friends should have been a clue. However, I thought everything was going great. It wasn't forever, just a few months, but enough that I had us on the path that my parents had paved, that Steph had followed. I'd finally found someone to get serious with."

Kate's hand had stopped, and she was now tracing patterns on my back. Her voice was barely above a whisper. "What happened, Drew?"

Bile rose in my throat, and I worked it back down. "One night my training session up at the station was canceled. We had some new recruits, and they were so green. Our chief had revamped our weekend plans as a result, and I had an unexpectedly free night. I headed back to the brewery in Fort Collins to meet some of our crew that I'd been with for years. I thought about letting Tiffany know about the change of plans, but I hadn't spent much time with the guys, so I figured I'd catch her later."

I took in a big breath of air and let it out slowly. Kate continued to rub my back.

"I walked into the brewery, and my best friend from the Hotshots, James, called out to me about how I needed to get the next round. I remember laughing and turning toward the group, only to see Tiffany standing next to him. At first, I thought she was there to surprise me. Then I noticed James's arm around her right as he bent his head to kiss her. My emotions went wild: anger and confusion battling for top billing."

Kate's entire body tightened around me.

Sweat had broken out all over me. I worked on my breath and continued. "I kept moving toward them even though everything in me was ready to run. Some part of me felt like I was being punked, like there had to be something else going on. Coming to stand in front of them, James finally stopped kissing her. He grinned at me and said he was so glad I was there so I could finally meet the girl he'd been telling me about for months, Tami."

"Tami?" Kate growled.

"Yep, my thought exactly. I played dumb because I couldn't figure it out right away and I felt like I was going to be ill. Suffice to say, in the next few hours with some quick conversations, I put together that Tiffany was actually Tami. She'd been unhappy with the pace of the relationship with James and thought she could make him jealous by dating another firefighter. She hadn't realized, she said, that we were friends."

"Bullshit. She wouldn't have given you a fake name otherwise."

"That's what I thought."

"So what did James say when you told him?"

I continued my gaze out the window.

"Drew, you told him, didn't you?" Her voice was so gentle, and I didn't deserve that.

"Yeah. It came out that night. At first, he seemed like he didn't believe me. We went back to base, and were going to talk more after we rested." I choked on the words, not wanting to go there, knowing I wasn't ready.

Kate could read me, it seemed. "That takes us to the stuff you're not ready to talk about yet, right?"

I nodded. "I think I'm still processing it all."

I felt her move lower to kiss the top of my head.

"If you want to go, I understand."

She immediately became rigid. "What? Why would I want to go?"

I numbly watched the snowfall. How did I explain how much I hated myself for this?

Kate wiggled out from behind me to sprawl on top of me and grab my face between her hands. "Hey." She brushed her lips against mine. *"Hey."* Her tone was stronger. "I don't blame you here. Does your friend? James?"

I closed my eyes. I couldn't meet hers. "No. Not now. Well, I don't think so. I kind of ghosted him for a while."

She was silent for so long I eventually had to look back to see what she was doing. And that broke me. She was watching me, tears streaming down her face.

I brushed them from her cheeks as more raced down. "Hey, it's okay."

She shook her head. "No it isn't. I don't know what else happened before you came home, came to Highland, but you clearly still blame yourself for shit that *is not your fault*. It's a good thing we don't live near this Tiffany/Tami woman because I'd like a word with her."

I couldn't help but laugh. Tiffany had at least four inches and twenty pounds on Kate, but I think Kate could take her, especially if she was as pissed as she appeared.

I leaned up and pressed a kiss to her mouth. "Thanks."

She tilted her head as she scanned my face, her tears drying up. "For what?"

"You're the first person I've told about what happened with Tiffany. I mean, the guys that were there know, but you're the first person who wasn't there. It helps that you are on my side."

"How in the hell wouldn't I be? I mean, *you* should be on your side. You dated a woman, you wanted a future with her, and you found out not only had she been lying about who she was, dating another guy the whole time, but she was actively using you." She was fuming, and it pulled me from my normal misery on this topic, giving me some perspective I desperately needed.

"Can we sit?" I asked, too distracted by her body on top

of me to have a conversation without reacting like a teenager who couldn't control his erection.

She scrambled back into the corner and faced me, her legs folded up under her on the couch. I sat back against the couch and draped my arm against the back of it.

"Okay, I did broach some of this with Jess last week, and we're delving into it more this week. Part of my struggle right now is I do feel guilty about sleeping with—hell, even dating—my best friend's girl." I held up a hand at the onslaught that was ready to spill out of Kate. "I do know that it wasn't my fault here"—I tapped my head—"but not here." I tapped my heart. "I'm working on that."

Kate looked at me and mimed zipping her lips and throwing away the key.

I laughed and continued my confessional. "Jess says that clearly this did a number on my ability to trust—others as well as myself. I have some assignments from her, one of which was to talk to James sooner versus later, which was one of the reasons I called him yesterday." I paused, debating how much to say. Though, at this point, I was just going for it. "It was easier because you were here."

Kate curled her hands into a heart, which she held out toward me but didn't utter a peep.

I reached over and tugged her foot toward me, remembering how comforting it was to hold it yesterday while I was talking to Murph. I needed that now.

"I do want to be honest, Kate." I looked up at her and found her watching me with wide eyes. "I like you. I like the idea of being friendly neighbors and more. But I have to be upfront. I'm not sure I'm ready for anything serious. I think I have some work to do with Jess to get that to be something I can trust again. Quite frankly, I'm a mess, and I'm certainly not a good bet."

She pointed at her mouth, clearly asking to talk, so I nodded.

She tossed the blanket to the side as she crawled toward me on the couch and came to straddle me, our bellies touching. Her elbows rested on my shoulders as she put each hand flat on the sides of my face, making me lock eyes with her.

"Well, hello," I said.

She grinned. "Okay, listen up, Drew Spencer."

I bit my lips to keep from laughing. She raised an eyebrow at me, so I spoke. "Listening, Kate Ashley."

If she had reading glasses, she would have just given me a teacher look over them as she raised her eyebrows. And suddenly, that was a fantasy I didn't know I had. Interesting.

"One, I'm not a violent person, but if I ever meet this Tiffany or whatever she's calling herself, I'll take her down."

Yep, working not to laugh still. "Noted."

"Two, no way in God's green earth are you even remotely responsible for this shit show except to have been misled by your lower brain. An affliction most men suffer from at some point in their lives. I'd tell you to cut yourself a break, but I have a feeling that would be a wasted sentiment. It will take time, but I'm sure with Jess's help, you will eventually get past this and whatever other shit you're blaming yourself for in there."

God, she was hot. So hot, even while I was struggling not to press her down on the couch and get lost in her, I was also trying to soak in her words and righteous indignation.

"And three?" I asked, because let's keep this pint-sized dynamo going.

She leaned forward and kissed my forehead, tip of my nose, each cheek, and finally my lips. Pulling back, she continued. "And three, I'm not ready for something serious either." She took in my skeptical look and gave me one right back. "You're working to trust yourself after the she-bitch. Well, Alex wasn't a bitch, or bastard, in his case. He's a great guy. However, I am still dealing with trusting myself to know what's a good match, I guess. I truly thought Alex and I'd be together forever, and then I woke up one day and realized I was in love with love, but not in love with him, or not romantically. I don't know how I did that, but I think I need to stay away from anything serious while I sort that out."

I was ignoring how tense my body got when she mentioned her ex, because what in the hell was that?

"So what are you saying?" My hands found their way to her hips because I wanted to grind her against me and I was fighting that instinct with everything I had.

She tilted her head and looked at me with a playful smile.

Oh boy.

"I thought it was perfectly obvious. You don't want anything serious, and neither do I. But clearly, we're attracted to each other, *and* we live across the hall from each other. So..."

"So..."

"So I think we should have fun and see where this leads but know that we're keeping it light."

Yep. My dick just jumped. He was on board because of course he was.

I looked up at this minx whose eyes were positively twinkling.

"So you're saying we should be friends, neighbors, with benefits."

"As long as those benefits include sex."

I laughed. "Well, of course they do." I looked down to

my lap where she was straddling me and shook my head. "And you think we can keep this easy? What do we tell people? Are we dating?"

She tugged her lower lip in. "I mean, sure? But not with the plan to get super serious, just to have fun."

"And sex, to have sex."

She laughed. "Yes."

"I mean, I'm sure we're going to get each other out of our systems quickly and go back to being friends right away, right?"

She nodded very seriously. "Right."

"It's not like every romance novel I've read for Ivy's book club with this trope has failed miserably at it." I gave her a skeptical look.

"Hush, we're different."

"Sure we are."

"So are you in?" She looked uncertain, and I couldn't have that.

I huffed out a laugh of disbelief. "Fuck yeah."

"Even if we fail miserably."

I pressed a kiss to her lips to get her to stop from biting that lower lip. "Even if."

Her hands pressed to my chest, then trailed down my torso to the hem of my T-shirt. "Well, then, what are we waiting for?"

Chapter 16

All Aboard

Kate

I grabbed Drew's T-shirt. "Well, then, what are we waiting for?" Where was this brazen woman coming from? No idea, but I kind of liked her.

Tugging it over his head, I tossed it to the side like it was yesterday's trash.

"Hey, now, Sully and Jake gave me that shirt when I invested in the brewery. Be kind." Drew's eyes were dancing with laughter. I was a fan of this look for him, so much more than the sadness that had been there earlier. But I couldn't stop to think about that. Stopping would mean further thought about the woman I now wanted to harm for deceiving him. It would also mean examining my motives and if I really thought we could be friends who slept together. That worked out so well for those who tried it. Ha.

But I couldn't commit to more right now. If I even remotely let myself think of trying for a serious relationship, I'd spiral. That would require thinking of Alex. About what went wrong. About my life plan that had been seriously derailed. About ignored warning signs. About, about, about.

Nope. Not going there.

Instead, I wanted to analyze the gorgeous man in front of me, shirtless.

"It's a lovely T-shirt. I'll commend Jake and Sully on the quality the next time I see them, but is that really what you want to talk about right now?" I raised an eyebrow in his direction and shifted in his lap.

His eyes crinkled in the corners. I wanted to kiss him there, so I did. Belly flutters. Yowza.

Drew ran his hand down my back. "No, I don't think I do want to talk about that shirt."

I worked my way down to his jaw. "What do you want to talk about?" I asked between peppered kisses on his bearded chin.

"Why you are still wearing so many clothes." He squeezed my hips.

"I can remedy that," I said. I pushed back from him to stand.

"No need to go so far, Kate." He said, reaching out for me.

"You wait right there, mister," I said, enjoying the feeling of power and playfulness I had with Drew. That was new for me, and I wanted to embrace it. Standing in front of him, I wiggled back and forth as I slid my teal leggings off and tossed them to join his T-shirt.

Drew licked his lips slowly as he looked from my toes, up my legs, and caught my eyes. His gaze was positively heated and made my core pulse. "Feel free to keep going," he said.

I slowly slid the white long-sleeve over my head. I heard the catch in Drew's breath as he realized I was braless below. As it joined the ever-growing pile of clothes, I looked back to him. Standing in front of him, clothed only in a lacy scrap of underwear, I should have felt exposed, vulnerable.

Instead, I felt powerful, and it was amazing.

He crooked his finger at me, but I gave his lap a pointed look.

He looked to his lap, then back to me with a smirk visible in that beautiful beard. "What are you saying, sweetheart?"

"Just saying now you're the one wearing too many clothes."

My heart jumped as he stood up and hooked his fingers in the waistband of his gray sweatpants. In one fell swoop, they were dropped and kicked to the side, making it all the more apparent that he had been going commando this morning. My first thought was if my underwear hid the immediate rush of wetness for him.

My second thought was holy shit, he was gorgeous. I mean, he was before, but yum. Let's get this show started.

As I did an internal cheer, high-fiving the devil and angel that were now apparently on Team Drew, he took matters into his own hands by stepping up to me, somehow getting my panties down my legs and off as he tossed me in a fireman's carry over his shoulder and headed toward his bedroom.

"Um, caveman? I can walk, you know." I called from my upside-down position.

With a slap to my ass, he said, "You were taking too long."

Gush. Who the hell knew that would be hot? Even so...

I slapped the gorgeous butt right in front of my face. Two can play at this game, bud.

He stopped and tossed me onto his bed. I bounced once

and looked up to make some smartass comment to him and stopped when I saw his face. There was no other word for it, his gaze was positively devouring me. Wow.

With a tug to my foot, he moved me to the edge of the bed. His fists bracketed my hips, and he brought his face to mine. "Still on board with this plan, Kate?"

I looked up at him in disbelief. "And if I'm not?"

"Then it stops here, and we can go finish the movie from last night."

I mean, he won no awards for checking for consent, it really should be the base level of human decency. However, to have him say calmly that we could go watch a movie while dealing with a hell of an erection, yeah, a point or two in his favor.

"And if I have no desire to stop this sex train?"

His mouth came to mine while he let out a laugh. I'd never kissed anyone mid laughter before. It was nice, light.

Pulling back, he met my eyes. "Then all aboard."

"Choo-choo?" I said on a snort.

He shook his head at me. "Lie back." He lightly pushed my shoulder, and I dropped to the bed but propped myself on my elbows to look down at him.

"I haven't gotten to touch you yet." I mean, he was there, beautiful, in front of me, and I hadn't laid a hand on him yet save his delicious ass that I wouldn't mind getting a hand on again.

"Patience, beautiful." He dropped to his knees, and my pussy positively fluttered. Good grief.

"Forget everything I just said. Clearly you have good ideas." *Shut up, Kate.* Why couldn't I stop talking?

"Are you always this chatty during sex?" He lifted one of my legs and began kissing his way up my calf, past my knee, to my inner thigh. His beard was a touch abrasive and all the way drop-dead sexy.

I squeaked, rocking my hips back and forth. I could feel the flush on my face, which I bet had spread to my chest and beyond, but I continued to watch because I couldn't look away.

At the top of my inner thigh, Drew hooked that leg over his shoulder and hesitated right at my mound. With a heated glanced in my direction, he started to lower, and then turned to my other leg.

Ahhhhhh. Dead. I was dead.

I thought about protesting, but even this felt too delicious, too decadent, so I worked on keeping those lips shut. I thought about suggesting that he put those fingers to work, my vagina felt so empty, but I also was lost in his touch. Somehow it was lighting me up everywhere.

He worked his way up my leg again, and goose bumps trailed his lips. When he reached the top of my inner thigh, he slid it onto his shoulder and met my eyes.

"Anything you want to say?"

Could you vibrate from want? I mean, at this point, I felt like it. Waves of sensation were rolling through me. Pulses were shooting down my core to my clit, and I was tempted to thrust it into his face. That felt a little wanton, though. But I wasn't sure I even could form words right now. I mean mouth-down-now was likely not what he was looking for.

"Please?" I gasped and then bit my lips because that was all I could do.

That smile that stretched across his beard told me he knew exactly what he was doing to me. He watched me for a moment, and I thought I would lose my damn mind if he didn't get on with the program until I felt his fingers trailing down my legs on either side and then spreading me so openly.

And he was there. Holy God.

My hips thrust up because I couldn't stop. He slid a hand up to hold me in place as he flattened his tongue to slide to my opening, then up, around my clit, and back down.

I growled as his tongue made another pass around the clit, but not actually touching it.

I could feel his chuckle against the most sensitive parts of me and started to work to be able to verbalize a retort when he decided to stop teasing and his mouth sucked me in. Finally.

Now all my previous sexual experiences would tell you that orgasms are glorious and stubborn little beasts. Even with my best partners, they took time to build up to. And even though I felt like we could have gotten to the good stuff quicker, we truly hadn't been at it long.

All this is to say holy shit. I worked to keep my breathing deep because the waves of ecstasy rolling through me went on and on as my body decided slow build up to an orgasm was a thing of the past. Too quickly, I became super-sensitive and pulled back.

Drew immediately moved to pepper kisses to my thighs and leaned to the side before crawling up the bed. He braced himself above me and kissed me long and hard. Pulling back, he looked at me with warmth. "Ready for more?"

Still deep breathing through the absolute warmth coursing through me, I nodded. "Want me to return the favor?"

He shook his head. "Not this time. It's been a while. Need to get in you, now." He rolled to his back, and I grabbed the condom he handed me. I rolled it on and then moved to straddle him.

He grabbed my hands to help me sit up as I notched him at my entrance. He moaned as he filled me in a thrust.

Sensations began building again immediately, and tears threated to spill over as I closed my eyes to try to control it. This was a lot. So much more than I'd thought. Emotions were flying through me as we rocked together.

"Jesus, you feel amazing," he growled as his hands slid up to cup my breasts. "Take what you need, Kate." He supported me as I rolled my hips, seeking a release that I wasn't entirely sure I was ready for. "Baby, open your eyes. I want to see you."

I faltered, not sure why looking at him was what felt like a step too far. Like it was somehow more intimate than what we were already sharing.

"Kate, beautiful, look at me." He tweaked my nipple. "I'm not going to last much longer."

"Me either," I said on a gasp as my eyes shot open to meet his. And I didn't. Once I locked onto his gaze, I shattered, riding him through waves of pleasure that detonated from my core and felt like something I wouldn't be able to come back from.

Before I could give it much thought, Drew joined me, wrapping me to him as I dropped against his chest. The pressure lessening as he slowed down his thrusts until we both lay there, gasping for air, sweat clinging to our bodies.

Drew's hands smoothed my skin, lightly trailing over and making designs that meant nothing and everything.

As we began to breathe normally, his hand came under my chin and brought my face up to meet his gaze. "We good?" he asked with a tone of concern.

"Absolutely," I said. What I should have said was that

he'd just rocked my world and destroyed it at the same time. How on earth was I going to be able to stay only friends with this man?

Because the truth of it all was that I wasn't. Not even close.

Chapter 17

Into the Woods

Drew

It had been a week, a goddamn glorious week, with Kate. Last Monday we'd fallen into bed together and stayed there for most of our snowbound day. We'd taken a break to watch movies, eat crap, and listen to music, but otherwise I found myself worshipping her body.

In other words, a version of heaven.

Tuesday morning we'd woken up to the sound of plows, and our bubble burst. I'd wondered if she'd distance herself or if I'd fall back on that, but no. Our friendship was still growing. We just happened to be a different type of friends, the kind who fell into bed together most nights too. Not a bad deal if you can find it.

As for the growing feelings I had toward her, I was pushing those aside. Healthy mindset, I was sure.

I'd met with Jess again and was out at Highland Woods today doing some homework for her. Or, as she'd probably say, for me. She said I needed to practice mindfulness, work to be present in the moment. Part of our conversation so far was to point out that I was dwelling too much on the past and worrying about not making more mistakes in the future. As a result, she'd directed me to head outside for a walk or run without my normal accompaniment of music or a podcast. I figured hitting one of the trails in the woods might make that easier, though the distractions around me might not have been what Jess had in mind. Hell, I figured it was worth a try.

I'd run out here with Jake many times. Steph even joined us when she was in town. It was relatively flat, so I could easily get some miles in and maybe grab a coffee at the café in the mansion when I was done.

Just as I was nearing the trailhead, I heard someone call my name. I glanced back to see Max and another guy walking down the snowy path in my direction.

"Hey, Max," I said when they reached me.

Max nodded his greeting. "Drew, this is Logan Traub. Logan, this is Jake Spencer's brother."

"Hey, Drew, good to see you in person." Logan bumped my fist. We'd talked over text in the past week but couldn't get our schedules to line up to have a real conversation.

Logan was about my height and I'd guess only had a few years on me, early to midthirties. He and Max were both dressed for the outdoors.

"You headed out on the trails?" I said, glancing toward the trailhead just ahead.

"Yeah, we were going to do a loop, checking on how everything's holding up after the snowfall of the past week," Max said.

"Max!"

We all looked back to the mansion and saw a guy waving at Max. "Need to run something by you," he called.

Max looked back to us. "Sorry. Blake has been working

on some numbers for our spring break volunteer planning." He looked over to Logan. "Rain check?"

Logan waved him off. "No worries. Let me know if you need anything."

Max turned and gave me a slap on the shoulder before jogging back to meet Blake.

With a glance to Logan, I gestured at the path. "Want to head out together? Maybe we can fit that conversation in now."

Logan tilted his head. "Sure, let's go."

We walked the first part in silence, the snow crunching under our boots. I wasn't sure on the final snow tallies from the storm last week, somewhere in the neighborhood of a foot or more, but some had melted since then. Barren trees lined the path against a brilliant blue sky, and there was a hush on the trail that was magical.

It was interesting. Highland Falls wasn't a large town, no more than ten thousand people at the most, but being out here in the woods was something else. Living in Colorado for just over a decade, I was used to spending a lot of time outside. Hiking had been part of my daily life. Hiking here was far flatter, somewhat easier, but just as special.

Actually, now that I thought about it, I hadn't spent near the time outside here as I had back in Fort Collins. Maybe Jess was on to something with this week's homework.

"So you texted and said you wanted to know more about the park?" Logan spoke up, reminding me that I wasn't alone.

"Yeah, sorry. Just thinking through something there for a minute." I ducked under some branches and then held them out of the way for Logan. I shook off my reflections to focus on Logan. "Well, it's like this. I was talking to Max and mentioned I wasn't sure what type of job I saw myself looking for in Highland. He suggested talking to you." I paused, thinking about what it was that I actually wanted.

Logan pointed toward the right at a fork in our trail. We headed that way over the packed down snow. "Are you thinking you want to work out here?"

He rubbed his hand over his beard, and I could practically see him mentally sorting through their jobs and, for this time of year, I'm sure what was a severe lack of openings.

I laughed, almost to myself. "No worries, man. I'm not asking for a job. Hell, I'd assume you all are low on full-time positions, especially this time of year."

Logan looked relieved as he glanced my way. "Good. I mean, we've been growing, but winter is a slow season. So how can I help?"

I paused as Logan crouched near some trees just off the path as I wondered what I did want from him—hell, I felt like I was spinning my wheels.

"Not sure. My degree is in environmental studies."

Logan looked up at me with a look of confusion. "Sorry, I just remember Jake saying you were a firefighter, and I'm pretty sure he said you were part of the brewery somehow..." His voice trailed off as he worked to connect the dots.

I stopped and faced him to give the overall info. "Quick bio, degree from CU, worked with a local firefighter group while at college. Joined the Hotshots. Did some training for them too. When Jake and Sully needed an investor to can their beer, I sent some funds their way—"

"Much gratitude for that. Their beer is the shit. Love it even more from my couch after a long day."

"Amen to that. Thought I'd stick in Colorado long-term, but it turns out that wasn't to be. Landed here and plan to stay, but not sure the brewery is my future."

Logan stood, brushing snow off himself as he did so. "Okay. So all that makes a hell of a lot more sense now with Max suggesting you talk to me, especially given your degree. Are you aware of what we do with the University of Illinois?"

I knew of the Big Ten university, of course, and that the park worked closely with them, but that was about it. "I don't think so."

"We consider them our partners, of a sort. We have several internship programs, we coordinate research on animals and wildlife, and over the past decade, we've been working on learning more about sustainability as it pertains to the park and how the public can apply it to their lives. Our goal is that this place will be net zero for energy and emissions in the next decade. We're hoping to be a model for the local community and beyond."

"That's great."

"And we've been working on growing some programs in conjunction with the university. Topics we're considering have ranged from gardening with native plants to composting to conservation to growing your own food, et cetera."

I nodded, thinking of the direction he was steering the park. "So are you thinking you could use help with the courses, planning, or the university?"

Logan looked off down the trail, lost in thought. I waited, listening to the birds calling to each other. Damn, I was glad it had warmed up since last week. We must have at least cracked thirty degrees at this point.

Finally, he looked back to me. "I'll need to talk to the

folks at U of I, but we're partnering with them to use a new grant for some of these initiatives. We've talked about creating a community outreach position. I think that might be something that would work for you. You'd have to interview, of course, after we post the position, but I have a feeling that could work out." Logan tugged off his stocking cap, stuffing it in his pocket. "What do you think? Is something like that what you're hoping for?"

My chest felt lighter, warm, like this was where I was supposed to be. For the first time in forever, I felt a sense of rightness. No, that's not right. I felt this way with Kate. But it had been a while since I felt a sense of peace when thinking about my future and where I saw myself. I'd take it.

"Yeah, I'm absolutely interested."

We hiked the trails for over an hour as Logan pointed out the different wildlife the park had over winter, the plants that were there, and where the spring growth would appear. As we did, my mind spun thinking of all the possibilities at the park.

"Drew?"

I looked over his way. "Damn, I'm being a shit hiking partner."

"No, just wanted to say I'm a good listener, if needed. Seems that the woods are a good place to work through shit."

I sat with that for a minute. "Just thinking about the position, the things we could accomplish. Got to use my degree a little with the Hotshots. Hadn't realized how excited I'd be at the possibility of really immersing myself in these topics again." My mind continued to wander. When Ivy first met Jake, she'd given him hell about the amount of water involved in brewing beer. Could I bring some sustainability practices to the brewery too?

I shook my head and laughed, looking to Logan again. "Hell, it's like all these connections in my brain are finally firing again after a long slumber."

"A walk in the woods can do that to you."

I nodded, and we continued along the snow-covered ground.

An hour later, we left the red trail at the point where it emptied out near the mansion. Just as I was getting ready to ask Logan if he wanted to get coffee, I saw my brother leaning against the building.

Logan nodded in his direction. "I think you've got company."

"Looks like it." I stopped and held a hand out in his direction. "Hey, thanks for the walk and getting me back on the path I want to be on."

"You bet. I've got your info now, and I'll give you a call once I check into the grant some more. You should hear from me in a week or so." He passed Jake with a slap to his shoulder and headed in.

Jake watched me head his way with a look I was beginning to hate, the concerned-big-brother look. I knew I'd worried them coming here the way I did and keeping shit to myself, but I hated that they felt like I was someone to worry about.

"Don't look at me like that."

"Like what?"

"No bullshit, man. I'm not going to break."

"Well, then start talking. I'm getting old and gray waiting for you to open up. Steph and I just want to be here for you. God knows you've been there for us, you ass clown."

"Ass clown? Really? What are we, twelve?"

"Well, when you behave as if you have to carry all your burdens on your own, the clown shoe fits."

I shook my head at him and gestured at the door. "Can I buy you a coffee?"

He gave me a skeptical look, then headed in.

The atmosphere of the café was excellent. It was in a long low room of the mansion that had the counter on one end, leather couches, assorted armchairs, and tables scattered throughout. One wall was floor-to-ceiling windows that overlooked the pond.

I looked over to the counter to see Logan had beat us in here and was talking to the barista, a woman about our age with long red hair.

"Drew, this is Allyson. She owns this place and the original, the Sanctuary, in town," Logan said as we came up to the counter.

I caught the way Allyson was looking in his direction before she turned my way and wondered what we'd interrupted. I'd seen Allyson before when I'd grabbed coffee in town but hadn't really gotten to know her yet. I'd have to ask Ivy if there was a story between her and Logan.

"Hey." I pointed to my left. "I'm this one's brother. I apologize or celebrate that, depending on your opinion of him."

Allyson laughed. "I'm friends with Ivy, so I celebrate Jake—well, most of the time. Welcome, Drew. What can I get you?"

Jake and I placed an order for a coffee each and then left Logan and Allyson to their conversation while we found some armchairs near a window.

Dropping into the nearest one, I relaxed. The hike hadn't been the mindful run I'd been planning, but it was time well spent all the same. I still felt a thrum of excitement, thinking of the conversation with Logan. We'd see what came of it, but for now, I felt like I had some direction for the first time in forever.

"So you going to make me pull it out of you?" Jake sounded irritated, which was unlike him.

"What?" I decided playing dumb was the way to go. Hell if I was required to confide the shit that was eating away at me.

Jake gave me a look that told me he was having none of it.

My look back was more of the same.

His sigh was ridiculously over the top. He stretched out, putting his feet up on a trunk in front of us that likely wasn't supposed to be used as a footrest, and took a drink of his coffee. With his gaze firmly locked on the water to give me some space, he let the bomb drop. "Just saying Margot is worried."

Shit. "Mom is worried?"

"And if you don't start talking, she's coming down to stay with you and make casseroles until you, and I quote, 'Act like his old self, dammit.' End quote. So it's me or Margot, take your pick."

"Dad isn't an option?"

"I could unload Steph. I'm sure she'd be happy to spend some time down here and leave Theo to deal with the girls' schedules. He might string you up, however."

"Hell no." Steph was an amazing sister. She was also completely type A and would want to organize my entire life in a matter of days. There would be no long contemplation of future plans. It would be all go, go, go.

Hell no.

Jess and I'd talked more about Tiffany over this week's

session as well as the aftermath which ended up bringing me here. She'd encouraged me to continue to face what I was running from but to do so on my own timetable. As she pointed out, my journey back to myself was a marathon, not a sprint.

So while I didn't want to get into all of it with Jake, I could begin to open up.

"I'm in therapy," I said, figuring it was as good a place as any to begin.

"So you said when you dropped that little morsel as you walked into brunch a week ago and have since avoided the topic like the plague."

"Dude, the plague comment doesn't track like it once would have before the Rona."

"We don't talk about that," Jake said. "Anyway, spill. Therapy is great. Did you feel like you couldn't tell us?"

"Hell no, I did tell you."

"Almost as an afterthought. Doesn't count."

I let out a sigh that only my siblings could bring out of me, a long suffering one, and spilled all the shit about Tiffany/Tami that I'd been holding back. To his credit, Jake sat there without commentary, staring at the water just like I was, which was the only way I could have gotten it all out.

"...so it fucked with my head and I'm sorting it out. Well, that and more shit that's tied to it but, no offense, that isn't anything I want to delve into right now. This was enough."

Jake sat there in silence for a few beats, and I... waited.

Clearing his throat, he gave me a side-glance. "I would be full of hubris if I thought I knew what you'd gone through—"

"What the fuck, hubris?"

He gave me a look. "What?"

My eyes narrowed. "I'm sorry, what the fuck is with the SAT-level vocabulary over there?"

We locked eyes, and I refused to look away until he gave in. "Fine. Ivy bet me I couldn't use it in a sentence today and sound like myself. Whatever."

I laughed and whipped out my phone to text her, but we had no fucking service out here. What the hell? I'd bet there was Wi-Fi, but I didn't want to deal with that right now. I'd share with the group later.

"Anyway, I'm just saying that is complete bullshit that you got played that way, but I'm confused why you're feeling any guilt. None of this is your fault."

I thought of everything I wasn't saying, but today was not the day.

"One, there's more, but that's for another conversation. But two, I feel like I've always trusted my gut. It's never led me astray. And then this shit went down. I don't know. It made me question everything. I felt like I hadn't just betrayed my best friend, even if accidentally, the future I thought was becoming clearer shattered. My gut failed. What was up was down; what was down was up. I lost my sense of direction, my guiding instinct."

"And then you lost your identity."

My head jerked as I turned toward Jake. "What?"

He continued to look straight ahead at the pond, almost like he was giving me a chance to process with him but on my own. "Your identity as a firefighter. I know you're holding back more, and I'll respect that—"

"Um, you weren't earlier. Threatening me with Margot?"

"You know that was a promise, not a threat. And you've unloaded some; we'll allow it for now."

"You will, will you?"

"What I'm saying is that your identity was tied to that group. Not only did everything else go belly-up, so did your job. It's a lot, Drew. Maybe take it easy on yourself."

I sat back into the armchair, the leather soft against me, enveloping me in comfort.

Fuck, he was right. So was this possible position with Logan a way to reclaim my identity? Or maybe forge a new one? And how did I make sure I didn't tie all of myself up into one thing again?

There was a lot to think about.

"So want to share your thoughts on the benefits of yoga on a sex life? Steph requested that portion of the brother heart-to-heart. I mean, no details"—he gagged—"but should Ivy call Kate to give her the lowdown on joining this clan?"

I choked on my coffee.

Jesus.

Chapter 18

Casual

Kate

I sat on my mat, legs crossed, eyes closed, listening to my own breath. Shifting, I concentrated on the sensation of the ground under me, hands pressed together, thumbs to my sternum. I needed to return to myself, but my mind would not stop spiraling. To be honest, it was beginning to piss me off.

Last night I gave in to Alex's reminder that I needed to call my parents again. While I knew he was right, avoiding them was making it worse, it had been more of the same. Disappointment. They strongly believed that I ran when I was scared, and in their minds, I had a history of this.

Running from responsibility.

Running from finishing a degree in elementary education.

Running from a relationship with Alex.

Running, running, running.

They had examples to back them up from childhood as well of course. It didn't matter that I knew my degree wasn't going to be fulfilling for me. I loved working with kids, but I had zero desire to deal with the shit show that was public education even ten years ago. Teachers were to be revered, but that wasn't what our society was doing. And as already established, while Alex and I were good as friends, the relationship was going nowhere.

But did that matter to my parents? Um, that would be a big fat no. They were, well... they were a lot. In my heart, I knew they meant well. They weren't warm and fuzzy people. They wanted the best for me and felt that pointing out where they thought I was lacking would help. That wasn't the way I was built, but I didn't know how to explain that to them.

And as well as I knew myself, as strong as I felt in my beliefs that I'd made the right decision, a small nagging voice said maybe they were right.

Maybe I ran when things got real.

Maybe I was a big fraidy-cat.

And then they started asking questions about how the studio was doing, and I got overwhelmed and couldn't put together a sentence to save my life.

I mean, when it came down to it, I knew they loved me, I knew they thought they were looking out for me, but damn it, I needed them to have faith in me.

Talking to them made me feel small.

I hated it.

Luckily, Drew had been there, sitting on his couch and texting with his siblings. After I hung up, he held me as I straddled him, my head on his shoulder. He hadn't said a word until I was ready, just rubbed my back and was there.

It was what I needed.

This morning, however, I'd woken up pissed. Why couldn't they just be there for me? My mind began to swirl, and I quickly got my ass to the studio to work out the feelings.

Breath work was where I started, knowing it was the one thing that would not let me down and would eventually bring me to the state of calm that I was so desperately seeking. Minutes passed as I eventually relaxed. Suddenly, I began to sense that I was no longer alone in the space.

Once I opened my eyes, I found that I was right. Kristine was quietly rolling out her mat as well nearby.

She came to a seat and took a centering breath as well. Without discussing it, we began to work through a flow together. I let her lead, following her though one series, then another, as my mind unwound and a feeling of lightness returned.

Before I knew it, my body and mind both felt loose, and we returned to our seated position to close out. Finding that center, I looked to Kristine to see her watching me.

"Yes?" I raised an eyebrow in her direction.

"Waiting to see if you want to talk."

I fought an eye roll that wanted to come up. "About Drew?"

"Oh, I'll talk about that glorious man anytime. However, I'm open to talking about anything. Why you were wound so tight when I got here, how we could find more income as a studio, you name it."

I debated what to dive into first. "Well, called the parental units again last night—"

"Ahh, enough said. I'm sure they were supportive, as always."

"About sums them up." A wave of sadness hit me when I thought of Drew's parents. What I wouldn't give for just a little of that with mine.

"I ran some numbers for the studio for last week. Maybe

that would be a good change of topic?" Kristine asked as she twisted in a stretch.

My gut clenched. Again. No one ever declared that running a small business was easy. If they did, they'd be liars. However, I had to be honest. I hadn't realized it would take up all my brain space.

We were two months in to our time at this space. Kristine had been teaching yoga in the community for two years, but in the studio, we were just in the infancy stages. We'd both come to this venture with an investment of funds, Kristine from her years without a space—in Highland and elsewhere; me with some of my savings. We had plenty of capital to float the business along as we got our bearings, but in no way did we want to operate in the red for long. And the first two months? We'd been in the red.

In the past week, we'd participated in one of the Main Street's events where local businesses offered a type of chocolate for each person who'd purchased tickets. Customers moved around the downtown, getting to know local businesses while having sweet treats. We'd had a sweets bar, complete with brownies, my irresistible chocolate tahini cookies—which sounded terrible, but were actually delicious—along with the chocolate-covered protein balls I'd made for Drew.

It had brought in plenty of new people, but time would tell if they'd buy a class or even become regulars. We'd brainstormed a few ways to bring in people beyond the event and were coming up empty. Just as I was ready to tell Kristine that I was at a loss, the door opened.

Ivy walked in with her hair blowing around her in a curtain. "Wow, it's freezing." She tugged the door behind her and turned to see the two of us seated. "Am I interrupting?"

"Nah, pull up a mat." Kristine patted the spot next to her. "Kate and I have been brainstorming how to bring in more funds."

"Ohhh, I hear you. This is a conversation Jake and I had a lot this fall. I was stressing." She shed her down jacket and kicked off her shoes before plopping to a seat, her long skirt billowing around her. "So where have you landed?"

I rolled back onto the mat. "Um, nowhere. We did the chocolate event this week and had a good turnout. We've sold some of my facial mist and essential oil blends. That's been some additional income, but not a ton." I looked up at the wooden ceiling and let my mind whirl. No luck. No brilliant ideas came to mind. "Just not sure where to go from here."

Ivy nodded as she looked around the space. "Well, you've only been here for two months, starting your third. What's your social media like?"

Kristine and I looked at each other as I swung back up to a seat.

"It could be better," I admitted. I mean, I wasn't a Luddite, but social media often gave me more negative feelings than I wanted to deal with.

"I hear you," Ivy nodded. "Maybe commit to a post a day on an account for the studio. You could both have access to it. That way, if you don't want to be on any platform much as yourself, you don't have to but are still reminding the locals that you're here."

"Great idea, Ivy. Free and not too difficult. We'll start there, thanks." Kristine rose. "Tea, anyone?"

Ivy and I followed her over to the teapot. Kristine got the water boiling and leaned on our counter where Ivy and I had sat on the stools on the other side. I realized, belatedly, that they were both watching me.

"Okay, that's creepy. What's up?" I looked from Ivy to Kristine back to Ivy.

They shared a smile then turned to me in unison. Oh boy.

"So," Kristine led with, then they both said, "Let's talk about Drew," at the same time.

Ahh. Up to speed. I worked to assume an innocent look.

"Nope, none of that, girly," Kristine said. "I've been waiting for you to spill the details. Where do you and Mr. Spencer stand?"

"What?" I shrugged my shoulders. "You know Drew came in for yoga several times over the past month. You also knew we'd had dinner at my place."

"And brunch with the family, a sleepover at his place during the storm, and... and... and..." Ivy trailed off.

Kristine finished up our mugs of tea and slid one to each of us. "Okay, I provided the beverage. Spill, girly."

Looking at their matching wide-eyed expressions, I burst out laughing and felt lightness fill me up. "Well, let's just say you were telling me to get back in the saddle, Kristine."

"Saddle being slang for sex with Drew Spencer? Full support." She raised a mug to me.

"Cosigned," Ivy said with a grin.

"Good grief," I said as I worked unsuccessfully to school my own smile.

"Mm-hmm, I see that look. Looking mighty satisfied, Ms. Ashley, if I do say so myself." Ivy positively cackled.

"And don't even try to drop the bullshit that it's just relaxation from a good yoga session, ma'am. I know better." Kristine wiggled her eyebrows at me.

I let my laughter fly, which felt amazing. "Fine, fine. Drew and I were snowed in together, and it was just as glorious as every snowed-in romance book has ever promised me it would be." I nodded toward Ivy. "I owe you a debt of gratitude for renting out your apartments upstairs to both of us."

Ivy waved away my words. "Heck no, the pleasure here is all mine. I love that guy. Anyone who dotes on my daughter the way he does is top of my list on the good guys. Besides, Jake and I have both noticed how much more relaxed he has been over the past few weeks. I'm assuming that's thanks to you."

I assumed a serious expression and head nod. "Yep, yep, doing God's work over here."

Kristine raised her tea once again, and the three of us clinked mugs.

"So..." Kristine drew it out. "Does this mean you're finally moving past dwelling on how everything ended with Alex."

I faltered, not sure how to discuss this.

"No, no, no, no, no." Kristine waggled a finger at me. "No I-lost-my-puppy-dog face. No going back, chickie."

"Alex?" Ivy asked.

I let out a sigh worthy of a teenager and then held up my hand to Kristine who appeared ready to spill it all. "Nope, let me."

I turned toward Ivy. "Hope you still have plenty of tea left, This will take a few minutes, maybe more."

She held up a hand. "Hold that thought. My brain is finally clicking into gears. I believe Addie said something about an ex-boyfriend in England."

I laughed, remembering the visit with the girls just a little over a week ago when Addie thought that Alex would've known the queen. Alex would love that. I'd have to tell him the next time I called, which I quickly penciled on my mental to-do list.

"Yeah, that would be Alex. We'd dated since college, heck, since shortly before Kristine and I met."

"Whoa." Ivy's face clearly registered her surprise at the length of our relationship. "So am I a terrible and nosy friend if I ask what happened?"

Ivy could never be a terrible friend. I couldn't think of a woman I clicked faster with than Kristine in college and this crew of strong women I'd met, Ivy included, since coming to town. I felt like my luck was finally turning around in that department. "No, of course not. I just realized one day that while I loved Alex, there was no romantic love left."

"Ask how that messed with her head," Kristine prompted.

I fought an eye roll again. Sometimes it could be a pain in the ass to have people knew you so well. "Shush, you." I looked to Ivy. "As Kristine is ever so subtly hinting at, my psyche is a touch messed up with the notion that I somehow didn't notice how Alex and my relationship had evolved and it's quite possibly made me gun-shy to try again." I glanced back to Kristine. "But *I'm working on it.*"

"As long as you're working on it with that gorgeous man who could double for some type of Nordic god, I'm good."

Ivy rubbed her chin. "Hmm, I wouldn't have thought Nordic with his brown hair, but maybe." Then she looked my way. "I feel like I should give you some of my moon water. It's supercharged with the moon's energy. Maybe we could do some type of ceremony for you?"

Drew had already told me that Ivy considered herself a green witch. Didn't seem like a stretch to find out that she collected moon water. I rolled with it. "I'm down for it anytime."

Kristine interrupted. "Okay, we're going to circle back to this moon water conversation later. Here's what I want to know. Are you giving this thing with Thor's body double a fair shot, or are you settling for less than you deserve?"

I fought the urge to raise my middle finger at Kristine or, heck, both unicorn horns. She pushed me, which I knew I needed, but it was still hard to face at times. "It's not like that with us." I hesitated, unsure as to how to explain Drew and my relationship, or whatever it was, with his own business remaining confidential. "Let's just say, without delving into things that are not mine to share, that we're keeping this casual for both of us because—"

Before I could finish, the door opened, letting in another gust of winter air. Drew poked his face in. He had on a gray-blue stocking hat that made his eyes pop, and the cheeks above his beard were rosy from the cold. His gaze met mine and absolutely lit up. He quickly jogged my way and spun me to face him before lowering his mouth to mine. The moment our lips touched I felt the cold and a jolt of energy as I melted into him.

A moment later he pulled back, letting our foreheads touch.

"Hi," he said, eyes locked on mine as he smoothed back a loose strand of my hair...

"Hey," I said breathlessly. Damn. That wasn't obvious. I'm sure no one noticed.

"Sorry," he whispered. "Probably should have checked before I greeted you like that in front of these two."

"Oh, don't mind us," Kristine said in a singsong voice. "We're enjoying the show."

"Yes, wave to the camera. I've got this on video for the sibling chat," Ivy said with her joy evident.

"It's absolutely fine," I said to reassure him. His eyes met mine and crinkled at the corner.

"In that case," he leaned in to press another kiss to my mouth. "I'm stealing Kate away from you two. Goodbye, ladies. Have a great afternoon. And Bookstore, behave."

"Never, you've taught me well!"

"Hey, Kate?" Kristine called as Drew grabbed my coat from the hooks by the door and slid it on for me.

I looked back to Ivy and Kristine. "Yeah?"

"That's anything but casual, chickie." Her smile was wobbly, like she was holding back emotion.

Damn.

I turned and headed out the door with Drew. I'd think about that later.

Chapter 19

Beards

Drew

Awareness gradually came to my consciousness in bits and pieces. My bed was warm, light streaming in the window. I stretched some before rolling to grab my phone and noted that it was just a little after eight. Also worth a thought or two, I'd slept through the night. Again.

I rolled to my back and thought through the past, what was it, week? No, today was the thirteenth. Kate had first spent the night with me after brunch. Counting back, that was the second. Holy shit, we were closing in on two weeks. In that time, I'd had one nightmare, which led to me sharing some of the shitstorm I had going on inside with her, then with Jess, and eventually with Jake.

And as Jess had predicted, it was helping. It was rude when people were right about things I'd been sure wouldn't work. But damn if she hadn't been on the money here.

Which begged the question: why wasn't I telling Kate or Jake about the final straw that brought me here? Jess had encouraged me to, but I put it off. Hell, I hadn't called

Murph again since our conversation when Kate and I'd been watching movies, even though he'd sent a few texts.

No answer there except I didn't feel ready. It was likely a cowardly way out, but there didn't seem to be another way. Not yet.

Rolling to my side, I looked at the empty spot in my bed. All night Kate had been there, and I'd wrapped myself around her like some baby koala. Now the sheets were cold. She didn't have class until four this afternoon, but it was possible she'd headed back to her place. I wondered if we'd been spending too much time together for her. She'd just gotten out of a relationship this fall after a shit ton of years with the guy. I knew we were casual, but maybe this was too much for her too soon.

I slid out of bed and made my way to the kitchen, ready for some coffee. As I reached the end of the hall, I quickly stopped. Seems Kate hadn't headed back to her place after all, unless it was just to get her mat.

She was set up in front of the large windows of my living room, her hair piled in a knot on the top of her head as she had one hand and one foot on the ground. The position reminded me of the standing splits we did in class, but instead of leaving the leg in the air straight, she'd grasped the foot and was doing some kind of quad stretch. I'd be on my ass in a heartbeat.

Some Adele song was filling the room at a low level. Her black leggings were my favorite, but today, competing for that top spot, was the awareness that she was in my T-shirt. It was baggy on her frame, but it still made me feel possessive, like I wanted to claim her in front of everyone I knew.

Mine.

And yes, I realized how perfectly ridiculous that was.

Instead, I quietly backed up and went in the kitchen to

grab some coffee, thanking the Lord for whoever thought up programmable coffee makers. Mug in hand, I went back in and leaned against the wall to watch her. It wasn't stalker-ish, much, but more the peace and joy that was evident on her face as she flowed through the poses.

A few nights ago that peace had been disturbed with a call to her parents. Hell, just listening in from my spot on the couch had made me text mine just to tell them I loved them. I'd never given much thought to the benefit of having the unconditional love that flowed from Margot and Sam, but I now realized it was a privilege.

Kate's parents didn't seem to realize that she was reaching for her dreams and was damn good at it. I knew she was stressed about the business, but I thought what she and Kristine were doing was amazing and the town bene-fited from it.

As I watched her move through a flow, I thought back to our conversation after she'd talked to her parents. I'd held her for a while as she told me about dropping out of college, finding yoga training, her work with a preschool, learning what she was good at.

We'd talked about her yoga practice, and I asked what she preferred, yoga where she was teaching a group or yoga on her own. She was like my mom when you asked who was her favorite kid—clearly me—she said she couldn't pick.

Kate had said she loved teaching classes because watching people find the benefits of yoga and having their lives improve brought her so much joy. But doing yoga on her own was personal. She didn't have to think about what worked for the group, what she'd planned, but she could listen to her body and do what it needed.

Which was what drew me to watching her. She was so graceful it was almost like some kind of dance. Her breath was even, but pronounced. I could hear her inhales and exhales, like she'd exaggerated them to give the sound a meditative quality.

I moved to the couch, not wanting to interrupt her, but also not wanting to keep creeping on her yoga practice. I didn't think she'd care, but I didn't want to startle her. Settling back into the corner, I took another sip of coffee.

From downward dog I saw her gaze come to me. "Hey," she said softly, moving to plank. "You didn't want to sleep in?"

"Nah." I placed my coffee on the coffee table. "I slept great. Woke up and couldn't go back to sleep."

"Want to join me?" she asked, lifting up to cobra.

"No mat."

"I have one in my place, just inside the door. Keys are on the table."

Why not? I headed over, grabbed the mat, and was back in minutes. Kate was still moving through a flow. When I rolled my mat out a few feet from her so we'd both have space, she glanced my way.

"Why don't you go to cat/cow pose and do some gradual movements? Tell me what spots you're feeling like working today."

"But I know your favorite part of yoga on your own is listening to your body. I don't want to take that away from you this morning."

She moved into a lunge. "I've been at this for over an hour, I'm good. Promise, though it's sweet of you to think of me."

"You were definitely not calling me sweet last night."

She leaned over and slapped my ass. "Enough, mister. Move around, let me know." And then she gave me a smirk and wiggled her eyebrows. "And for the record, I like that version of you too."

I dropped into cat/cow pose as Kate had taught me over the past few weeks. First, I found my breath and worked on longer inhales and exhales. I began arching my spine, then pushing my stomach down. That led to figure eights, and the tightness was evident. Jake and I'd began upping our running miles this week, debating if we wanted to do a race this spring. Clearly, I hadn't stretched enough.

After another stretch, I glanced Kate's way and found her watching me.

"Hips, glutes, hamstrings, quads?"

"How did you know?"

"Well, I know you are running more, and you had somewhat of a hitch when you were moving through your figure eights, like you were doing mini stretches."

"I was trying to lean into the discomfort," I said, trying again. That was a lesson I took from class back in January. Hell, I think Jess would also say it was good advice for life, but in many ways, outside this practice, I was running like hell from anything that made me feel uncomfortable.

Something to think about later.

I lost myself for the next hour, following Kate's voice as I moved from pose to pose. I'd been to enough classes now that I didn't feel the need to look at her when she was describing a pose but instead could visualize what I needed to do and move to it. It made it almost like a meditative practice, but one that was also stretching out some tight running muscles.

Before I knew it, we were cooling down and rolling up our mats. It amazed me that we'd been friends now for only a few short weeks, but I felt like I'd know her for years. Kate headed back to her apartment, and I had a slow morning and a leisurely afternoon where the only item on my schedule was to chat with Jess. Around four I headed to the brewery to get ready for a few hours of work.

Walking in, the smell of hops and the early scents of dinner greeted me. I shed my coat and headed into the bar area. Our hostess, Lauren, and some of the guys were busing tables, getting ready to begin dinner prep, though we had a while before most people would come out. Late afternoon sun was coming through the giant windows and hitting the barn wood and bricks around the room, lighting it with a warm glow.

After saying hello to the crew setting the tables up for the night, I went over to the guys. Sully was stationed behind the bar, pouring a beer. Jake was bellied up and appeared to be giving him shit. They both turned to me and Jake burst out laughing.

"Where in the hell did you get that shirt?" Sully asked, scanning my torso.

I gestured at my SHE WANTS THE B T-shirt with a beard silhouette on it and then gave these two a shrug. "I mean, it speaks the truth, right?"

Jake was typically clean-shaven or a day or so out. Sully let his go a few days more than Jake before shaving. Neither grew a full beard.

"Didn't answer the question. Where in the hell did that come from?" Jake squinted at me, like he was trying to discern something.

Max appeared from the direction of the bathrooms. He took a glance at my shirt and held up his hand in response.

I slapped his and turned back to Jake. "Kate."

All three guys looked at me with skeptical glanced. "Kate?" Jake said.

"Damn, knew I liked her." Sully held up a glass in my direction with a nod to the taps.

"Fire and Rain," I said in response to his unasked question.

"She might give Maggie a run for the money in the strong-willed department," Max said. Sully slid an IPA his way after passing me my West Coast IPA.

The piney taste hit immediately, but then mellowed as I took a drink. You had to love a job that fully supported a beer or two while working, though my job description was different than most. Make no mistake, when we were busy, it could be exhausting. But Sully and Jake had built a ridiculously competent staff. I ran the bar during my shifts, and they all took care of their sections with an ease born of years of experience. They had a lot of loyal staff here, and it showed.

I thought about what Max had said as I looked back at the guys. "Not sure I'd say strong-willed, more someone who likes to laugh and didn't think I'd wear this."

Jake took out his phone and snapped a photo, I'm sure for our group text. "Well, she clearly didn't know you well enough then."

I shrugged. "I mean, if she wants to tell the world that she's a fan of the beard, who am I to deny her that opportunity? If people want to interpret that in a more rated-R way, not my concern."

Sully shook his head. "You better hope Lou and Verdell don't come in tonight. She'd love that shirt."

"Hell, Lou probably gave Kate the idea at a yoga class," Max said.

Miss Lou was the town busybody. I had no idea if she was in her seventies or eighties, but she was trouble, and her husband, Verdell, was a damn saint.

"Okay, now that you're all here, we need to talk." Sully looked at each one of us with a serious express.

I looked to Max on my left and we exchanged glances that indicated neither one of us had any idea what this was about.

"Spill, Sullivan," I said as Max raised his glass in my direction. It was better to just be assertive with this group. We clinked and turned back to the other two. "Is this serious, or are we having a heart-to-heart on new menu ideas?"

Max spoke up. "Oh, if this is menu-idea time, where's Pete? I've got several."

"You two think with your stomach all the time. And we're not changing the damn menu until spring. Easy." Jake was grumbly today, though to be fair, a lot of the menu concepts fell to him and Pete. The rest of us just told him what we wanted to eat, and he had to make it happen.

"No, idiots. I wanted to check in on what you're all getting the girls for the holiday. I figured we'd avoid one wife/fiancée/girlfriend being pissed at one of us that way."

I looked at him with what must have been confusion. "Two points of order here: one, am I included in this conversation? I mean, Kate and I just started hanging out. And two, what holiday?"

The other three groaned in unison.

"It's your fault for not raising him right," Sully said to Jake.

"Novice," Max said as he shook his head at me.

I looked to Jake, waiting for him to fill me in. He was texting because of course he was.

"Hey," I began.

He held up a hand. "Nope. Steph and Ivy need to be in on your ignorance or they won't forgive me for my lapse." He texted for another minute, then put his phone down.

"There. Now where do we start. Hmm..." He seemed to be considering something and then leaned over and slapped me upside the head.

"What the hell?" I rubbed.

"Okay, I wish I had Ivy and Steph here for this, but I'm going to do my best. In reference to your aforementioned points; one, you and Kate have been inseparable for almost two weeks. From what I'm gleaning from that T-shirt, you have some carnal knowledge of each other and not just a one and done. So I think it's appropriate to go with the label of girlfriend. Might not be serious yet, but are you sleeping with anyone else?"

"What? Of course not."

"I rest my case. Two, it's Valentine's Day tomorrow, you imbecile."

Shit. I immediately began to sweat.

"I mean, am I supposed to get anything for Kate?" I looked from one face to another. Jake and Sully shook their heads at me like I was some poor fool. Max shrugged.

"Emma told me that Valentine's Day is a commercial holiday and not to get her anything."

"Oh, Harp, you idiot. My sister is the world's biggest romantic. You didn't actually listen to her, did you?" Sully asked.

Max gave him a look. "Hell no. I've known your sister since she was five. Do you think I don't know her by now?"

I was impressed. "What did you get her?"

"A framed picture of her favorite spot at her parents' at sunset."

Sully whistled. "You took a picture of the creek?"

Max puffed up his chest. "Nope. I had the photographer that owns the photography studio Click head out and do it for me. Wanted to get the light just right."

"Damn, that's good," I said, lowering my voice. I looked to Sully. "How about you?"

He rubbed his hands together. "A full day booked at the spa in Bloomington, scheduled the week before she heads back to school from maternity leave. And a monthly massage for the rest of the year."

Maggie and Sully had just had their daughter, Ellen, at Christmastime this year, and Maggie was due to head back to teaching seventh grade in mid-March.

"That's a great gift."

"Yeah, Maggie would really love to go to a concert, but I know that staying up that late while she's still having to nurse El in the night would drain her. So I figured a gift that let her have some time to herself would work. She's done so much." He looked to Jake. "How about you?"

"For Addie, I got a tiara and a fluffy pink boa."

Absolutely tracked. She'd love it.

"And for Ivy, I bought her a fiddle-leaf fig."

I met Sully eyes and laughed at his expressions. I hadn't known what it was until hanging around Bookstore. "It's a plant," I said to him as I looked to Jake. Ivy had been talking about getting one of these forever, but she wanted a mature one and they weren't cheap, especially to Ivy who liked to save all the pennies. "You know she's going to flip if you got a big one. Cost, man."

"Got it from a guy in Champaign who had too much stock, and he cut me a deal for a few growlers. And you're right; she will flip. Damn thing is crazy tall."

Hell. These three all had amazing gifts that fit their girl perfectly. "What the hell am I going to do? I've known Kate for a few weeks. Not sure that warrants anything at the level of what you all are doing."

"But you clearly need to get her something, I mean, she

got you a kick-ass shirt for the hell of it." Max pointed out. We both stroked our bearded chins and grinned at the other two with their bare-ass faces.

I breathed out and thought of what I knew about Kate. She liked hanging out with friends, but loved quiet evenings in when we hung out.

"Want me to call in the big guns?" Jake asked, holding his phone up.

I gave him a questioning look when he returned it and said simply, "Steph."

I immediately felt a weight leave my chest. While she would give me shit, she also knew what the hell she was doing. "Hell yes."

He got to work.

Lauren came over to talk to Sully briefly about the night's specials, and we went over the staff changes for the evening before Jake interrupted.

"Steph says that there's some funky blanket-like towel at the gift shop in town that Kate said she wanted but didn't want to spend the cash on right now. They were talking about it at brunch, and she'd looked them up online to see what she meant. She suggests that, some essential oil from Ivy in a rollerball, and you need to cook her dinner." Jake looked up from his phone.

I could breathe deeper with a plan in place. "Hell, that would all be a piece of cake. I've got this."

"Cake would be good. Baking for her? I'm thinking that could be a home run." He glanced down at an incoming text and then looked to me. "And your guitar. She says play her a song or two."

"Done."

Movement at the door had me looking to the large opening to the dining room. Ivy and Kate stood in the opening with Emma, all three clearly just coming from Kate's class. Kate looked my way, her eyes locked on my T-shirt, and she burst out laughing. She turned to the two women with her and gestured my way, talking at a rapid rate.

I couldn't look away. Her face was bright with joy, and her eyes positively hypnotized me.

Jake leaned over, pulling me out of my trance. "Not your girlfriend my ass."

I was so screwed.

Chapter 20

Valentine's Day Surprises

K*ate*

I trudged up the steep stairs to my apartment, dreading spending the afternoon and evening alone. I mean, it was ridiculous. Drew and I had only been doing whatever we wanted to call this for a few weeks. He was under no obligation to make Valentine's plans with me. Or that's what I was telling myself.

In reality, I was hurt. Last night we got to talk briefly at the brewery, but I'd already known I wouldn't be staying with him. He had the dinner shift and was covering for someone who was out, so he hadn't gotten home until late. I had an early yoga class, so I'd stayed at my place. And in no conversation last night or text this morning had there been any mention of today's holiday.

Damn. I'd walked in after class last night and seen him in the ridiculous T-shirt I'd bought him on a whim and been so certain that was a sign, but that begged the question of why on earth I was hoping for a sign. I wasn't in this for a relationship; we'd already talked about this. After everything with Alex, I needed to catch my breath, do some reflection—in other words, get my shit together.

Alex. It had been far too long since we'd talked, which I didn't want to make a habit. As I hit the landing, I tugged my phone out and swiped through messages until I found our thread where he reminded me to talk to my parents. Well, that had gone well.

Me: *Called my parents. That went as well as you'd expect.*

There. I felt better having sent off a message. Before I took another step, there was a reply.

Alex: *Remember, you can't control their reactions, just that you put yourself out there. Good for you, and screw them if they don't appreciate you. Was Kristine with you when you called?*

I paused, then went with it.

Me: *No, Drew was.*

Alex: *The neighbor that is possibly more?*

I bit my lip.

Me: *I mean, I'm leaning toward for sure more?*

Alex: *I'm glad you weren't alone when you talked to them, and I'm happy you're reaching for more. You deserve this, Kate. Own it.*

Me: *Thanks. Talk soon?*

Alex: *Count on it.*

Feeling more at peace, I headed into my apartment and stopped just inside the door.

"What in the world?" I murmured, looking around. At my voice, Drew came around the corner from the kitchen.

"Welcome home, beautiful." He slid my yoga bag off my shoulder and put it in the corner where I kept it. "Come on in." Taking my hand in his, he tugged until I cleared the door, which he shut behind me. "Hope you don't mind. I had Ivy let me in so I could set this up."

My eyes went from one spot to another. "What—?

His lips found mine for the lightest of kisses that left me wanting more. "Want me to give you a tour?"

I nodded as I rose up on my toes for one more quick kiss.

"Okay." He moved me toward my couch. "Here we have our movie-watching spot set up complete with comfy pillows, blankets, and excellent snacks."

"What are we watching?" I said, looking at the display and noting that Netflix was open.

"Your choice. There's the new romance book that has been made into a series. I have it cued up, but your call."

I paused, my eyes catching two things. "Hold on. One, is that the blanket from the Mercantile?"

"Good eyes. I might have heard a rumor that you wanted it."

My eyes threatened to tear up. This man. Instead, I refocused on what was important. "And two, what are those brownies?"

"Homemade. My aunt makes the best brownies in the world. I happen to have her recipe."

I groaned as my mouth watered. Yep. I'd be eating those. Powdered sugar on brownies? Sign me up. My eyes snagged on a plant on the end table. "A houseplant?"

Drew wrapped his arm around me. "That, gorgeous, is a golden pothos. I have it on good authority that these are hardy plants, *and* I figured it could stand in for the golden retriever or doodle until you're ready for a pup."

My eyes watered. "Is the good authority Ivy?"

"Yep."

"Hi, Goldie," I whispered, naming the beauty. I glanced back to Drew. "Do you want a dog?"

He gave me a funny look, but then said, "Yeah. I've always thought I'd get one once I was settled."

My fingers ran over his chest before I glanced up at him. "Do you care on breeds?"

"Nope."

"Have you thought of names?"

His expression was sheepish as he looked away. "Yeah."

I leaned in. "Daisy."

"Daisy?"

He nodded. "Margot's favorite flower. She had them planted all around our house. Said they're simple, but dependable and beautiful."

"Like Margot."

"And you."

My breath caught. "What's next on this tour?"

He led me to the kitchen where a variety of things were laid out on the counter. "Here we have the makings of homemade pizza, recipe courtesy of Emma, pizza stone borrowed from Ivy."

"So what you're telling me is that this evening is going to end with me gaining ten pounds?"

"Totally worth it."

He continued down the hall to my bedroom. "And here you will find pajamas that the woman at the store promises me will be the softest things you ever put on."

I ran a hand over the top. It was crazy soft. There were cozy socks included. I noted the rollerball next to it. "And this?"

"A relaxation blend from Ivy."

I turned in his arms to face him. "Drew..."

His hands came to my hips. "Kate."

I felt a feeling of guilt or worry in the pit of my stomach. "This is too much. Honestly. I made you some of those chocolate-covered protein balls that you like, and now I feel like a fool, like I somehow failed a test..." My voice trailed off as I worked not to kick myself.

"Nope, not needed. Honestly, I've never bought anyone anything for Valentine's Day before—"

"What?"

He shook his head at me as he leaned down to press a kiss into my forehead before standing back up. "I told you, no serious relationships until last year, and that shit show didn't start until after the big day. Actually, if the guys hadn't talked to me at the brewery last night, I wouldn't have had anything for you, which I would have felt terrible about."

"Well, at least you would have been the one feeling like a failure then." I gave him a small grin.

"Seriously, I love those protein balls, you know that."

"So which one of the guys do I owe a thanks for all this?"

"Honestly? All of them. Well, Sully brought up the topic, they all shared what they were getting their girl-friends, then Jake had the foresight to ask Steph what you would like. I added the soft pajamas, but that's partially for my own benefit."

"How so?" I thought I deserved points for ignoring the girlfriend comment, even though my heart rate had to be at elevated levels that would notify my watch.

"See, while supersoft, these pajamas also cover more skin than your typical one, so I might be able to control myself a little better during the movie."

I kissed the underside of his jaw. "We'll see about that."

Drew peered down at me. "So are we ignoring the label I just threw down?"

Yep. My watch must be very concerned for my heart right now. I was too. "Um, what label?" Cowardly, I know. But seriously, what if he was talking about something else? I was not going there.

Drew gave me a look that said he knew exactly what I was doing and he was having none of it.

He sat down on my bed and tugged on my hand until I was sitting on his lap. I put a hand to his chest and looked into his eyes, blinking back moisture in my own.

"Are you Santa? Am I supposed to tell you what I want for Christmas?"

"Kate, let's talk about this." He squeezed my waist. "No bullshit, beautiful. Honestly, Sully was talking and asked what everyone was getting their significant other and used the labels of wife, fiancée, and girlfriend. Being totally transparent here, I balked at first."

He looked at me with warm eyes, like he was gauging my reaction. I didn't know what he saw, but I knew my heart felt like it was going to come out of my throat.

"Jake pointed out that I've been seeing you and only you for two weeks, we met a month ago, and you are the only woman I've thought about, or wanted to think about, since then."

I looked down to my lap. I didn't want to hurt him, I couldn't hurt him. Staring at my hands, I willed myself to give voice to my fears. "Drew, it's just, I'm not sure—"

He cupped a hand under my chin and brought my eyes up to meet his. He didn't look upset. If anything, he looked concerned. "If you're ready? You're feeling scared?"

I nodded in his grasp.

"Me too."

A tear escaped the corner of my eye. Then another. His thumb came up and brushed it away.

"So what do we do?"

He leaned forward to brush his lips over mine. "Let me ask you this. Do you want to see anyone else?"

I shook my head. The thought actually made me nauseated.

Another lip brush. "And you want to keep on seeing me?"

I nodded vigorously. I mean, hell yeah.

He kissed the tip of my nose. "So what if we don't put any pressure on ourselves? We're seeing each other, we're not seeing anyone else, and we don't have to decide where this is going, if anywhere, right now?"

I had to be honest, part of me had a little twinge of sadness, like I *wanted* to define where this was going. But a bigger part of me was not there. I was firmly in the land of scary feelings when I thought of any future plans.

Clearing my throat, I looked up to Drew. "That works for me."

"You've been through a lot this week, Kate. I know you're stressing about the business, then there's the conversation with your parents where they were less than supportive of you, again..." His voice trailed off as he brushed my hair behind my ear, and I nodded.

Tipping my chin up so I met his eyes, he brushed his lips. "We're still learning about each other. How do you usually deal with stress?"

"You mean other than my parents' theory of running from it?"

His finger slid around my chin. "Nope, we're not disparaging you, beautiful. Are you a pro/con list maker?"

I smiled. While we might not know each other well, he

did know me. "Yes. Well, that and..." I trailed off, unsure how he'd take the admission.

"And?"

"Well, I mean, I usually talked it out with Alex." I looked into his stormy eyes, pretty sure he wasn't the territorial type. If he was, that would likely be a deal breaker.

Instead, he nodded. "Makes sense. You all were together for a long time." He looked to the windows, then back to me. "You two still talk, right?"

Uncertain, I nodded.

"That's good, right? I mean, you said he was a good guy."

"Yes, he is. You're really all right with that?"

"Why wouldn't I be?"

My chest was lighter. "It's just some guys wouldn't want their girl talking to her ex."

His smile was a beacon of light inside his beard. "My girl?"

My cheeks heated. "I mean, you called me, you know..."

He leaned forward to kiss my nose. "I know, Kate. I'm good with that label. And I'm good with you talking to Alex anytime you want or talking it through with me, but you know what I'm abso-fucking-lutely looking forward to?"

I tilted my head and looked at him. "What?"

"When you trust yourself enough to believe in your decisions deep into your core, no one else needed." And with that, he gave us a much-needed subject change. A squeeze to my hips, he slid me off his lap and stood. "Go ahead and check out the pj's."

I looked from the bed, to him, and back to the bed. "What?"

He'd taken a few steps toward the door and stopped to look back at me. "Pj's and then food."

"I mean, I thought—" I glanced back toward my bed.

"You thought we were going to have sex all day?"

My face heated. "I mean, not all day, but at least once."

"Oh, don't worry, beautiful. I just want to spoil you first, and I'm beginning by making you a pizza. But the two of us heating up these sheets? That will be happening later; it's just not the only thing I want from you." He winked and headed back toward the kitchen.

I looked to my bed and soaked in his words, all of them. I mean, I felt terrified and warm at the same time. How in the hell did that work? I felt like in Drew, I'd found someone who really saw me, all the way to my core, and that scared the shit out of me.

We were doing this. Okay. Letting go of everything heavy for now and stepping into the light, at least for now. And when was later happening anyway? I stripped, sliding the crazy-soft pajamas on, and left my bra off. Maybe I could make later happen sooner and think about the rest of these worries another time.

Worked for me.

Chapter 21

Not Out of the Woods Just Yet

D*rew*

Dawn came and I watched Kate in her sleep. She looked so peaceful, beautiful beyond all that I'd ever imagined. Her long brown hair had been in a side braid but had come loose sometime in her sleep or last night before bed.

Jesus. She was the most responsive lover I'd ever have, bar none. She'd come back from changing into the pajamas I'd bought for her, and it had been clear by her visible nipples that she wasn't wearing a bra. Judging by her smile, I'd known that was purposeful.

We'd still had dinner, watched another classic, *The Goonies*, and she'd given me a protein ball by feeding it to me.

And that was all she wrote.

I'd flipped her over the arm of the couch so that she was on her belly and tugged her pants down so I could devour her from behind. Once she was out of her mind, I'd grabbed a condom from the coffee table drawer that we were now using for that purpose and slid all the way in.

Pure heaven.

Which had of course freaked me way the fuck out. To the point that when we were done and lying together, Kate had passed out cold from a little wine and a crazy schedule all week. I'd carried her to bed while she remained in a hard slumber. But I hadn't slept, not then, not ever last night. Not one minute. I watched her, and my mind raced.

My anxiety was next level, and I was struggling to pinpoint the reason for it. But by morning, I knew that lying in bed and stewing about it wasn't helping.

With a whisper of a kiss to her cheek, I slid out and got dressed. In her kitchen, I programed her coffee maker so that it was good to go once she woke up and grabbed a scrap of paper to leave her a note.

What to write, what to write?

Finally, I settled on a short, but honest, note.

K-

Feeling stressed this morning. Heading to the woods to burn some energy, then the brewery for a shift. Text if you want to meet up for dinner. Taking my protein balls with me. Love them.

D-

PS – Coffee is ready to go, just hit the Brew button.

Bile rose up in my stomach. I'd almost signed in with an *L* above my name. That's how we'd left notes for my family growing up. Before we'd had cell phones, the three of us had been in and out of the house all summer long. Our neighborhood had a shit ton of kids, so we were only required to be home by dinner and let my mom know where we were. Notes were written with our initials for shorthand along with an *L* for love.

I'd almost written *Love, Drew* at the bottom of the note,

and it felt terrifyingly right. Hell. I was not ready for this, right? I knew damn sure she wasn't.

Before I could have a complete mental spiral, I grabbed the protein balls from the fridge and snuck off to my place where I texted Jake an SOS and asked him to join me for a run at Highland Woods. After tossing on some cold-weather running gear, I quickly hopped in my old-ass Bronco and drove out to the park.

As quickly as I'd made it out here, Jake had been faster. He stood against his truck in the parking lot, scrolling on his phone.

"That thing needs to be retired," he said with a glance at my vehicle as I slid out.

I patted the hood and shot a look his way. "Bite your tongue."

He shook his head. "It's older than you."

I rubbed my hand over the side. "Not by much, and she's taken me this far. We're sticking together."

My dad had this Bronco when we'd all been born. It was the car I learned to drive in, what I continued to drive from the time I got my license until today. The only thing I would have preferred was my grandfather's blue-and-white Bronco from the seventies, but that sat in my parents' garage to only venture out during pristine conditions. Really, it was their fourth child and, quite possibly, my dad's favorite.

And I completely understood where he was coming from.

"Have a trail you want to tackle today?"

I thought about it. "Let's hit the one along the river," I said, no idea what color that one was marked on the trail map.

Jake nodded, shifting our path slightly to the trailhead that was in the meadow.

We reached it, and he tapped his Garmin to track our run. Our initial pace was easy, shoes crunching in the snow. It was warmer here than in town, the barren trees creating their own wind block around us as an eagle soared overhead.

After five minutes, Jake broke our silence. "We going to acknowledge the SOS text?"

I kept running, my heart beating in my ears. "Spiraling."

"About?"

"Everything." *Pause.* "Nothing." *Pause.* "Kate."

We ran on, our strides matching over the uneven ground.

"Seems like you're right on track then."

My head shot to look his way, only to stumble over a root. Jake grabbed me before I could go down. I righted myself, and we continued on.

"What do you mean, on track? On track for more hours of therapy? Sure."

I was starting to break a sweat. It was cold, but the sun was warm. I also quite possibly over layered.

"Nah. I mean, I don't deny that therapy is beneficial or that you need it right now, but I'm saying I've been around this town during this past year. First with Max, then Sully, then me and even Nate with Elle; we've all had our moments to varying degrees."

I soaked in that statement as we continued down the trail. Following that train of thought, I knew where they all landed.

My breath stuttered.

"Fuck, Jake, I'm not sure that's the path Kate and I are on." The sweating was full force now, and I was pretty sure it wasn't entirely the result of the run or extra layers.

Jake stopped us in the path and looked at me. "But is

that what you want? Deep down? Isn't that why you're freaking the fuck out and we're on this damn trail before eight in the morning?"

I put my hands on my thighs and worked on my breath. Fuck.

Looking up from my vantage point, I saw Jake watching me, his hands on his head as he caught his breath, but his expression was watchful and... something. Maybe like he was waiting for me to figure it out?

Hell, that was going to be a long wait.

"I don't have a plan here," I said as I rose up to look him in the eye.

"Don't need one."

"You sure about that?"

"Man, don't make me be all sappy."

"Now I've got to hear this. What?"

"Follow your heart, you fuck nugget. If Kate's the one for you, work this other shit out and don't stop until she knows what she means to you. Life is too short to waste any of it."

Yep. Heart and stomach clenched in unison. Shit if that wasn't a terrifying idea. "What if I'm wrong? I thought Tiffany, Tami, whatever the fuck her name is, was it. Look how wrong I was."

"You're going to have to get your therapist to give you some insight here. Or maybe let me slap you upside the head. She fucked up, you didn't. You can't control others, and as scary as it sounds, you're going to need to trust Kate."

I closed my eyes as I turned away and let that idea wash over me. I did trust Kate, I truly did. She was a good person.

I didn't trust myself.

No, that was bullshit. I trusted Kate; I just wasn't sure if I was ready to hand over control of my heart yet.

Though, honestly, it might be too late.

Opening my eyes, I noticed someone standing up the trail from us sitting on a bench made from trees. I looked to Jake and nudged him, nodding in the direction of the man. "Is that Logan?"

Jake's head spun in that direction, and he nodded. In unspoken agreement, we dropped our conversation and headed his way.

Reaching the bench, Jake cleared his throat since it didn't seem like Logan had heard us. Logan looked over and wiped a hand over his face, standing up. I immediately felt like we'd interrupted something private.

"Hey, guys." Logan looked over at us. "Out for a run?"

"Yeah, we won't intrude. Just wanted to say hello," I said with a glance to Jake. Looking back at Logan, I debated what to say, but then with the shit I'd been dealing with lately, I hated to not offer an ear. "You good?"

Logan looked back to the river and took in a deep breath. I knew that feeling and wished I knew him better and could offer up more. Turning to meet our eyes, he nodded.

"Yeah, thanks. It's just, well, it's a hard day. An anniversary of a hard day. I like to start it out here, but I don't love talking about it."

I held up a hand. "Not prying. I get that, more than you know. We need to finish our run before my lunch shift at the Homestead."

"Thanks. And I had on my to-do list to call you this week. We're a go for the outreach position. I'm posting it on Wednesday. If you want to shoot a resume my way, I'll get you on the interview list."

For the first time that day, my chest loosened. "That

would be amazing. I have your email, and you'll have a resume tomorrow."

He nodded and we parted ways.

As we headed down the trail, my mind pinged from Kate to Jake's comments to the grief that was clear on Logan's face to the job opportunity.

After another mile, Jake cleared his throat. "The job Logan mentioned, that was the one you were telling me about?"

"Yeah."

"That's fucking cool," he said as the trail took us closer to the river.

I nodded, thinking of all the possibilities.

Jake came to a stop at the top of a bluff. The river stretched out in front of us, a thin layer of ice visible in parts. We stood there for several minutes, letting our breathing slow as the birds called to each other all around us.

"You good?"

"Yeah. I think you're right. I need to trust her."

"And yourself."

Fuck. I swallowed the lump in my throat, my voice barely audible above the sounds around us. "And that."

He bumped his shoulder into mine, and we headed back down the trail. Winding our way through the park, we picked up our pace so that talking wasn't necessary, but our footfalls allowed my brain to wander, processing everything that was said and the shit that wasn't.

Logan must have headed back already because we didn't see him again. Once we reached the meadow, Jake's phone chimed with several texts. The park was notorious for shit cell service with all the trees, but the meadow with its wide-open space was one of the rare spots where it wasn't an issue. He pulled his phone from his armband, and his face split into a wide grin.

"What?"

He shook his head and handed me the phone.

Ivy: *Tell Drew that I've decided to kidnap Kate for the day. I'm at her yoga class, and we've decided she's spending the day with Addie and me. Dinner at our place. Drew is invited. Otherwise, I'm pulling out his baby pictures.*

I looked to Jake. "Not sure that's a threat; I was a fucking adorable baby."

He rolled his eyes at me. "What do you want me to tell her?"

I shrugged. "Bookstore is welcome to hang out with Kate, though that's not really my call. And I'm glad to have you cook for me after my shift if that's cool."

"Of course it is."

Hours later, I walked up the back walk to Jake and Ivy's. My day had been spent with a seriously long nap after my run to make up for my lack of sleep, then a late lunch shift at the brewery. I'd messaged with Kate earlier and said I'd just meet her here since she'd hung with Ivy and Addie for most of the day.

Walking in the back door to their place, I was hit with amazing smells and loud music. My stomach took me directly to the oven, and I opened the door. Chicken stew and biscuits. Excellent. That shit was amazing, especially when it was cold out.

I closed the oven and followed the sound of Addie's laughter. Coming into the living room, I couldn't help but join her. Kate, Bookstore, Jake, and their dog, Chief, were all wearing tiaras and/or feather boas. Addie had on bright red lipstick, purple sunglasses, a navy T-shirt dress with the solar system on it, and rainbow leggings. She seemed to be directing the adults in some dance music to...

I listened carefully.

Ah, Fleetwood Mac. Sometimes Addie got their name mixed up, but they were certainly her favorite band.

Jake looked my way. "I don't want to hear it."

"Looking beautiful, bro." I snapped a photo for Steph.

"Uncle Drew!" Addie ran at me and jumped when she was still several feet away, trusting that I would catch her.

And of course I did. "Hey, Ads. You keeping these people in line?"

"It's a dance party. You need a costume." She squirmed to get down and then began spinning immediately.

I nodded. I'd do anything this pint-sized warrior asked of me.

"Ads, it's just about dinnertime," Bookstore said before leaning over to kiss me on the cheek. "Hey, Drew."

"Bookstore."

Jake scooped up Addie and headed toward the kitchen.

I turned to Kate and felt like I promptly lost my breath. Interestingly, that seemed to be my normal reaction to her. I loved that she wasn't dressed up to be here, but comfortable in who she was. The long-sleeved white T-shirt was almost sheer, which made me think of things that didn't need to be thought of right now. Her jeans had some holes in them, rolled up at the bottom. She had already kicked off her shoes. Her long loose braid over her right shoulder only served to remind me of last night on her couch.

Hell.

Her smile widened as she moved in front of me and rose up on her tiptoes to whisper in my ear. "Now, now, now, Mr. Spencer, you look like you are thinking some impure thoughts."

"Do we need to stay?" I growled out.

"Drew," she said in a warning tone before kissing my cheek and stepping away.

Ivy laughed out loud—of course she did—as she hooked her arm with Kate's and the two of them ducked their heads together, conversation flying, as they made their way to the kitchen.

Jake was right. I couldn't control any of this; it was already too late. I was gone for her.

Now what?

Chapter 22

Friendships

Kate

I sat in a cross-legged position, observing our Monday morning class. We had a core group of regulars and then a smattering of people who dropped in depending on their own schedules. This morning there were twelve of us practicing together, including Drew.

For the past hour I'd led the group through a variety of poses, moving around to adjust as needed. Drew's smirk, barely visible from his position in downward dog, told me we'd reenact some of this later.

I'd refocused. This man. It had been six weeks since he first took a class from me, almost a month since we started whatever we wanted to call this, and my desire for him was only amplified from where we started. Yeah, that "let's get it out of our systems" idea had worked about as well as it did in my romance books. I cared about him, deeply.

I had no idea what to do with that.

A week ago we had dinner at Jake and Ivy's place after I'd woken up alone. He'd spent the night but left me a note that said he was feeling anxious and needed to go run. At first, if I was being honest, I felt hurt that he couldn't talk to me about what was going on. But he'd taken the time to make sure I'd be able to have coffee, and he'd left me a note being vulnerable that he was struggling. It was then I came to the frightening realization that I wanted more. I wanted to be the one he turned to, but that wasn't what we'd agreed on.

In the meantime, I'd avoided talking to Alex, who'd messaged me back. I knew I was being a cowardly. Looking deeply, I didn't want to talk to him because then he'd see that I was holding back and push me to face reality. Hell, it was why I'd steered clear of any conversation with Kristine. I was running scared because I knew I wanted something with Drew that I didn't know how to ask for, and after Alex, I wasn't sure if I wanted to reach for more again.

In a low moment over the past seven days, I'd realized that I'd started to see myself as someone who maybe wouldn't get a happily-ever-after, someone who didn't get the relationship that lasted until we were old and gray.

While that made me angry with myself, I wasn't sure how to change that mindset. I was leery of letting myself start something because I couldn't see the future. Would it last? Would we stay together? If not, what was the point?

I let out a cleansing breath. My students were in Savasana, letting their energy calm and set them up to face their day. I might need to do the same.

"As you slowly come back to awareness, begin to find the movement that feels right to you. Maybe rotate your hands, your feet, as you make your way to your side, then come to a seated position."

I let them take their time as one by one they joined me in a seat. The lights of the studio were low with some daylight coming from the outside through the large glass windows.

Once everyone was ready, I continued. "Press your hands together, thumbs to your forehead. I wish you the best in your day. Namaste."

There were murmurs around the room as folks moved to gather their items. The people who'd borrowed mats and props returned them to their spots. Drew gave me a nod from the back and then headed out the door. He was opening the Homestead this morning, so I knew he had stuff to do.

Kristine came up as I was rolling my mat. "Want to grab an early lunch today?"

I glanced up from my spot on the floor. She looked worried. I was sure that had something to do with my avoidance, and that was on me. I'd work on it.

"Sure. I was meeting Ivy and Emma at Goodman's for lunch. Want to join us?" Goodman's was the deli down the street, and I'd been dreaming about their desserts since Ivy had suggested it yesterday.

"I'm not intruding?" Kristine looked unsure, and I wanted to kick myself.

"No, of course not. Listen, I'm sorry I've been keeping to myself."

"So you acknowledge it."

"Yeah. I'm sorting some stuff out, and sometimes that's made more difficult when I'm around people who know me well."

"Because we don't let you tell yourself false narratives?" Kristine raised an eyebrow my way.

"Fair statement."

"Can I butt into this girl talk?" I turned to see Lou Williams, one of our regulars.

Oh boy. Any conversation with Lou was bound to be an interesting one. Lou was looking lively today. She was a small dynamo, somewhere in her late 70s with a tight cap of gray curls. Today's yoga clothes included leggings that had stripes on one side, polka dots on the other, and a T-shirt that said SMASH THE PATRIARCHY. Her eyes twinkled with energy, as always.

"Of course. Are you here to fill us in on the latest in town?" Lou was always in the know, a byproduct of running the coffee shop for years in Highland.

"Well, the main gossip of late has been you and the younger Spencer boy, but you know that already." She gave me a wink. "Unless you want to share any new intel."

Jesus. "Nope, I'll let you speculate."

"Dangerous decision. Anyway, I'm sure you noticed Jeanie wasn't with me today."

Jeanie and Hattie were constant companions of Lou's. Hattie didn't attend yoga with Lou, but Jeanie usually did. The two women lived in one of the assisted living centers in town, and Lou usually picked Jeanie up to bring her here. I was impressed with their dedication; my new students weren't typically their age. We modified several poses, and I'd added a chair yoga class with them in mind.

"I did see she wasn't here. Is everything okay?"

"Will be. She hurt her wrist last week. Started to tumble after slipping on some snow and ice. She grabbed on to a car nearby and righted herself but got herself a little strain. I was wondering if there was any of that chair yoga you do online? I figured I could go visit and do that with her a few times this week so she can keep her joints moving."

"Great idea." I thought about the yoga classes I knew online. Most of it was geared toward younger people. "I can't think of anything off the top of my head, but I can just tape myself doing a class and put it on our social media. Would that be helpful?"

Lou brightened. "Yes. They have Wi-Fi over at the Arbors. When do you think you'd have one up? I'll let her know. She'll be thrilled. Maybe I'll get some of the other old people out there to join us. It would be good for them."

Shaking my head at Lou calling the others, but not herself, old, I decided to ignore it. As for getting a class up, I could do that pretty easily. I didn't have anything going on the rest of the day beyond lunch. "How about I get something taped this morning and have it up by this afternoon?"

"You're a doll," Lou said, then leaned in and whispered. "Now we have some time. How's that gorgeous man of yours? He's gained some flexibility in his hips since he started coming to class. That's got to help out in the bedroom." She gave me a knowing look.

Kristine started laughing as I groaned. "Lou, you're terrible. Not talking about this with you. Get out of here so I can get your video done or I'll have to call Verdell to come wrangle you."

"He gave up trying to control me back in the sixties." She winked and headed to the door. "Thanks, ladies."

I looked at Kristine. "She's a menace."

"And we love her for it."

Too true.

A few hours and one uploaded video later, the two of us were walking into Goodman's. I heard our name and looked at the side room to see Ivy, Emma, and Maggie there. Since we'd called our order in already, Kristine and I headed in to join them.

"Maggie, I didn't know you'd be here." I leaned over to give her a hug around the baby nuzzled against her in a sling. Maggie and Sully's little girl, Ellen, was just over two months old. I knew she was headed back to teach in a few weeks and wondered how she felt about that.

I took in her appearance. Her strawberry blonde hair was in a pile on the top of her head. She looked tired, but blissfully happy.

"This little one has been more chill in public of late, so I figured we'd venture out. I needed some time with adults." She patted the baby's butt in the sling as she moved back and forth, swaying as she spoke. "Besides, we're having one of our author visits at the school tomorrow, so I wanted to check in with Ivy and Emma."

I nodded, knowing how much these three valued this project. I believed Emma had spearheaded it, bringing a diverse group of authors for young people to town over the past year. It had been cool to see the town come together. Whenever a new author came, the bookstore and library featured their books and held book clubs for the adults in the community around that author's books. I think there were six or eight scheduled thought the school year.

"Who is coming this time?" I asked. I didn't read a lot of young adult books, but I'd known a few of the people they'd brought in.

"Jason Reynolds," Emma said. "He's amazing. I can't believe he had any availability. He does so much."

That name was familiar. Thinking about it for a minute, I took a guess. "Author of *Long Way Down?*"

Maggie nodded. "Have you read it?"

"Heck yes. That ending..."

"I know. My students have so many questions. I'm heading in tomorrow with the baby to be there for this. They are going to flip."

Emma, Ivy, and Maggie's names were called over the speakers, indicating their orders were up. Emma and Ivy moved toward the counter. "We've got this," Ivy said to Maggie, pointing for her to sit back down. Kristine and I grabbed the two empty chairs to join her.

"So are you looking forward to going back to school?" I asked as we all settled in.

Maggie peeked into the sling to check on Ellen, then settled back in the chair. "Beyond the author visit tomorrow? Well, yes and no. I'll miss the time at home with this peanut, but I don't think I have it in me to be a stay-at-home mom. I mean, hats off to them; that's super impressive. I kind of have the best of both worlds in that I can do that in the summer. However, right now I'm looking forward to being back in the classroom, talking to my colleagues, helping my students work through their own issues. It helps that my daycare is amazing."

Emma and Ivy returned as Emma joined the conversation as she and Ivy began passing out their food.

"You really did luck into it," she said to Maggie, then turned our way. "A woman named Kris recently moved to the area. Her husband is farming out near Sully's. She's using their farmhouse to start a daycare. In a few years, if it all pans out, she wants to run a preschool based on the philosophies of Reggio Emilia."

I looked to Kristine, and she shrugged as our names were paged. "I've got it," Kristine said, heading off toward the counter.

"Reggio Emilia?" I said to Maggie and Emma.

Maggie nodded. "I went to a preschool with the same philosophy when I was young. It's similar to Montessori or the Waldorf approach. Basically, the kids explore what they're interested in. Spaces are open for exploration and teachers are guides, not directors. I'm excited to see what she does with the daycare with that philosophy in mind." She continued to pat Ellen in the sling.

"That sounds amazing. Maybe I should reach out and see if they'd like to incorporate yoga into the daycare if she has any preschool-aged students. I love working with kids."

Kristine came back and handed me my spinach salad before sitting down with her sandwich. We both had iced tea and some of their house-made dill pickles. "Yoga into another preschool class?" she asked, clearly overhearing the last part of our conversation.

"Yeah, new place that Maggie is bringing Ellen."

"That would be great; you do such a great job with littles."

Looking to the group, she said, "Thanks for letting me crash your lunch."

"You're invited anytime," Ivy said. "Though I know it's hard to take time off when starting a new business. How's it going? I feel like I haven't checked in since our conversation two weeks ago."

Kristine nodded as she put her sandwich down. "Well, we worked on our social media accounts, trying to post daily at the very least, and have seen an uptick in followers and customers. More would be great, but it's a start."

I nodded as I finished a bite of spinach salad. The crisp bacon was an excellent salty contrast to the hard-boiled egg. "Yeah. Today I put up a short video doing chair yoga on our Facebook page for Lou's friend, Jeanie."

Emma looked my way. "Jeanie with the cute gray bob, always in her Birks?"

"That's her."

"She hasn't been in the library for at least a week. I was going to call the Arbors to check on her."

"Lou said she had a small accident but will be fine.

However, it means she can't come in for class for a few weeks, so I'm going to post some classes online for her. I put the first one up just an hour ago, but we've already had lots of positive feedback. I hadn't counted on anyone watching it besides Lou and Jeanie."

Maggie looked pensive for a moment. "You know, there's that super popular YouTube channel with yoga on it. I wonder if you couldn't do that on a smaller scale for our community."

My mind lit up with possibilities as Kristine said, "Interesting idea. What are you thinking?"

"Not sure. Selfishly, I was thinking how much I miss your classes. Realistically, I could come now, but it's hard to figure out if Sully or I can be with Ellen. Once I go back to school, that will be even more difficult. It would be awesome if I could support your studio and get yoga classes back into my schedule somehow."

Hmm. I tapped my mouth. Support the studio through online classes. We could figure that out. I met Kristine's gaze, and she nodded. Something to work through later.

I looked to Emma and decided to switch topics. Enough about us. "How are wedding plans going?"

Emma's face lit up, and she began to talk all about the plans for a small wedding at her parents' farm in June. We then grilled Ivy. She and Jake had gotten engaged at Christmas but were planning a low-key wedding this summer.

An hour passed quickly, each woman at the table sharing an update on their life, things they were struggling with or working on, giving advice, cheering each other on. I found myself getting emotional.

"Hey, you okay?" Kristine leaned over to ask me.

I sniffed, wiping a stray tear from under my eye. "Sorry, it's silly."

Ivy reached across and squeezed my hand. "What is it?"

I felt a flush heat up my neck and face. Looking around the table, I lowered my voice. "I didn't think I'd ever have this."

Emma, Maggie, and Ivy looked confused. Kristine squeezed my arm, knowing what I was talking about.

"All through high school and, with the exception of Kristine, college, I looked for girlfriends. I found a lot of nice woman, and they were all happy for me to be their friend, but it was lopsided friendships."

"How so?" Maggie asked.

"I'd text, call them, check in with them on how they were doing, invite them to lunch, out for drinks. We'd go, and it would be a great time. But it was always me reaching out to them, never the reverse. I felt like an afterthought. Heck, apparently, I *was* forgettable. Once I stopped actively reaching out, I'd never hear from them."

I looked away. It was hard to admit that you weren't that important to other people. However, I knew it wasn't really my issue. They just weren't the friends I was meant to have. That didn't mean it wasn't a hit to my self-worth.

With a glance to my right, I squeezed Kristine's hand. "It made me value the friendship I had with you even more." I looked back to the group. "My mom used to always say if you had one good friend, you were set. And I decided I had that and stopped trying for more. However, if I'm being honest, I've been lonely. I hate to say that because I've had Kristine and Alex, but I didn't want to ask too much of them because what if they left?"

Kristine looked at me in alarm, and I raised up a hand to stop her. "I know, it's silly, but that's how I've felt."

"You can't get rid of me, Kate. Alex either." Kristine squeezed my hand back.

Looking back to the group, I wiped away a tear or two that had escaped. "But you all have welcomed me in since I moved here, so has Nic and Elle, and I can't tell you how much I value it. It's been nice."

"Back at you, sister," Maggie said. "Emma and I were just talking about our circle earlier today. How would you all feel about a monthly book club? Not as part of the bookstore or library, but for us and a few more women, though anyone is welcome. We can rotate where we hold it each month."

"Sign me up," I said as Kristine responded, "In."

"Elle is too and Nic," Ivy said. "I told them about it at the bookstore today."

Emma munched on a pickle. "Grace and Gabby from my library want to join. We might have to have a chat with Tim, he's going to want to come."

I laughed thinking of Emma's coworker. He was a riot. "I'm down for Tim attending anytime."

Maggie spoke up. "Sully said he can provide the beer for our meetings, which means the guys will be on driving duty."

Ivy held up her iced tea. "To book clubs, beer, and girl-friends."

"Hear, hear." We all clinked glasses.

Ivy looked over at me. "And please know, I had much the same experience finding my own friend group until I came here. This place is magical, I swear on it. We could tell Shelly over at the Main Street offices that Highland should have a new slogan. Move here and you find your happily-ever-after—friends *and* significant others."

My eyes widened. "Oh, I'm not sure we should go there just yet."

Ivy gave me a measured look. "Shouldn't we?"

"Now we're getting down to the good stuff," Emma murmured.

"Heck, this was another reason I came," Maggie said. "So Kate, at what point in the romance arc are you and Drew now?"

I looked at her confused. "What?"

"Denial? Seems a little late for that," Maggie muttered.

Ivy looked at me with a kind expression. "You have to realize they've been watching several couples pair off over the past year. Maggie's getting impatient."

"Well, I'm just saying one of you people could get pregnant so I wasn't the only one dealing with leaky boobs right now," Maggie said.

"Working on it," Ivy replied, raising her eyebrows.

"Woo-hoo!" Maggie reached over and high-fived her.

Emma worked to calm the crew down; fellow diners were looking our way. "All we're saying, Kate, is that this goes a lot better if you just relax and let the relationship happen. We all had our own baggage that got in the way for a while. We love you and Drew together."

"Oh, they are one hundred percent at the not-giving-up-the-baggage-just-yet stage," Kristine said with a glance my way.

"Hey!"

"I speak the truth," she said with a shrug.

I couldn't argue that.

Maggie leaned forward, hand holding Ellen to her chest. "Kate, I'm speaking from experience here. *Let it happen.* Let that Norse god rock your world and enjoy the ride. Once you decide you're open to what comes next, you can relax and enjoy it."

"Oh, I've enjoyed the ride," I said because apparently my inner middle schooler was coming out to play. "I'm just working on the being open to the idea of what comes next."

"That a girl." She gave me a nod.

I sat back and looked around the table as the conversations flew. So this was what I'd been looking for: friends who celebrated with you, complimented you, bragged about you, and held you accountable in the softest of ways. It was all I'd hoped for and a hell of a lot more.

I met Kristine's gaze and smiled. She returned it because I knew it had been a journey for her too.

Chapter 23

Words of Wisdom

Drew

The brewery was quiet in the lull between lunch and dinner. Mondays were slow anyway, but this time of day was especially so. I wiped down the bar, checking to make sure everything was stocked for the rush sure to come this evening.

My attention caught as a man entered the bar area. He came toward the middle and pointed at a stool. "Can I order from the menu at the bar?"

"Absolutely." I grabbed a menu and slid it in his direction. With a gesture toward the taps, I asked. "What can I get you?"

"All those brewed here?"

"No. We have several but also support other breweries in the Midwest."

"I'm not choosy. Pick your favorite that you all make."

"Sounds good. Where do you stand between stouts and IPAs?"

"Both are great, but I'm leaning toward stout today."

Nodding, I drew a pint of Barn Owl Stout and set it in front of him, giving him the space to figure out what he wanted to eat. I knew he wasn't from the area. While Highland Falls had apparently become more diverse since Sully grew up here, it was still sadly lacking. Add that to a town that was less than ten thousand people, and I knew the majority of the adults at least by sight, especially with my job here. A six-foot-tall Black man with an impressive mane of dreads absolutely would be notable in Highland Falls, so clearly, he was new to town.

I grabbed a glass of water for him and headed back down the bar. "Need any help deciding?"

"Yeah, man. It all looks good. What do you recommend?" He scanned the front and back of the menu.

"I'll give a few suggestions of my favorites. The nachos with steak are unreal. Sweet Thai bone-in wings, also great. There's a buffalo chicken sandwich on there that I get often. And Pete, our chef, has been experimenting with smash burgers of late and they kick some ass. Add sweet potato tots or fries to that, and you're in business." I reached over for some rolled silverware to put in front of him while he debated.

"Let's do the smash burger and those tots."

I nodded and turned to put his order in the system.

"Nice beer," he said as he took another drink of the stout. "You one of the brewers?"

"Nah." I leaned against the bar across from him. He was my only customer, so might as well settle in. "My brother and his buddy started this place; they're in charge of the beer. I invested in the canning portion of it this past summer."

He nodded, and I got the feeling that he really soaked in

what I was saying. Sometimes when you talk to people, you could tell they were waiting until you were done talking so they could say something. It was the opposite here, like this man wanted to hear you.

"Name's Jason," he said, reaching his fist across the bar.

"Drew." We bumped hands. "What brings you to Highland Falls?"

He laughed. "You know I'm not a local? Is this one of those places where you all grow up here and know everyone?"

"Nope. Just moved here myself from Colorado this fall. I'm from the Chicago area before that."

"Story there, man. But I'm here for work. I write for young people and am doing a visit with the middle school tomorrow and a small group at the library tonight."

"Ah, you working with Emma at the library, Ivy at the bookstore, and Maggie at the school?"

"Whoa, it is a small town," he said. "Not used to that. I'm from DC. And yes to all three, though I've mainly been talking with Emma Sullivan."

"All three are good people and friends of mine. Emma is the sister of one of the brewery owners, Maggie is his wife, and Ivy is the fiancée of the other brewery owner—who is also my brother."

He rubbed a hand over his beard. "Dang. Might need you to draw a map of that."

"So you like writing for kids?"

"Absolutely. Kids have so much empathy, compassion. We have a lot we could learn from them if we're open to it."

I nodded. "Maggie, who works at the middle school, has been on maternity leave. I hope you get to see her. She agrees with you there. She's always telling me how we'd all be better off if we'd follow the examples of her students."

"Well, she's right." Jason took a sip of his drink. He sat back as one of our servers slid his food in front of him. I grabbed some condiments he might want and put them near him on the bar.

"So Drew, what's your story? How do you go from Colorado to here? Were you working at a brewery there too?" He took a bite of his burger as he was waiting for my answer and let out a moan. After chewing, he said, "My compliments to—Pete, was it?"

"Yep. I'll pass them on. To answer your question, went out to Colorado for college, fell into working as a firefighter, did a stint with the Hotshots out West for close to seven years, and just moved back."

A few drink orders came in for the one other table in the place. I filled them and set them to the side for Tom to grab, then turned back to Jason.

"I knew it, man. There's a hell of a lot more story there."

I shrugged, filling up his water. "Not much. Made some missteps, working on righting myself now. Starting over, I guess."

"Never too late." He moved on to the tots. "I know in this situation," he gestured from himself to me, "It's usually the customer seeking advice from the bartender, but I've been told I'm a good listener if you want to talk about those missteps." He tossed another tot in his mouth. "And when you're talking to this Pete guy, these are worthy of some love too."

"Noted." I grinned; there was something about him that made you feel immediately at ease. "As for missteps," I shrugged. "What can I say, I fucked up."

A voice came from our side. "Or you could say you were human and we all fuck up."

Jason and I turned to the side, and I felt myself step back in shock.

"You look like you've seen a ghost, Spence."

James was standing in my brewery. Here. In Highland Falls. I was at a loss for words.

"James." He held a hand out.

"Jason." He held up a fist instead, which James bumped. Jason took a last drink of his beer and stacked his silverware and napkin on his plate. "This was excellent, man, but I've got to head off to the library to start getting ready for tonight. What do I owe you?"

I waved him off. "Pleasure to get to know you. This one is on me. Thanks for visiting our town and the work you do with kids."

Jason nodded his thanks and headed out while I came around the bar to greet James. He immediately pulled me into a crushing hug, slapping my back repeatedly. Eventually, he let go, and I headed back to my side. "I'll be off in about twenty minutes, but what can I get you while you sit your ass down and tell me what in the hell you're doing here?"

He laughed. "Dealer's choice."

I poured him a Fire & Rain. "You want food?"

"Have you ever known me to turn it down?"

I ordered both of us an early dinner.

"This is good," he said, drinking another sip of the West Coast IPA.

Before I could reply, Daryl, the bartender on next, came to relieve me early. I quickly went over anything he needed to know, then told him I'd be joining Murph at the high top in the corner.

With a beer for myself, I nodded for James to follow me to the table.

"So you just took a wrong turn and ended up a thousand miles from home?"

His light grin turned more serious. "Worried you were still dwelling on the past; thought I'd come out and make sure you'd moved on."

I looked down to my beer.

Murph knocked on the table, and I looked up to meet his gaze. "Let's break it down. What are you still struggling with the most? The girl? The fire? I'm tired of dancing around this."

I worked on deepening my breath. Jess had pointed out in a session that when I got anxious, it immediately became shallow and caused the anxiety to spiral. I'm sure if she was here, she'd tell me it was time to lay it all out since she'd been asking me to do that for weeks. I'd finally been able to process it with her but had been taking baby steps facing it anywhere else but in a session.

"Honestly? I think it goes together." I focused on box breathing for a moment before continuing. "I think before last spring, I trusted myself. I felt like my gut would tell me who was worth spending time with, who wasn't. In a fire situation, I could see what needed to be accomplished and work to protect our crew while getting the job done. In four weeks, that was all shot to shit, and I was left with zero confidence in myself and a whole lot of doubt."

I couldn't meet his eyes.

"Drew... Drew. Look at me please."

I'd never heard Murph's voice so quiet. I pushed myself to meet his eyes.

"Hear me when I tell you this. One, as I've said repeatedly, you did me a favor with Tami. She'd completely snowed me. I'm grateful you showed me her true colors, even if it was unintentionally."

"I see that, but what does it say about me that I trusted her? That I was falling for her?"

Murph raised his eyebrow at me. "Um, what does it say about me doing the same? Are you telling me I deserved that?"

I shook my head.

"Then why are you telling yourself that you do? You made an honest mistake. Go easy on yourself."

Shit. I sat back in my chair and stared at him, unblinking. I hadn't thought of it that way.

"Now that last call we were on." He grabbed my forearm as I looked away, sick to my stomach. "Spence, the smoke was everywhere, the wind shifted, your escape route looked like it'd disappeared. It was a shit show. It is not your fault that you all got cut off from the rest of the team."

I looked up at him with my heart in the pit of my stomach. "You don't understand. I wasn't focused. All that had just gone down with Tami. The recruits with me were so green. It was my job to lead us, and I almost did—to our death. If you all hadn't figured out what had happened and charged in to get us, we would not be here having this conversation."

Murph squeezed my forearm. "I hate to be the one to break this to you, Spence, but you actually aren't a damn superhero."

"What?"

"No one is perfect. Not our chief, none of the other guys on the Hotshots, not me, not you."

"The stakes are so high out there, James, there's no room for error. I fucked up. Maybe I should have taken myself off duty that day. I knew I wasn't in a good space."

"You know damn well that we needed you. And since

you don't remember, let me share now you did a shit ton of good work that day, before and after that misstep. Yeah, you and the rest of the guys could have done things differently that day. If we went through the crew, that's happened to many of us before. Once you guys were back with us, you continued fighting the blaze for the rest of the day and into the night. You *helped* us beat it back. We saved that farm on the ridge with your help. So stop being an asshole to my friend. Stop treating yourself the way you'd never treat any of us. Have some fucking empathy, man. You're human. Deal with it."

For the first time in months, my breath came easier. "I don't know how to tell you how much I needed this. I'm just sorry you had to come a thousand miles to tell me."

"I mean, if you'd just talked to me at any point, we could have gone through this, you damn idiot."

I laughed. "Deserved. I kept telling myself if I talked to you I'd find out that all the guys had lost respect for me. That was hard to take on, since I'd lost it in myself." I let out a breath.

"So that's why you left?" James asked.

"Partly. Also, after we got cut off, I started having nightmares."

"About that?"

I nodded, my mouth going dry. "I'm in the smoke, the recruits are with me, but I can't get us out and you all aren't coming in. I wake up shouting for you all as the fire rages."

"Fuck, Drew, you should have told us. We have therapists you could have talked to." Murph's expression was serious.

"I did. I mean, I finally called the chief a month or so ago and told him what was going on. He gave me the name of a therapist that he knows of, and I'm doing telehealth with her."

"Helping?"

"Slowly."

"I'll take it." James finished off his beer as Tom brought our food. I'd gotten both of us the same meal Jason just had. "Now that we have the heavy stuff out of the way, how's life?"

I felt the grin spread across my face before I could answer.

"Ho-ly shit. What's her name?"

"What makes you think there's a her?" I asked, fucking with him.

"Because I've never once seen you look like that. Spill, sir."

"Kate Ashley."

"And..." He popped a tot in his mouth and groaned. "Damn."

"I know," I said, having one of my own. So good. "Kate's a yoga instructor here in town. I took a class from her around six weeks ago, and we became friends, then neighbors, and now we're dating."

"What was that?" James asked, eyes narrowing.

"What do you mean?"

"When you said you were dating, there was a moment you didn't look happy." He pointed at me with his fork.

"Put that weapon away." I took a bite of my burger, thinking of how I should answer this. Fuck it. I was laying it all down tonight; might as well continue. "When we started this all up, we both said we were keeping it light, nothing serious."

"Why in the hell did you do that?" Murph looked at me like I'd lost my damn mind.

"Well, you might be aware that I was struggling with trusting myself. And my recent relationship choices hadn't exactly panned out." I took another bite of my burger, wiping the juice off my beard before it dripped too much.

"Jesus, you fool." He gave me a pitying look.

I rubbed the bridge of my nose with my middle finger. "At any rate, Kate was just as reluctant to jump into something serious for her own reasons."

"And now that you know you're in love with her? What does she want to do from here?" He asked, waving his burger at me.

"Love?" I sputtered. "What in the hell are you talking about?"

"Dude, not to get too deep into feelings because I know nothing about them, but you were positively glowing when you talked about her. You looked exactly like my sister when she met her husband. It isn't hard to read. So answer the damn question: what are you going to do now?"

My attention was distracted by the woman in question entering the brewery. She and Kristine came into the bar area, shedding their winter coats as Kate unwrapped a scarf from her neck. She scanned the bar as she talked to Kristine, until her eyes met mine and she beamed.

"Wild guess. Is that goddess her?" James asked, dropping his burger and wiping off his hands on his napkin.

"Yes, but—"

"And the vision to her right?"

"Her business partner, Kristine. But, hold on—" It was no use. Murph was headed right for the two of them, and I was left wondering what in the hell had just happened to me.

Love? Really?

Kate looked from Murph who had pulled her into a

hug, to me. She shook her head and laughed, her eyes lighting up with humor at whatever he just said. Likely a joke at my expense. Her eyes crinkled as she stayed locked on my gaze, and I found myself moving toward her without a thought.

Yep. I was fucked. Now what was I going to do?

Chapter 24

Geodes

Kate

Kristine was clearly having the best night ever. We'd arrived at the Homestead an hour ago to grab some dinner after class. Selfishly, I'd wanted to see if Drew was still here. He'd had a shift, but I hadn't been sure what time he got off. I needed to see him. We felt like we were settling into something good, but I also sensed I was waiting for the other shoe to drop.

Walking in here, I'd seen him sitting with someone I didn't know. I couldn't look away; his face was relaxed. I didn't know how to describe it except to say I wouldn't have been able to tell you before this moment that he'd been holding on to some tension, but with it released, it was obvious and I wanted to know more.

The man sitting with him was all kinds of gorgeous. He had wavy brown hair, tan skin, and blue eyes. He'd said something to Drew and then immediately headed our way. When he reached us, he stopped toe-to-toe with me, and his face had been positively dancing with amusement. I got a sense that this man was loads of fun.

"Kate? You're a tiny little thing to have tamed that beast."

"Excuse me? Beast?"

"Sorry, name is James Murphy. I worked with Drew, who *can* be a beast in terms of stubbornness, in the Hotshots. Just heard about you over some kick-ass tots. Have to say I've never seen him light up when talking about someone he's dating." He got serious for a moment as his voice softened. "And I'm damn glad to see it."

"A friend from the Hotshots?" My mind raced through the names from any conversation with Drew. My eyes locked back on James as I let out a breath of air. "Wait, you were close. Weren't you..." I wondered how to ask what I needed to in a sensitive way.

"...the one that had the girlfriend with an identity problem?" He smirked.

I burst out laughing and allowed him to pull me in for a hug. This was huge. I could tell Drew was still struggling with blame in that situation. The fact that James came all this way likely said a lot.

Stepping back, I tilted my head to look at him. "Did he know you were coming here?"

"Nope. Figured if I told him, he'd find a way to take off. Surprised the ass and we worked through some shit. Now I think the two of you need to join our party and lighten the conversation." He turned to Kristine. "Drew says you're Kate's business partner. Can I interest you two in joining us?"

Kristine did not hide her appraisal of James as she gave him a seductive smile. "Lead the way."

Interesting.

Hours later, we left Kristine and James to close down the brewery, or at least to continue to flirt with each other without an audience. James was staying at the same Airbnb Drew had used when he first came to town. The two of them were clearly ready for some alone time, so Drew and I decided to leave them to it.

As we walked the streets of Highland, I stayed lost in thought while Drew led me to our place by our linked hands.

"Penny for your thoughts?" He said with a squeeze to my hand.

I let out a breath of air which puffed out in a cloud. It wasn't late, near eight, but I felt like it had been a full day, and I had so much I wanted to tell Drew I didn't know where to start. Including the fact that I wanted, no *needed*, to process my day with him.

"Just thinking about my day," I said as I followed him in the door next to the bookstore and up the stairs.

"Want to come over and debrief?" he asked with a nod to his place. "Or I can come to yours."

"Pj's, then yours," I said.

He nodded his agreement and started to turn toward his door before tugging me back to lay a kiss on me that made me tremble at my core. My mouth opened for his, and his tongue slid in as a tidal wave of feeling swept over me. My arms wrapped around his torso, and I raised up to my tiptoes, debating if I should try to climb him.

Too quickly, his hands found my hips and set me back a step. I looked to him, working to catch my breath. "What in the world was that for?"

He winked. "Looked like you needed a preview of what was to come."

I turned and went into my place, leaning back against the door the moment I closed it. What was I doing again? Ah. Pajamas. Got it.

I made quick work of shedding my clothes from the day. Scanning my drawer, I smiled and picked something out just for Drew. Within minutes, I was back at his place and stepping in.

He wasn't in the living room or kitchen. "I'm back." I called, raising my voice so he'd hear me in his room.

"Grab a drink if you want one," he said. "Be out in a sec."

Looking in his fridge, nothing was jumping out to me. Instead, I grabbed a mug and nuked some water. Drew had begun keeping the tea I loved here, and right now I needed the warmth.

A few minutes later I was leaning against the counter with the mug cradled in my hands, eyes closed, as I worked to find my center.

"Uh-oh."

My eyes opened to see Drew leaning against the opposite counter, his eyes scanning down only to come back and lock on mine.

I tilted my head to the side. "Yeah?"

"Well, one, don't think I missed that this is the getup you wore over here when I first moved in. Count me as a fan."

I wiggled my hips in the blue lounge jumpsuit that was unbuttoned to show off my navy lace bralette.

"Thanks."

"Two, tea."

"Nice alliteration. Want to share more?"

"You often cradle a mug of tea when you're stressing and need to re-center yourself, or that's what you tell me. So I'll repeat, uh-oh." He walked the steps to cross to me, effectively surrounding me with his arms at either side.

I peered up to him, wanting to stroke his beard, muss his

hair, kiss his lips off. But I also wanted just to cuddle into him. I was in so deep it scared the hell out of me.

"Could we maybe sit on the couch?"

He kissed my forehead. "You bet." Before heading in that direction, he grabbed a beer from the fridge, opened it, then led the way.

Once at the couch, Drew dropped into the corner and spread his legs with a chin lift to indicate I should plop on down. I moved to sit between his legs, my back to his front. He pulled a chunky knit blanket from nearby and draped it over my legs before encouraging me to lean back.

"Comfy?"

I nodded against him.

"Okay, babe. Spill. What's going on in that gorgeous head of yours?"

Tears pricked my eyes. "I'm selfish."

"Come again?"

"You clearly had a conversation with James today. We should be talking about that."

His lips found their way to my neck. Over the past few weeks, he'd learned my body so well he could like map out my favorite spots, and this was absolutely one of them. "Babe, we can talk about that in a minute. Tell me about your day."

I took another drink of tea, staring out the windows, seeing nothing. "Really, it was mostly good. Class went well. I posted a yoga video to our Facebook page for an older lady in town who can't get to the studio right now. We've had a lot of feedback on it that people would like more of that."

"That a possible revenue stream you two would like to explore?" His lips continued to trail up and down my neck. Goose bumps trailed his lips.

"Possibly. Probably. No, definitely."

He tugged the rubber band off the end of my braid and started working my hair loose. I let out a deep sigh as I melted into him. I was a huge fan of anyone playing with my hair.

"What else?"

I closed my eyes as he massaged the base of my neck. "I got emotional with the girls at lunch."

He moved to massaging my temples. "How so?"

"It was about friendships."

His hands stilled. "Friendships?"

I nodded, wanting desperately for him to continue the massage but unsure if I should continue taking from him without giving something in return. Luckily, his hands started moving again, and my head became a rag doll.

"What about friendships?"

I shrugged. "I don't know. I think I have some fears buried that the reason I didn't have a lot of women friends was that I was somehow lacking."

"Babe."

I wanted to giggle. His voice was filled with disbelief like he couldn't believe it. "That's it, *babe*? Is that a complete thought now?"

He squeezed his arms around me, resting his chin on my shoulder. "I mean, of course you aren't lacking. You're amazing."

I worked to blink back more tears. "I mean, objectively, I know I'm a nice person. I'm kind. I think I'm a good friend. But for the longest time, like the majority of my life until I moved to Highland Falls, Alex and then Kristine were the only people who were a friend *back* to me. Others came and went, were kind even, but it was like I was an afterthought. I wasn't worthy to be in their inner circle, but if it was a larger group, they might think of me then. It's hard to not let that eat away at you."

"So you had Kristine..."

"Yep."

"...and Alex."

My heart thudded. Drew knew Alex and I had been friends for a long time, that we still talked, but we hadn't really had a conversation about it. I was terrified if we examined my relationship with Alex, if Drew really saw everything that was swirling in my brain, he'd know that I was too much and decide he was done with me.

Quite frankly, I wasn't sure if I'd blame him.

Unaware of my swirling thoughts, Drew squeezed his arms around me, then both hands raked through my hair as he continued to massage my head. "I think we should talk about Alex."

Deep breath. "I don't know that we need to."

"I think some of this might be connected."

I turned to kneel in front of him, leaning over to set down my tea. Meeting Drew's eyes was hard, I felt vulnerable, but I also wanted him to see me.

"How is Alex connected to my feelings of friendship?"

He cupped my face in his hands. "Before I tell you what I'm thinking, know that I don't believe this. I'm just worried that maybe you do. Okay?"

I nodded, placing my hands on his thighs and bracing.

"I think you saw yourself as unworthy of friends and maybe also fearful that it didn't work with Alex because you weren't worthy of a long-lasting relationship. And your parents don't help in this regard."

I sucked in a breath. I mean, I'd been telling myself something similar, but what did it say that Drew saw that?

He pulled my mouth to him and pressed a kiss to my

lips again before pulling back. "Don't go there, Kate. Remember, I think that's bullshit. But for you, is there any truth to that?"

I nodded as tears spilled over my lids and I was helpless to make them stop.

He brushed them away as fast as he could. "Is there anything I can say to reassure you that isn't true?"

Helplessly, I whispered. "I don't think so."

"Then I need to show you."

Drew scooped me up and headed down the hall. One we reached his room, he laid me down on the bed more gently than I'd ever dreamed possible. He grabbed the back of his T-shirt and tugged it over his head. In another beat, his joggers were on the ground and he was standing before me, gloriously nude.

His eyes met mine, and he smirked. "Babe, I wish you'd get with the program. Why are you still wearing clothes?"

I got with the program.

After kicking my jumpsuit to the side, Drew fell onto me, his mouth meeting mine. I felt like I was drowning in emotion, but I didn't want to come up for air. His hand slid down to my core as his fingers entered me.

"Fuck, you're ready."

"More than," I said as I arched up.

He leaned over to my bedside table and grabbed a condom. Making quick work of it, he asked, "Preference on position?"

"Whatever gets you inside me the fastest."

He laughed. "Oh no, Ms. Ashley. We're savoring this."

"Savor me the second time," I said, beyond impatiently.

Drew ignored me, leaning down to capture my mouth as he slid inside. He started slow, rocking up inside me, hitting the spot in the front of my vagina that promised all good things. Slowly, maddeningly slow, he continued to thrust, building up the pressure that threatened to destroy me. The entire time, his eyes were locked on mine. When I turned my head to the side, he followed me, kissing me as he turned my head back to face him.

"Do you feel that?" he asked, his eyes locked on mine.

"Yes." I gasped. I couldn't lie, the connection was unreal. I felt vulnerable and laid bare while also feeling like I was a part of something beautiful.

"You"—he leaned down to pepper kisses over my cheeks, down my neck, across my breasts—"are worthy of everything good in this world, Kate Ashley. Friendships, relationships, everything."

I closed my eyes, tears streaming as my orgasm crested closer and closer, emotion and sensations threatening to destroy me.

Drew ran his tongue along the underside of my breast, then pressed worshipping kisses on each nipple and locked eyes with me. "I fucking love you, Kate, and I need you to know that. Do you understand?"

I mutely nodded as he thrust again and I broke, stars blinding, as he continued until he found his own release.

I wrapped my arms and legs around him, dreading the moment he left me to deal with the condom. I felt like a geode broken open, my insides spilled out for the world to see.

"Be right back," he whispered with a kiss to my nose. I lay there, unable to move, as he disposed of the condom and came right back. Drew slid back in the bed, tossed the covers over us, and rolled to his side, tugging me to him as he spooned around me. His arm wrapped around my waist, and his mouth came to my ear. "Sweetheart, two things you should know. One, I'm in this with you, far more than I ever planned on, but that is what it is. And two, you've got me as your biggest cheerleader by your side. I'm here, and I'm not going anywhere."

I kept my back to him as tears streamed down my face and I blinked at the wall. Drew loved me. He'd dealt with so much, worked to face his fears, and was ready to be all in. And what had I done to work on myself? Nothing. But that wasn't stopping him. Drew saw me, the good and the bad, and that scared the hell out of me.

Chapter 25

Punch to the Gut

Drew

I drove out of the park, my thoughts jumbled. True to his word, Logan had posted the position for the park, and I'd gotten my shit together immediately. Today I dropped off my resume and application. I could have done it online, but I wanted to check in, and my dad's old-school mindset reminded me that I shouldn't miss an opportunity to make a good impression.

As per usual, my phone vibrated with texts once I reached the stop sign at the edge of the park and returned to the land of decent cell reception. Glancing down, I saw one from Bookstore. With a look behind me and to the cross-road, I saw no one in the vicinity. I clicked to make a call on speakerphone, tossed the phone in the passenger seat, and started driving while the sound of ringing filled the vehicle.

"Wow, an actual phone call instead of a text. Should I feel honored or are you asking for bail money?" Ivy's voice filled the Bronco.

"Such faith you have in me, Bookstore. Why on earth would I need bail money?" I glanced around at the sky. We were days away from the first of March, but it looked like we were going to have more wintery weather anytime. The clouds felt ominous, like something was on the horizon.

"Not sure, baby Spencer, but if anyone could do it, it would be you."

"Thanks for the vote of confidence. Calling because I'm headed back from Highland Woods and saw your text. Lunch date with you and Addie still open?"

"Yep. Her school is closed today. Some frozen pipes are giving them a headache. Nic is filling in with me at the bookstore. I'm home with Ads."

I thought of my day. It stretched ahead of me with nothing planned. Unlike my mindset a month ago, that didn't fill me with dread but with a lightness. Damn, the yoga was working. Kate might not let me hear the end of that. "Want me to watch her? I'm not working at the Homestead and don't have any plans."

"No, but thanks. It's been a while since we spent the day making blanket forts and hanging out. I'm looking forward to it."

I turned onto the road that would take me straight into town. "I don't want to crash that. Want me to catch you all a different time?"

"No, not at all. Jake will be here for lunch too, and Addie is super excited to hang with her big boys."

I grinned, heading down the street to park at my place. "I'm just pulling up at my apartment. Need to shower, then I'll be to you all."

"Great. See you shortly."

She disconnected just as I turned off the car.

Thirty minutes later I was jogging up the back walk to Jake and Ivy's place. Opening the door, I bellowed for Addie.

"Ads?"

"Drewwww!"

It was a toss-up whether the pounding of her little feet or her voice alerted me to the incoming missile first. Either way, I braced to prepare.

Addie came through the hallway from the upstairs and living room at a sprint. Sparkly purple tutu flying, she leaped for me when she was still three feet away, arms out, trusting me to catch her, which of course I did.

Damn, I loved this pint-sized dynamo. The thing about Addie was that she was present in every moment, no pretenses, just owning who she was and loving with her whole heart.

As much as it pissed me off, I knew I'd missed some of that with Emily and Jennie. I'd been in Colorado when they'd been born and hadn't spent anything like the months I'd been with Addie in Highland Falls with them. That was one thing that would be changing now that I was living in the same state. Watching them a few weeks ago was just the beginning. I'd already talked to Steph and Theo about finding a way to spend time with their girls at least once a month. A six-hour drive round trip was worth it because before too long they'd like want to hang with their friends more than their uncle.

I guess in some ways I had a hell of a lot to be thankful for when thinking of the bullshit that had sent me packing from Colorado. Hell, James and I had met up for a daily run for the past three days since dinner Monday night. He'd just taken off to visit friends in Chicago, then was going to swing back down here before heading home. Wasn't sure if him staying a few extra days had been thanks to me or if he'd hit it off with Kristine more than she'd let on. Kate said Kristine had left it at

James being pretty to look at, but she wasn't ready for more than that.

Murph wasn't used to having to work for it. I had a feeling he'd be back.

But spending time with him this week had helped to sort so much of my shit. Yesterday's session with Jess had cemented the changes I felt taking place. It seemed messed up that a conversation with Murph had been what I needed. I'd told Jess it pissed me off that if I'd just talked to him back in the summer, I might have gotten here earlier. She reminded me that it likely wasn't *just* the conversation, but that I'd done a whole lot of growth over the past few months and the time had been right to face my past.

But my clear mind also highlighted the fact that Kate was, if anything, more freaked about what was happening between us than I'd ever imagined she'd be, and I had no idea what to do about it. I'd told her I loved her on Monday.

Damn. Let's sit with that for a moment. I, Andrew Francis Spencer, told a woman I'd loved her for the first time at the ripe old age of twenty-nine.

And she hadn't said it back.

My younger self would have been flipped, certain the radio silence meant I was alone in these feelings. For some unknown reason, I wasn't. I knew to the depths of my soul that she felt the same, but she was holding back. She'd made excuse after excuse to avoid me for the past three days. I was giving her the day, then wading in. I wasn't going to lose her.

I'd be lying if I said I wasn't scared though. Not about how she felt about me, but how she was feeling in general. I knew the shit that was swirling around her in the past year had knocked her confidence, but I couldn't get her to open up and talk to me about it. I mean, I wasn't an expert here, but I felt like that was a problem. Then again, what in the hell did I know about relationships?

Tiny hands came to either side of my face. "Drew, stop spinning, I'm getting whooshy."

I shook my head. Good Lord, Ads. Focus, man.

"Sorry, Ads. No need for us to get whooshy. What do you want to do today?"

Addie held her chin in her hand like she was contemplating the great problems of the universe. I reminded myself that laughing right now would do me no favors. "Well, we could color, or I could do your nails. And then there's making cookies. We have so many options, Drew." She gave me big eyes.

I looked to the doorway from the hall. Ivy was standing there, watching the two of us, with a soft smile on her face. Sometimes I felt like she and Addie had been part of our family for so much longer than four months. I was damn glad Jake had proposed at Christmas so that they were going to be permanent fixtures. Smartest thing he'd ever done, not that I'd tell him that.

"Ads, I want to talk to Uncle Drew real quick, then you can play. Okay? How about you start on a blanket fort?"

Addie tapped me to be put down so she could take off. "Okay, Momma, but can I watch a movie while I build?"

"You bet, peanut."

She was off in a flash; this time Chief was trotting right behind her. I noticed he was back up to speed after a run-in with a vehicle three months ago. That damn dog made us all weepy with the way he protected Addie. There was never a dog that had loved a girl more.

"Can I get you a drink?" Ivy walked over to the fridge, but I waved her away.

"I know where everything is, Bookstore." I opened the

fridge to grab a beer from the brewery. I didn't usually drink with lunch, but today seemed like it might call for it. I raised an eyebrow in her direction when I looked her way to see her fidgeting. "Spill."

Ignoring me, she grabbed a mason jar glass and poured herself some iced tea. I noted the other mason jars in the window ledge that looked out into the backyard, each filled with water and labeled with a date on a piece of tape. Knowing Ivy, this was her moon water, collected during a full moon and filled with some type of charged energy. I remembered the first time she told me about it when she and Jake were still dancing around their attraction to each other. Maybe I could ask Kate to gargle with it? Wondered if those magical properties would help solve this shit.

A look back to Ivy told me she absolutely had something on her mind. She was now sitting on the island and regarding me with a speculative look. I leaned against the counter opposite to her and took a drink, thinking I'd wait her out. It didn't take long.

"Why do you look so relaxed when Kate looks like a mess?" She seemed ticked, but she'd certainly gotten my attention.

"Kate looks like a mess?"

"Yup."

"Not my fault, Bookstore."

"Guys never think it's their fault." She gave me a knowing look.

I took a sip slowly, savoring the fact that I was going to knock her on her ass. Not that I wished her any ill will; I loved Ivy. She was like a sister to me. But just like my sister, she did bust my balls when she felt it was deserved. And here? It simply wasn't.

Looking at her over the can, I shook my head. "Put away the glare, Ivy. It's not warranted."

"I'll be the judge, Andrew."

I worked to hold back a look. "All I did was tell her I loved her. I told her, but she didn't reciprocate, which is fine. That's not why I said it. But do you want to tell me how that makes me the bad guy?"

Ivy gasped. "Drew! What did you do that for?"

I put down my beer, growling. "Seriously? I'm actually aware of my feelings, verbalized them, and was mature and everything. What's wrong with that?"

Ivy put her tea on the counter and slid down to standing so *both* hands could come to her hips. Uh-oh.

"Drew Spencer, you know Kate has been working on letting go of her relationship with Alex." She whipped up a hand to stop me, though I was going nowhere. "Not that she still has feelings for him beyond friendship; it's just that she feels like she failed and is a little emotionally fragile."

"I know this, Ivy Jameson."

"She loves you, Drew, even if she isn't ready to acknowledge it."

"Also clued in to that, Bookstore."

"So you should know she needs to get some closure with Alex and let go of that relationship before anything more can happen."

"I'm good with that, Bookstore. I'm fine with her talking to Alex anytime. They text and everything. I'd never get in the way of that."

She rolled her eyes at me and looked to the ceiling, muttering to the goddess in heaven who created me with far too much confidence or some nonsense.

Looking back to me, she whispered, "She needs to talk

to Alex. That's been her person that she processes her life with for thirteen years."

I looked her straight in the eye and said, "I agree."

I laid it all out. "I just want her to one day get the confidence to process not with Alex, not even always with me, but herself. I want her to know that *she* is smart, that her decisions are wise, and give herself some goddamn credit for once."

Her eyes widened.

Good. Glad we both knew the score.

Hours later I dragged myself up the stairs to my apartment. I'd been the horsey for Addie for so long, my knees wept. My nails were now a sparkly purple. We'd built forts, watched cartoons, made brownies, and had an amazing time.

And the whole time I'd had part of my mind on Kate.

At the top of my stairs I looked to my door, then hers. Ivy thought I should let Kate have some space, at least for now. I was against that idea. I mean, I did want her to feel empowered enough to make her own decision, but with the winners she lucked into for parents, I really didn't want her to feel alone.

I took a step toward my place when Kate's door flew open. I turned quickly and felt like I had a punch to the gut. She was beautiful, of course. Black leggings, gray tank, denim button-down, hair in a messy bun, Converse All-Stars, backpack thrown over her shoulder, and swollen eyes with a red nose. She'd clearly been crying, and not just a little.

"Kate." I took a step toward her and stopped as soon as she held her hand up.

I watched as she closed her eyes, then looked back to me as her door closed behind her. The only way I could think to describe her appearance was broken, and it killed me.

"Please don't come closer." Her voice warbled.

"Are you okay?" I mean, clearly the answer was no. Ivy told me she was a mess, but I hadn't understood the level.

"No, yes, maybe? I mean, I'm trying to deal with my own shit. I hadn't. I thought I did, but the truth was I'd shoved it down for months—hell, maybe years—and now I can't move forward unless I do."

"Okay." I nodded, acting like I was following all this, when in truth I was all sorts of lost. "How can I help?"

She bit her lip and looked up at me with a tentative glance. Taking a deep breath, she said, "I need you to let me go."

My heart clenched. "What?"

Her eyes closed as she took another fortifying breath, then looked at me, a little stronger. "I'm flying to see Alex." She braced, like she was going to run if I even took a step toward her.

I willed myself to be strong, to be what she needed. I mean, the woman was going to England with a backpack, not moving boxes. I could do this. However, I couldn't lie; this was difficult. Standing here, hearing the woman I loved say she was going to her ex-boyfriend, was a punch to the gut. Alex was her sounding board, I knew that, but I wanted to apply for that role. Hell, I thought I had. I wanted to beg her to stay or ask to come with her. But I couldn't. I wouldn't. If this got her where she needed, where we needed, I could do this. I had to trust her.

Though I felt like I might combust.

Instead, I looked at her and said the only thing I could. "Okay." Pause. "Have a safe trip. Text when you land."

Kate's eyes widened, like she thought I'd fight her. Hell

no, I was going to show her that someone had faith in her decisions, even if it killed me. I just wanted the woman to find the confidence in herself that I'd seen before, that I knew she had.

She nodded, seemed to hesitate like she wanted to move closer, but then turned and walked down the steps. I heard her whisper thanks as she moved from my sight.

I stepped into my apartment and let the door close behind me before I broke.

Fuck. What did I just do?

Chapter 26

Easy on Me

Kate

"Excuse me, is there something I can get you?"

I looked up into the kind eyes of the flight attendant and felt shame. Or was it guilt? Damn, I needed to refer to Brené Brown's book again. I think it was shame, and it was flowing through me. Four hours into my flight to London and I hadn't stopped crying yet.

I was a mess. A hot mess.

Fortifying breath. "No, thank you."

She nodded and moved down the aisle. I dropped my head back against the headrest and worked to center my breathing.

Not helping. I stared at my lap, willing the tears to stop. Could you become dehydrated from crying?

A wadded-up tissue appeared in my line of vision. I looked to my right and saw the older woman who was in the window seat. We'd gotten lucky and had an empty seat between us. She'd fallen asleep as soon as we pulled away from the gate, which I'd been grateful for. One less person to see the state I was in.

But maybe I hadn't been as quiet as I'd assumed.

Her skin was paper thin, covered in age spots and wrinkles, though her nails were painted cherry red. I looked from her hand to her kind blue eyes behind bright red frames.

"Darling girl, you need to use this." She motioned below her own eyes.

Shit. Mascara. Great, now I wasn't only the girl having a mental breakdown on the plane, I also likely looked like a raccoon. Super.

"Thank you," I whispered, taking the tissue and mopping up my face.

"Now tell me what caused the waterworks." She lifted the armrest between her and the empty seat and then rotated to face me. "I'm putting my money on a man."

I laughed, which I would have told you would be impossible ten minutes ago, but her kind face was working some kind of magic. "Based on life experiences?"

She shrugged. "You don't reach eighty years old without realizing that men are clueless. So lay it all out. What did he do?"

I let out a sigh worthy of all the crap I'd been holding in. "Honestly, it's not a man, it's me."

My seat mate made a noise of affirmation, which led me to keep going.

"I'm thirty-two. Shouldn't I have figured out life by now?"

She patted my hand. "Sweetheart, the thing you learn as you get older is that none of us have everything figured out. We're doing the best we can with what we know. As we learn more, we do better. Unless you're a clueless ass; then you ignore the lessons you learn along the way."

"Maybe I'm a clueless ass."

"Oh, honey, clueless asses don't shed tears, worried they have screwed up. They take all the ignorance that foolish people have stored up in spades and keep on going, ignoring any flags going up around them. Trust me, you are not clueless."

She picked up her hand for a moment to unbuckle, slide over, and then put my hand in hers once again. I'd lost my grandmas when I was pretty young, but just for a moment, I let myself soak in what it would be like to have one in my life and clutched her hand like the lifeline it was.

"Darling girl, my name is Betty. Tell me everything."

And so I did. My history with Alex, my realization that I hadn't really had friends, beyond him and Kristine, until now. My recent foray into being a small business owner. Drew. It all came spilling out like a runaway train. Through it all, Betty continued to make noises of support while patting my hand.

"...I lay there in bed after he told me he loved me, and I just *couldn't* say it back. Betty, what in the world is wrong with me? I do love him. I know it, he knows it, but I didn't say it." I took in a gulp of air. "And then I ghosted him for days while my feelings welled up like a tide that was going to drown me until I packed it all up, texted Kristine that I was heading to London, and walked out the door and right into Drew."

Betty laughed.

"It's not funny," I said somewhat desperately.

"Oh, sweetheart, it kind of is. I mean, what goddess puts the new guy across the hall from you? Do they read romance books in the Great Beyond? Because that's a heck of a trope."

I arched an eyebrow at her while thinking Ivy would be a fan of Betty's since they both apparently were followers of the goddess above.

"Forced proximity, dear. When it's in a snowstorm is my favorite. How about you?"

"You read romance?"

"Who doesn't? Best form of genre fiction there is."

My face heated. "Actually, we were snowed in when we first got together."

Betty scanned my face. "By the looks of that blush that is even spreading to your neck, I'm going to say that being snowbound did you some good."

"Betty!"

"Hush, child. One, I like my romances steamy. There is no time when you're my age to deal with this fade-to-black nonsense, though if that's your jam, you do you. There's a book for every reader and all. But let's deal with your heartache. Did you get it all out?"

I looked down at her hand, not able to meet her eyes. "I hurt him," I whispered.

Betty squeezed my hand, and I reluctantly lifted my head to meet her eyes. "Do you know that for certain?"

My heart sped up, and I felt a little nauseated. "He didn't ask me to stay. He didn't talk to me. He just told me to have a safe trip and to text when I landed."

Then, to further state my case of myself as villain, I pulled out my phone, opened my texting app, and showed it to Betty. "And then he sent me *this*."

Betty took the phone and moved it so that she could better see the picture I was forcing upon her. She read the text below the picture of my pothos:

Drew: *Grabbed Goldie to take care of her for as long as you're gone. We'll both be here when you get back, and we're rooting for you.*

"Is Goldie the plant?"

I dropped my head against the seat to look at the ceiling. "Yes. Drew got it for me because I've always wanted a dog. A golden retriever or goldendoodle…" My voice trailed off. I really was a fool.

She chuckled. "So he's leaving you to do what you need to do and trusting you to do so. Heck, he's rooting for you. He sounds remarkably well-adjusted. I'd hold on to that with both hands, darling."

I closed my eyes, Drew's face swimming in my mind as my chest constricted. "I feel so lost, Betty. What do I do?"

We sat in silence for a few minutes. I wondered if Betty was regretting her seat placement, but then she cleared her throat.

"When I met my Frank, we were both in our late twenties. I had sworn up and down that I'd never marry. I was thrilled with life as a single person, even though it wasn't the norm back then."

"Is it now?"

"Touché. Well, it should be. Whatever works for you, embrace it. If it works for someone else, celebrate for them. We're all far too concerned about things that are none of our business.

"At any rate, Frank and I had a wonderful relationship, and it was a whirlwind; from meeting to wedding day was less than six months—"

"Whoa."

"I know. In the end, maybe that was for the best. Ten years after we got together, I lost my Frank in an accident."

My eyes shot to hers, but Betty was watching me with a steely strength.

"I'm so sorry," I whispered.

"Nothing to be sorry about, dear. I loved him desperately while I had him. Just because our time together was short doesn't mean it wasn't beautiful or that it wasn't important for my life."

I had a hunch of where this was going. "But Alex and I weren't separated because of a tragedy, and we never married, but our relationship failed."

"Did it?"

I looked at her, wondering if she was confused. "I mean, yes? We broke up after thirteen years."

"Listen to yourself, darling girl. Thirteen years. Over a decade. And you're still friends, clearly. You're flying to him when you're facing a crisis."

"I don't love him, not like that anymore. I'm just going to London..." I paused and thought about it. "Honestly, I don't know why I'm going to London. Habit maybe? He was my person for so long. When I was facing a big decision, I ran through my choices with him." I looked down to my hands and studied them. "Even when I felt like we needed to break up, I talked it through with him. When I wanted to drop out of college, to change careers, Alex has been my sounding board..."

I looked to Betty and confessed my fear, "My parents aren't what you'd call supportive. They think I run when I'm scared." I looked around the plane. "And now, I guess, I'm proving them right."

More tears. I was going to need an IV to rehydrate.

"Oh dear. One, I wish you had more support from your family. That being said, when you've run, to borrow the belief of your parents, did you regret what you supposedly ran from?"

I thought about that for a moment. Slowly, I met Betty's eyes. "No, I didn't. College wasn't for me. Continuing in school for that degree would have been a waste of money. And leaving a job that wasn't working for me was putting myself first."

"As was leaving a relationship that had run its course."

I nodded.

"Maybe your parents don't see it, but I think you're running from what you know isn't serving you, which is exactly what you should do." Betty paused, then grasped my hand tighter. "And I think you need to listen to what you are sharing. You clearly don't think of Alex in a romantic way anymore, if only because the way you look when you talk about your Drew makes it crystal clear how you feel about him.

"Maybe you need to examine why you feel a relation-ship is only successful if you're still together. Did you learn about love when you and Alex were together? Did you grow? Did you experience life together? Have adventures? Maybe Alex was the person you were supposed to be with for then, just not forever. He gave you the tools to take into this next relationship. Maybe that means you will be blessed with marriage and kids, maybe not. But life isn't only worth living when everything is coming up roses. Life is hard, and sometimes you need to take a moment, soak in the world around you, and learn from it as you move forward. That's where you are now."

I thought about that. Maybe?

"And as for your friendships with women, I've discov-ered that finding my true friends in life—whether that's with men or women—it's like panning for gold in a river. They're hard to find, and there's a heck of a lot of rocks that trick you. But when you find those relationships that just work, where people are there for you just as you are there for them, hold on. It's not easy, but life is so much better when you find those ones you click with. Sometimes you find those people quickly; more often it takes some time. That just makes you treasure them all the more."

I let out a long breath as a weight rolled off my check. "So it isn't something wrong with me that made Alex and me not work out or my earlier friendships fail?"

"Oh goodness, Kate, is that what you think?"

I nodded mutely.

"Oh honey, I don't think there is anything wrong with you at all."

The flight attendant came up at that moment to give Betty some information she'd requested about gates at Heathrow.

I whispered to Betty, "I'm going to listen to some music," so she wouldn't think I was ignoring her. She nodded and continued to talk to the flight attendant while I popped in my air pods and put my head on Betty's shoulder. I was adopting this woman to be my personal grandma. I'd let her in on the secret later. But for just a moment, I needed to process things on my own.

Glancing at my playlist of downloaded songs, I tapped on Adele, then "Easy on Me."

As the familiar lyrics washed over me, I let Adele's voice soothe my battered spirit. Soaking in the words with my eyes closed, I suddenly sat up and glanced down at my phone.

I clicked to start the song over.

Again.

And again.

I'd always listened to this song as Adele was telling someone else to go easy on her.

But...

What if it could be a message to herself? Like a love letter to the broken, but beautiful, person you are. That we all are, at times.

That might be the lesson Adele needed. And maybe I did too.

As the music swelled, building to the chorus, I felt everything swirling up inside. I'd worked so hard for years to have everything together. To push it all down, move along, not acknowledge what was going wrong.

But leaving college had been me taking a tentative step toward acknowledging myself. Career switch, same thing. And finally, choosing to leave someone I loved, but wasn't in love with, forced me to acknowledge it all.

It hadn't been running away but being brave and making the right decisions for myself. I knew that deep in my core.

Adele sang on about good intentions, and I didn't bother to disguise the tears flooding my cheeks. I felt like a damn had burst and it was all being released. However now it felt like I was cleansed from the inside out.

The song ended, and I replayed it. Again. And again. For at least thirty minutes.

Finally, I pulled my headphones out and looked to Betty who'd been knitting by my side in the middle seat while I listened, not even moving back to her original spot, making sure I knew I wasn't alone.

"It's not my fault."

"Nope."

"And it's not Alex's fault."

"No, ma'am."

"And it wasn't a failed relationship."

"You're getting there, sweetheart."

"And I don't need him to make decisions. I can trust myself."

"Go, Kate!"

"And I *am* worthy of love, in friendships and relationships."

"Goddess knows that's true."

"I need to be kinder to myself."

"We all do."

"And I love Drew Spencer."

"Of course you do."

I looked over this kind face and said the only thing I had left. "Thank you."

"Thank yourself."

I dropped my head to her shoulder and fell into a deep sleep for the rest of the flight.

Almost four hours later, Betty and I moved through the airport. We'd already exchanged phone numbers so I could keep her abreast of how everything worked out. But I also wanted to stay in contact with her. She lived in the Chicago area, so we'd already made plans to meet up when she got back from London.

We headed to the baggage carousel to pick up Betty's suitcase. "Are you even going to go see this Alex, or are you just going to buy a ticket home?"

"Honestly, I need to get some food and figure out my next steps," I said just as I heard my name called.

Betty and I turned as one to see Alex steps away before he pulled me into a hug.

"Kate, I'm so glad you're here," he said into my hair.

I peered around him to Betty whose grin was Cheshire cat large.

"I'm guessing this is Alex," she said with a laugh and a twinkle in her eye.

Well, hell.

Chapter 27

All I Want

Drew

I strummed my guitar, my gaze firmly locked on the windows in front of me in the light of the day. It hadn't even been twenty-four hours since I saw Kate, and I could think of nothing else.

Over and over I'd played "All I Want" by Kodaline since I'd woken up this morning, if you could call what I did last night sleep. It was sappy, I knew. And Steph and Jake would never let me hear the end of it, but it said everything I was feeling inside, and somehow playing it was helping. Kind of.

Because the truth of the matter was that my heart was breaking. Why in the hell did anyone willingly put themselves into this position?

The rational part of my brain thought for certain that Kate would go to London, talk to him—I couldn't say his name right now; it made me nauseated—and then hop back on a plane to me.

The part of me that was afraid, the part I was leery to even give voice to, was scared she was never coming back.

If she loved me, like I thought she did, why would she leave me?

Part of me feared that she was running, but that made me think of her parents. For whatever reason, she felt like she had to go to London. I needed to trust her and pray she found what she needed.

I hit the end and started again just as the door burst open. It said something about my mental state that I didn't even jump up, but tipped my head back to see who was barging into my apartment.

An upside-down glance told me my siblings had invaded.

I didn't acknowledge them, but instead righted myself and continued playing.

"It's worse than we thought," Steph said.

"Well, to be fair, Nic did say it was this song, over and over, for the past three hours," Jake said.

I snorted. "It hasn't been three hours."

"She said it started up at seven, and it's ten in the morning now." Jake dropped onto the couch next to me.

I looked to Steph who was folding into the corner on my other side. "You were up early if you got down here by ten."

"Left as soon as Jake called."

I gave that a moment. Nic called Jake, or more likely, Ivy. Jake was worried and called Steph. She hopped in her car and drove straight down. Soaking that in, I'd assume they were worried that on top of all the shit out West, of which they still didn't know it all, I got dumped and now was going to break down even more than I already had.

While they were meddling, they were also the best.

"I'm okay."

"The blisters that you're going to be getting on your

hands will say otherwise." Jake held out his hand for the guitar. I was honestly glad to hand it over.

I dropped my head back to rest on the couch, considering my ceiling as I thought of how to alleviate their concerns, which weren't completely unfounded. Jess's voice in my head reminded me to share my truth.

Keeping my eyes closed, I went for it. "You know about Tami/Tiffany. What I haven't shared yet is that after that shit show went down, my Hotshot crew was called out to help out with what we thought was a standard fire. I was with a few of our new recruits, and the wind shifted. We got cut off from the rest of the crew and turned around in the smoke. Thanks to some quick thinking on the part of some of the regular team, we got out. But it was tense there for a while." Visions of smoke and shouts for help played out against my eyelids as I let the memories wash over me. Curling my toes into the rug beneath me, I reminded myself of where I was. *I am safe*, I told myself over and over. Damn if it didn't help. "After, well, I struggled. I blamed myself. I had nightmares about being trapped, not able to get out. So when you offered up the chance to invest in the brewery, I took it and decided it was my opportunity to get out."

"Jesus, Drew, I'm so damn sorry." Jake put his hand on my right knee.

Steph slid closer to my left side, dropping her head to my shoulder after kissing my cheek. "Baby brother, I'm so glad you are okay. I wish you'd shared everything you were dealing with when you came back, but I'm hoping the fact that you are now means good things."

I soaked in the feeling of being sandwiched between them. I truly did feel safe, which said a lot.

"The shit that was causing me anxiety is lessening. One of the guys on my crew and a good friend came out earlier this week. We talked. He stuck around, and that—well, that helped me see that I shouldn't be shouldering the blame and guilt that I was."

"Of course you shouldn't be." Steph was threatening to go all protective mode, I could hear it in her voice.

"Down, Steph. I know. I've been seeing a therapist recommended by my chief. Jess has helped. Talking to James has helped—"

"Can we meet him?" She squeezed my leg.

I knew they wanted to be supportive, and I loved them both a whole lot for that. "Sure. He'll be back down in a few days before heading home, but we're also planning something this summer, possibly."

Jake cleared his throat. "And how does Kate fit into this?"

I didn't lift my head and kept my eyes closed. My heart hurt. It motherfucking hurt. How was that possible? "Kate is in London."

"Oh boy," Jake said under his breath.

"Why is that worthy of an oh boy?" Steph hissed at him. Wasn't sure if she thought I couldn't hear her, but since she was less than two feet from me, clearly, I could.

"That's where her ex lives."

"Shit."

"Exactly."

"Am I needed for this conversation?" I lifted my head up and looked from one to the other. They didn't even have the decency to look remorseful.

Steph apparently decided to jump on the grenade first. "So she dumped you."

"Nope."

"What?" She looked confused. "No? Then why on

earth are you playing a song about wanting your love back and looking like someone who got their dog run over?"

"Too soon, Steph," Jake said from my right.

"Too soon for what?"

"Chief? Four months ago? Too soon."

"Jesus, Jake. Your dog was a fucking hero. And he didn't get run over, he just got nudged out of the way."

"Nudged? Are you kidding me? Did someone remove your heart along the way and Theo forgot to give us the memo?"

"So melodramatic."

I stood up and headed for the kitchen. This was more than I wanted to deal with right now. I figured they could continue to banter without me.

I should be so lucky.

Instead, I was like the Pied Piper of my siblings, and they fell in behind me like little ducks.

"You're upsetting Drew," Steph said.

"No, that would be you."

"Are you getting into plants?" Steph called. "This is a beautiful pothos."

Glancing behind me, I pointed at the plant. "That's Goldie. It's Kate's. I'm watching it while she's gone."

I opened the fridge, debating the contents. Too early for beer? I mean, Kate was in London. That was six hours ahead of us. Could I drink one in solidarity with her? And honestly, ten a.m.... I'd had earlier starts to my day while tailgating in college with friends before a game.

Steph hissed to Jake, "He has her plant. That means she's coming back, right?"

I was twenty-nine. It was too early. Closing the fridge, I grabbed some whole beans to grind to make coffee. Grabbing them from the cabinet, Kate's box of tea fell out and dropped onto the counter.

And I stared at it.

And stared at it some more.

Part of me knew Jake and Steph were still standing beside me, but they'd stopped talking, so I was just going to soak in the quiet for a moment.

"Did we break him?"

"You broke him," Steph said.

"I'm not broken," I said, in fact wondering if I might be. I mean, I was staring at a box of tea, wondering if I'd have to throw it out because the person I bought it for would never be here again to drink it.

So much for positive thinking.

"Let me make the coffee," Steph said, grabbing the beans. Jake steered me back to the couch.

Ten minutes later we all had a mug in our hands and my two siblings were on the couch, facing me and waiting.

Fine. Let's get down to it.

"Monday night, after I had the emotional conversation with James, Kate and I came back here. To sum up and leave out the stuff we aren't discussing, I told her I loved her and she didn't say it back."

"I'm so proud I could burst." Steph had tears leaking out of her eyes. Interesting; the woman rarely cried.

"I know she and Alex are close, that they talk through shit together. It makes sense that she wants to talk to him, but I thought she might give him a call, not go all leaving on a jet plane on me."

"John Denver is hugely underrated," Jake said to Steph.

"Not. The. Point." I practically growled.

He had the decency to look abashed. "Sorry. Continue."

I took a swig of coffee. I needed fortification. "At any rate, I'm fine with her friendship with Alex, but I also think Kate needs to know that she can stand on her own. She doesn't need Alex, Kristine, or even me to affirm her decisions. I want her to have confidence in herself, but I knew she was struggling. I came home from lunch yesterday with you all. Bookstore had told me to give Kate space. I debated the merits of that idea—"

"Ivy is always right."

"Whipped," Steph and I said in unison.

"*Anyway*, Kate walked out of her apartment and told me she was going to see her ex."

"And you said…," Steph prodded.

"I said okay and told her to have a safe trip and text when she landed."

"Yowza."

"Yikes." Steph grimaced.

"What the heck is wrong with that? I gave her the space to make the decisions she needs. I trust her to go and do what she needs to do."

"Do you?"

I looked to Steph. "What?"

"Do you trust her?"

"Of course."

"Then what's up with the three hours of a song that's all about breakups, missing what you lost?" Steph tilted her head as she watched me.

Fuck.

I worked on what I did with Jess, sitting with my feelings, recognizing them, and worked to see them as separate from me.

Taking a breath, I looked back to Tweedledee and Tweedledum and chose honesty. "Okay. Deep down, I'm terrified that she's going to go to Alex to talk and decide they have all this history and should never have broken up."

"And yet you didn't tell her not to go. Why?" Steph pushed.

I sat with that, pushing past my initial responses to look deeper. I closed my eyes and worked to find the truth. "Because I have to trust her. I have to give her wings."

Now Jake just looked confused. "You mean airplane wings?"

Steph laughed outright. "No, doofus. He means the quote about giving those we love wings to fly, roots to come back, and reasons to stay." She looked my way. "But did you give her reasons to stay?"

"I texted her that I grabbed Goldie and said the plant and I would be here when she got back."

Steph leaned over, putting her hand on my knee, her eyes locking on mine. "See, you did give her reasons to stay. She might not see it yet, but you laid it all out. Now you have to wait."

I looked to the door. I could wait, I really could, and for the sake of my aching heart, I hoped she'd be home soon.

"It's five o'clock somewhere. Who wants a beer?" I stood up to head to the kitchen. Coffee wasn't doing the trick.

"That's my boy," Jake said with a laugh.

I had this... At least I hoped I did.

Chapter 28

Love You Always

Kate

"I'm assuming this is Alex?" Betty's voice came from behind me as I stood frozen in shock, wrapped in Alex's arms.

He pulled back, stretching his hand toward Betty. "I'm sorry. Yes, I'm Alex. Kristine hadn't mentioned that Kate was traveling with anyone."

Ah, mystery solved as to how Alex had known I'd be at the airport. I bet Kristine's fingers got a workout firing off messages as soon as she'd received my text. I'm sure if I took my phone off airplane mode, I'd see several replies filling my screen, which was all the more reason not to do that. I didn't want anyone from Highland Falls impacting my decisions right now. Including one tall Norse god who I missed more than I could express.

Nope. No. No waterworks right now. Wish Betty well on her trip, talk to Alex, get a flight back home. Or maybe get the flight before we talk so that I used my time well? Then again, I needed to allow time to get through security.

A realization that Betty and Alex were waiting on me to respond to something shook me out of my mental to-do list.

"I'm sorry, what did I miss?" I asked, looking from one to the other.

Betty came closer as Alex dropped back to allow us some privacy. "You good, Kate?" Her kind eyes scanned my face, looking for what, I had no idea. "Looks like your next steps got decided for you."

"I'm good, Betty. I told you he wasn't a bad guy."

She murmured her agreement. "He's also not *the* guy, right?"

I nodded.

She squeezed my arms in support. "Are you okay with me heading off?"

"Oh, of course." I felt terrible I'd kept her from her plans. "You didn't need to stay."

"I didn't mind, Kate. You know how I said that finding lifelong friendships is like panning for gold?"

I watched her, giving a small nod.

"You are proving not to be a rock."

I laughed out loud. Betty was proof that once you hit a certain age, you had no time for filters.

"Thanks, Betty."

"No thanks needed, my dear girl. I think I might need to come see this tiny town of yours when I'm done visiting my friends here. Small-town living isn't something I've tried out before."

The idea of introducing Betty to my friends was enticing. I think she'd love them. Though I didn't know if I should introduce her to Lou. I had a feeling they would be a dangerous combo.

"That sounds good."

"And until then, you're going to put up more yoga videos so I can work on joining you for a class online."

I laughed. "You bet, Betty." Yeah, no worries, she'd fit right in.

Betty pulled me in for a hug before looking over to Alex. "You take care of this girl, you hear?"

Alex gave me a smile before meeting Betty's eyes. "Absolutely."

Her eyes on me, she brushed my hair back before whispering in my ear. "Feel the world around you, Kate. Experience it. It's up to you to choose."

I closed my eyes and nodded. "Going easier on myself, Betty. Thanks for the wisdom."

We stood there for several moments, rocking back and forth in each other's arms, before she stepped back.

"Okay, enough of that. I'm getting on in years and need to leave this airport. I hope you find what you came for."

I gave her a small smile. "I think I have but might as well finish the trip."

With a wink, she turned and walked away. I missed her already.

Alex cleared his throat, and I turned his way, willing away the emotional waves filling me up inside.

His voice was light, like he was trying to decide how I was feeling when he finally spoke. "When you said *talk soon* the other day, I didn't think you meant in person."

A laugh bubbled up unbidden. "Yeah, about that..."

Alex reached out and pulled me against him again in a tight hug. "I'm just glad to see you, surprise or not."

My head moved in agreement of its own accord. Alex was a good friend, but now that I'd sorted myself out, I didn't even know where to begin with him.

Stepping back, he scanned me. "Okay, physically, you look like you're all in one piece. Emotionally?"

"Improving since a transatlantic flight I just hopped off of."

"Good. And Kristine says this neighbor you told me about, Drew was it? That he could be a body double for the next Thor movie?"

My face flushed. "Well, his hair is darker and short like in *Ragnarok*, but yeah."

Alex looked fierce for a moment. "A good guy?"

"The best." My heart ached. This was still strange.

"Nope, Kate, not allowed to go there. You know I'm dating too. This is as it should be." His expression was a knowing one.

"What?"

"If Drew can give you what you deserve, then I'm fucking delighted. So not to be rude, but if he's all that you and Kristine are indicating, then why are you here? Felt like seeing Big Ben? Parliament?"

"Nah, we'd never make it out of the traffic circle."

"Kate..."

My eyes welled up. Quite possibly, I should look for a Gatorade. Surely I was approaching dehydration levels. "Originally I came because I thought I needed you to help me sort out my brain."

"And now?"

"Well, Betty"—I gestured to the direction that she'd gone—"pointed some things out to me in our conversation on the flight over. And quite frankly, I did some soul-searching. I think, in some part of my subconscious, I'd thought there was something wrong with me. That it was to blame for our failed relationship, for my lack of good friends beyond you and Kristine. I think I was worried that what

Drew and I've begun was doomed to fail because of some deficit I had."

Alex knew me well and hadn't tried to interrupt even though I could tell he was practically biting off his own tongue.

"And now?" he asked after I stopped vomiting out my feelings.

"Now?"

"Now do you realize that entire line of thinking is bullshit? Some of it, unfortunately, planted by your parents?"

I had a burst of emotion as I realized I did and I had worked through that all on the plane. Thanks, Adele.

I looked Alex in the eyes, feeling a huge wave of relief wash over me. "Yeah, I do."

We stood in the middle of the hustle and bustle of the baggage claim as we looked at each other, years of understanding passing between us. Finally, Alex nodded with a huge smile, like he was making up his mind.

"Okay. Let's talk about next steps. Do you want to stay here or get a return trip today?"

I must have looked surprised because he continued instead of waiting for me to respond.

"Not that I don't want you to stay; I'd love to visit. But I also can tell that you've made some decisions, and I don't think I'm the person you need to talk to anymore. Kristine already texted me the options you have leaving today. So if that's the plan, let's get you a ticket and maybe some food or a drink in the restaurant before security. If you want to stay, let's get the hell out of the airport." He was looking down at his phone, scrolling through what I'm sure was a detailed text from Kristine.

I said the first thing I could think of. "Thanks."

His head jerked up to meet my gaze. "Thanks?"

I stepped closer, laying my hand on his arm. "Thanks for being a good friend for over a decade, one of my best. Thanks for reflecting on our relationship and realizing with me that we were better off as friends instead of taking the easy route out and heaping the blame on me. Thanks for being a huge supporter in my life."

Alex's expression moved to one of caring and warmth. "Sweetheart, just because we have changed how this thing between us is defined does not mean you can get rid of me that easy. We thought we'd be growing old together one way; now it's just shifted. I want the best for you, just like I know you do for me. So no, you aren't getting rid of me. I'd already planned a trip back to see you once stuff settled down here for work. Now I'm even more anxious to come. I need to meet this guy so I can give him my full approval."

"You're that confident that Drew will have your approval?"

He laughed, his eyes crinkling around the corners. "I mean, between me and Kristine, who's harder to impress? And he already won her over, so that's all I need to know. Well, that and the fact that you're here. In the world of Kate Ashley, that means you're ready to dive into the serious waters with him that scared you for a moment." He gave me a considering glance. "Am I right?"

I nodded and cleared my throat. "I think I was scared because in a matter of weeks, I could tell this is something that could level me if it didn't work out." Alex gave me a quirked eyebrow. "I know, I know, but I also have to realize that it could be worth every risk."

"The best things are," he said. Then, holding up his phone, he asked, "Okay. So stay and visit or figure out what flight you need home."

A tear slipped down my cheek. "I do want to visit you sometime, truly."

Alex brushed the answering tears away that were falling. "None of that. It isn't like this is goodbye."

"Nah, you're just a three-hour drive and eight-hour plane ride away."

"Yep. Practically next door." He watched me for a moment, then nodded toward the exits. "So how about we go get you a ticket home?"

I sighed as a weight left my chest. "Yep. Let's do this."

Six hours later I'd filled up on food in a restaurant before security with Alex. We were saying goodbye. Again. Or see you later. Whatever.

"Are you going to be all right?" His expression was serious.

"I'm good. Swear."

He tugged me into a hug that threatened to squeeze the life out of me. I felt him kiss the top of my head as he spoke so that I could hear him above the noise of the people around us. "Thank you, Kate Ashley."

"For what?" I asked his chest, which I was smashed against.

"For being the best friend I had in college and beyond. For teaching me how to be in a relationship. And for showing me what I need to look for in future ones."

I leaned back to meet his eyes. "Are you looking for one right now?"

He shook his head, his blue eyes twinkling. "Nope. Having fun with casual meetups right now."

I squeezed his waist. "But one day..."

"One day, but I'm not in a hurry."

I grinned at him. "Too much good sex right now?"

He shrugged. "Can't say it's bad, that's for sure."

I pulled him back in. "I'm happy for you."

"And I for you."

I moved back, looking over at the direction I needed to go. "I have to leave. Take care, you."

"Back at you. I'll visit soon and send you sunsets in the meanwhile."

I nodded, knowing that we would still be friends, but something was being put to rest here, and it felt good—but final.

"Love you always, Alex."

"Love you always, Kate. Now go get him."

Lightness filled me up. "I plan on it." And with a wave, I turned and headed back to the man who was calling my heart home.

Chapter 29

Starting Over

Drew

Standing at my window and looking at the streets of Highland, I felt a tension in my gut that wouldn't lessen. Steph and Jake had stayed with me for lunch and the early afternoon but finally left to go on a run that I passed on and then swing by the brewery. Steph said she was staying for the weekend and I could just suck it up and deal with it, which tracked.

I think they'd known I needed some time to process on my own and made their own excuses for their errands to give that to me, which I appreciated. I knew I'd been right to let Kate go. I'd known this was something she needed to do. Didn't mean it wasn't hard.

My ass vibrated, which wasn't as fun as it seemed, but likely a check-in from my siblings. I tugged out my phone.

Nope, not my siblings.

Murph: *Chicago is a place I could get used to. Plan on being up here through the weekend, then will head back your way. Thinking of staying through Wednesday, then heading back. Want to meet up for dinner Sunday?*

I felt like I lived in a vacuum. Not more than thirty hours ago, Kate left to fly to London. How was that possible? I didn't know what day of the week it was or what I'd be doing tomorrow, much less whenever Sunday was, but I should figure it out.

Pulling up my calendar on my phone, I was reminded that it was currently Friday, early evening. Hell, dinner would probably be good on Sunday. If left to my own devices, I might just mope in here indefinitely.

Me: *Count on it.*

James gave my text a thumbs-up. I was just putting my phone back in my pocket when I felt it vibrate again. I pulled it out to see an unfamiliar number. Reading the first line of text, however, I quickly opened my phone to see it all.

Random number: *Sorry for the possibly intrusive text. My name is Alex. Kate said you knew she came to see me.*

I read it, then read it again, then saved Alex's contact information while deciding what to reply.

I also saw that he was typing.

Another text came through.

Alex: *FYI, Kristine gave me your number.*

Made sense. Kind of. Wasn't sure what he was gaining by messaging me. I wanted to ask if she was still there, if she wanted me to text her. I'd resisted so far. I didn't want to place any pressure on her.

Alex: *I just wanted to say, she's more centered than I've seen her in years. She's also one of my closest friends, and I hope that you're cool with that because I have a feeling you aren't going anywhere, unless you two aren't in the same place.*

My emotions were all over the place at that message. One, it made me fucking glow that he thought Kate was doing so well, *especially* after how she looked walking out of here yesterday. Two, the fact that he thought I wasn't going anywhere, well, that was just God's honest truth. But three, hell no on the whole "are you in the same place" bullshit. At least I hoped we were.

But that wasn't something I wanted to have a chat with her ex about. Seemed like an invasion of Kate's privacy, so just no.

I thought about it for a minute, then replied.

Me: *Yep, you've got Drew here. Glad Kate seems good to you. And yeah, I know she considers you a close friend too. Works for me. Be well.*

I looked that over before hitting send. A large part of me wanted to ask if he was with her now, but if Kate wanted me to know, she would have told me. So I was letting that go.

Alex sent me back a thumbs-up, and I tossed my phone onto the couch and picked up my guitar. I started to play Kodaline's "All I Want" again but knew Jake and Steph would groan, possibly pelt me with a pillow. I shifted through the songs that felt right and landed on Stapleton's "Starting Over." I played it once, fumbling through a chord progression, and then began it all again.

It was on the second time through that it happened. The door opened, and I repeated my actions from the morning, tipping my head back, expecting to see my siblings once again.

It was Kate.

Kate, who was still in the same clothes I saw her in yesterday, but not crying. She looked... I didn't know how to put words to how she looked. Tired, certainly, but, maybe, resolved? At peace? Whatever it was, I started to put my guitar down.

She shook her head as she closed the door behind her and moved in my direction. "I know I don't have the right to ask, but can you play that song again?"

I looked at her watchfully. "Sure?" I went back to the beginning.

Kate walked around the sectional to curl up next to me. She must have tossed her shoes on the floor, or maybe she'd stopped by her place before coming here. It didn't matter to me, I was just so happy she was there.

Looking from her feet to her face, I noticed she was bobbing her head to the music, her face relaxed in a way I'd never seen it.

I got to the end and wasn't sure if she wanted me to play something else or just start this one up again. Before I could ask, her brown eyes met mine.

"I saw Alex."

"I know."

She looked at me quizzically. "How?"

"He messaged me." She started to speak, but I interrupted. "Kristine."

"Ahh. She's been busy."

I snorted, thinking of what the past day had been like for Kristine. I wondered if she set a record for texting. Had she filled in all their friends here? Likely.

"I also met a lady on the plane. Betty."

"Okay," I said slowly, wondering where this was going.

"Well, it's like this. In talking to her, I realized some things about myself." She looked up at me with wide eyes. "Namely that my parents are simply wrong. I'm not running from the right things, but everything I've run from is something that *wasn't* working. By leaving it behind, I took care of me. And I don't need Alex to make my decisions. Honestly, I don't even need you."

I started to interject, but she held up her hand and I shut my mouth.

"Hold on. Not that I don't want your input, just that I can trust myself to do what I needed."

"You can, Kate. And I'm happy to support you however you need or just sit by your side." I itched to move across the couch and pull her to me, but I had a feeling she wasn't done.

"For the longest time, I was afraid to admit I was lonely. Like it was something shameful, some character flaw, something I'd done. Who the hell knew that moving to this tiny town and opening up to the women I met would bring me exactly what my heart desired, including something with you."

"You realized all this by talking to some lady named Betty? I want to meet her and buy her a drink."

"And Adele."

"The singer?"

She nodded.

"You know that it's okay to be lonely sometimes. That isn't a reflection on you, just that you haven't met your people."

"Yeah, I think I've got that now."

"Well, I hope I get to see this Betty one day."

Kate laughed. A glorious sound that I felt down to the marrow of my bones. "Well, you might get your chance. She says she will come visit me before returning to Chicago. After her London adventure, that is."

I tightened my grip on my guitar, wanting so badly to hold her but unsure where we stood. "She sounds full of life."

"Yep. And she's got to be eighty years old with some kick-ass red-framed glasses."

"Sounds like she'd get in some trouble with Lou." I had no idea what I was saying. I was fighting every instinct that was screaming through me right now. Should I ask her where we stood? Should I give her space? Should I touch her? Should I—?

"Drew?"

I looked to her. "Yep?"

I watched as she took a deep breath, then locked eyes with me. "I love you."

I couldn't breathe. She continued, thank God.

"I'm so sorry. I should have said it back Monday. I should have talked to you this week. I should have at least said something before leaving the damn country."

The guitar needed to go. I set it aside and started to reach for Kate's hand, but she trumped me by sliding across to straddle my lap. Much better decision on her part.

"I can't explain what went through me. Monday night we spent time with James and Kristine. You felt different, like you relaxed finally. I realized you had done so much work on yourself since we'd met. You'd taken up yoga, worked with Jess, and then laid down your worries to your friend. You'd been a damn adult and faced your fears, your insecurities, and had ended up on the other side. And as afraid as you'd been to trust your heart to someone else again, you'd done it. You'd told me how you felt... and I felt? Like a coward.

"This week I spiraled. I knew what I wanted with you, but I felt like I didn't deserve it, or even worse, maybe I had some type of deficit that made it so I couldn't have it. I should have talked to you, but in my brain if I'd shared this with you, it was like telling you I was a bad risk. So I fled."

I smoothed back her hair that was escaping the bun on the top of her head. "I wish you'd talked to me. I think I could have set you at ease."

She shook her head. "I think I had to do this myself."

I agreed, but it didn't make me wish I hadn't been able to help.

I tipped her chin so that I could look into her eyes. "So you love me."

Her grin was beautiful and immediate. "I love you."

My smile matched hers. "And I love you."

She closed her eyes and soaked that in. "You do."

I leaned forward to brush my lips against hers. "What do you want from us, Kate? I'll give you anything."

Her eyes opened, and they swam with unshed tears. "You will, won't you?"

I nodded.

"I was thinking the song you were playing was a pretty good message. Want to start over?"

I shook my head.

Confusion flitted across her face. "But I—"

I leaned forward to kiss her again. "I want to continue. Where we've come from is important. We don't need to start over; we already did that when we came to Highland Falls. We found each other while we were starting over. What we need to do now is we need to keep going."

She let out a sigh that seemed like she'd had the weight of the world on her shoulders and it had just left. "So we continue."

"Yep."

"As something casual?"

"Fuck no. As something serious." My hands found her hips as I wondered if what I was going to say would make her run, but fuck it, I wasn't holding back. "As in someday soon I want to talk to you about ring sizes. As in I need to meet your parents, though I'm not super excited about that."

"They mean well. They're just antiquated and overly critical. They love me, but they weren't raised to be super affectionate."

"Well, they need to learn that or keep their mouths shut. Moving on, where was I? Oh, as in we need to decide if this is where we want to settle. As in I need to know your opinion on kids because I'd like some, but if you're not about that, then I'll get behind you."

"As in you want a future with me?" Her eyes were wide.

"Yes." No hesitation. No elaboration.

She had a small gasp, then looked unsure. "Do you think we could get a dog?"

I grinned. "After all that I just laid out, you want to talk about dogs?"

She shrugged. "I mean, you know I've always wanted one."

I stood up, letting her slide down me. "Poor Goldie, so unappreciated."

She gave me an impish grin as she looked to the plant on my side table. "Thanks for taking care of her. And Drew?"

"Yeah?"

"I'm good with all that."

I grabbed her hand and then headed out of the living room.

She tugged back. "Where are we going?"

I glanced back to her but didn't stop moving. "You look like you might fall asleep standing up. We're getting you showered and in bed."

I stopped when I saw her expression fall. "What?"

Her face heated up, the blush spreading from her

cheeks to her neck. "It's just that I hoped, I mean, it's been five days, and I wanted..."

I sorted through her stammering and grinned. "You wanted to have sex."

She looked to the ceiling. "Well..."

I couldn't disguise my desire. "After."

Her eyes met mine with a heated look. "Are you going to help me shower?"

My cock responded immediately. "Absolutely."

Forty minutes later, we were in my bed, naked. Much to Kate's dismay, we hadn't had sex in the shower. I didn't want to start over, or continue, with her by heading to the hospital after one of us got injured for trying to fuck against the tiles. Maybe when we looked for a place of our own, we could find a shower with a bench seat. She couldn't complain, though. I'd risked my knees to go down on her and get her where she needed to be.

And now she seemed ready to pass out.

We lay on our sides under the covers while I ran my hand over her hip, pulling her back to nestle her ass against me. "Did you sleep at all in the past thirty hours?" I pressed a kiss to her shoulder.

"Some on the way out, most of the way back." Her voice was soft, like she was floating between worlds. "But don't change the subject. You said we could have sex."

"Babe, you're exhausted. We don't need to right now." I trailed my fingers up and down her arms, watching goose bumps follow my path.

Her voice was quiet, but emotional. "I am exhausted, but I wanted to."

Far be it from me to deny her. "Let me grab a condom." I started to roll away, and she reached back to stop me.

"Do you have to? I haven't slept with anyone but you since Alex, and I've been tested. I also have an IUD."

I froze. Damn, this day was getting better and better. "I'm clean. I was tested after the shitstorm last year and haven't been with anyone besides you since."

"So..."

My hand stopped caressing her, and I slid down to lift her top leg and hook it over mine. "Is this good?" I asked as she was opened to me.

"Yeah," she whispered.

As I slid my hand over her hips and into her folds, I could feel how ready she was for me. Notching my cock at her entrance, I slid into her from behind, overwhelmed by feeling. This wasn't a position where we were going to be able to move much, but that was the point. It was intimate, soft, and sexy as hell.

Kate's head dropped back against me, leaving her neck exposed, her hips tight with mine. My lips found the sweet spot near her collarbone, and I sucked on it lightly while thrusting into her.

Jesus. She was clenched around me, making mewling noises that drove me mad. I'd thought this would be a longer session, taking more time to get off because of the position we were in. Looked like I was wrong and damn happy to be so.

Kate reached back to lightly squeeze my balls, and I almost lost it. Seemed that I was going to need to be more hands-on. I slid my arm over hers to find her clit. "Slow down, lady. Need to get you there first."

"Feels too good," she got out breathlessly. "I'm almost there."

Already? Damn. Another caress from her, and I began tight circles.

We moved together, connected from head to toe, and I worked to hold off my own orgasm as I felt the first flutters telling me Kate was on the way to hers. With one more thrust, I lightly flickered my fingers back and forth over her clit and she exploded.

Thank fucking God because I followed her right over.

We lay in the quickly darkening room as the sun set and streetlights went on. I got up, grabbed a washcloth that I dampened with warm water to clean her up, then tossed it on the floor and slid back behind her. Within minutes, Kate's breathing evened out, and I knew she was close. I pressed another kiss to her temple and settled behind her. It was only a little after seven, so I knew I wouldn't sleep yet, but I had zero issue lying there with her while she did.

"Drew?"

"Yeah?"

"Just wanted to say, starting over, continuing, whatever, I'm glad I'm with you."

I shook my head. This woman. Tilting my head down, I kissed her neck and then spoke into her ear. "Love you, Kate Ashley."

"I love the shit out of you, Drew Spencer."

I squeezed my arms around her. "Glad to hear it."

Chapter 30

Daisy

K*ate*
Sunlight hit my face, bringing me out of my deep sleep. Drew was curled around me and I felt immediate peace. Leaving my eyes closed, I went through the past week. The doubt, fear, insecurity, all leading to my panicked flight to London and back in less than a couple of days. An excellent way to rack up some points on my credit card, but not the most well thought out of decisions. Drew's arm tightened around my waist, and I snuggled back into him.

It had all been worth it.

"You awake?" His voice had a gravelly quality in the morning that I loved.

"Mm-hmm." I didn't want to move or leave this bed. Instead, I wanted to bask in his embrace, the warmth of the sun, the security in our path forward. Was it too late to see if hibernation was an option? How much did we really need to interact with the world anyway?

The rumble in Drew's chest at my back told me he was laughing at me, albeit silently.

"What's so funny?" I asked, still not opening my eyes. I was committed.

"You. You've been in this bed for fifteen hours. Any plans on leaving soon?"

I reached back, grabbing his ass, and squeezed. Eyes still closed, I worked on an innocent voice. "I think I could convince you to stay in here with me."

The rumbles stopped in Drew's chest as he leaned over me, kissing my neck which made me arch back toward him. His mouth came to my ear as he threw the cold water on my plans.

"My parents are at Jake's, and so is Steph."

I shot up in the bed and looked to Drew. "What? Since when?"

Drew's eyes looked down at my breasts, then back up to my eyes with an arch to his eyebrow. I grabbed the sheet to pull over me and snapped my fingers at him. "Focus, Spencer. When did your parents get here?"

Drew propped his head up on an elbow as he watched my panic unfurl. "I mean, I am focusing, Kate. Not my fault that you're giving me something new to focus on."

I glared. It was warranted.

He laughed as he grabbed my waist and tugged until I was lying on top of him as he rolled to his back. He smoothed my hair behind my ears and leaned up to give me a soft kiss.

"Steph came down yesterday after Jake threw up the SOS sibling signal. They were worried about me." His gaze was watchful, waiting.

Shit. "Because they were concerned about you after the heartless woman you were dating took off to another country to visit her ex-boyfriend?"

Drew's hands came to either side of my face so that I

couldn't look away for him. Shame was churning inside me. We'd worked everything out last night, but apparently, I still had some guilt built up over my behaviors this week.

"Sweetheart, it isn't like that. The three of us needed some time anyway to hash through the reasons I ended up in Highland Falls. This gave us that opportunity."

I was silent for a moment. When we'd come to bed last night after our shower, we'd had soul-connecting sex. Seriously, I hadn't realized it was a thing, but I was now a believer. Then I'd drifted off. Drew had lain by me, playing with my hair, looking at his phone, and just ensuring I knew he was there. At some point in the evening, I'd woken up, and he'd shared more about why his friend James was in town and everything that had gone down with the Hotshots that brought him to Highland Falls.

My heart broke for him and what he'd gone through, but also, I felt so damn proud of him and everything he'd faced in therapy in the past few weeks. Mostly, I was just so grateful that he was okay and here. I hadn't realized he had told Steph and Jake about it, mainly because I wasn't aware Steph was in town.

"How did that go?"

"Oh, you know. Steph wanted to go all Mama Bear; Jake was growly."

"So they were supportive in their own unique ways."

He snorted. "I guess you could say that."

I lay on top of him, lost in his eyes. Then I got to the point. "And they were also being supportive because I'd left."

His gaze didn't leave mine. I could tell he was debating how to say what he needed to. "Yes, they were supportive for that reason. And yes, I have to admit I wasn't doing especially great. Kate, I knew you were doing what you needed to do. That wasn't a line of bullshit I fed you on that landing. It's just when you've given your heart to someone and they're on another continent seeing their ex, worry can creep in. But you don't need to stress. While they were supporting me, they were also rooting for us. Steph even said you'd be back, so there's nothing to fear there."

I worked my lower lip between my teeth, wondering how to ask what I needed to before saying fuck it and letting it fly. "So Margot doesn't hate me."

Drew's smile spread across his face. "Far from it. I messaged all my family last night to explain that you were home and my parents decided on an impromptu trip down today to have brunch. You know she loves a brunch. She also had to bring something for me from home."

I nodded, soaking in the feeling of being encased in Drew's arms.

With a kiss to the underside of my chin, he spoke against my skin. "We good, beautiful?"

I let out a bunch of air and fears at the same time. Surely, I'd lost ten pounds in the past few days because I was releasing all these misconceptions that had held me back. I felt lighter and more myself than I had in years.

"I'm ready. Just let me grab some leggings and a T-shirt. I need five minutes tops." I started to slide off him and out of bed when I realized he hadn't said anything.

Looking back, I saw that Drew was watching me with an amused expression as he bit his lower lip, like he was holding back a comment.

"What?"

"Um, babe, you kind of—" he gestured toward my head.

I couldn't decipher this without coffee. "You're going to need to be more specific than that."

He shook his head, but then sat up. "Well, it's like this.

You're rocking some excellent sex hair right now. So you can go for the leggings and tee, but unless you want Jake and Steph to tease both of us until the ends of time, you might want to whip up one of those braids or a bun to contain that beauty."

I laughed as I ran my hands through my hair. It had been wet when we got in bed, then there was the damn fine sex, then sleeping on it wet. I could only imagine what it looked like. "Noted. So maybe ten minutes will be more like it."

In the end, I was wrong, it took closer to fifteen minutes before we were on the road. We detoured by the Sanctuary because I had a snow globe to drop off for Allyson. There was a set of shelves on the walls in the coffee shop with her full collection on display, many purchased from friends and customers in their travels as gifts for her. When I'd see a super touristy London one at an airport gift shop, complete with Big Ben and a red double-decker bus, I had to grab it for her.

Drew led me through the door as I stared at our clasped hands while he threaded through the space to the counter. My thumb idly slid against his. When would holding his hand get old? A year? Ten? Twenty? I hoped never. His firm grip made me feel cherished, safe. I never wanted to take it for granted.

Lost in thought, I didn't realize he'd stopped walking halfway through the café until my front slammed into his back.

"Oof."

Drew turned, his mouth sliding to my ear. "Sorry babe, but wanted to see if you knew the story before we barged in up there." He nodded to the counter.

Glancing around him, my gaze locked on the scene he

was talking about. The place wasn't too busy yet for a Sunday morning. I was guessing it would be picking up here soon. Drew, however, was looking at the counter. Allyson was behind it, coffee cup cradled in her hands. She took a sip, her long strawberry blonde braid hanging over her shoulder as she gave a beautiful smile to the man sitting in front of her, Logan. Logan looked, as Betty would say, like she hung the moon. I didn't know if either of them were aware of anyone else in this place.

Fascinating. Wonder if Allyson would feel like sharing at the next yoga class.

Drew's eyes were on mine when I glanced back at him. "Nope, no idea, but I think that would be a good match, at least from what I know. Thoughts?"

Drew shook his head, and we began walking again. "Nah, just glad there will be another couple for the local gossips to watch."

"Aww, sweetheart, you don't want Ms. Lou following you anymore."

"Menace," he said with a laugh.

Reaching the counter, I cleared my throat and watched Allyson's cheeks heat up as she looked my way. Yep, she had a lot to share. This would be fun.

After surprising Allyson with her gift, which she loved, we finished our trek to Jake and Ivy's, walking in their back door and into the familiar chaos that was Drew's family.

Addie was dancing around the kitchen island with her little hands waving in the air as she cheered, "Dance party," her rainbow tutu flying up around her. Chief was happily trailing her as the sounds of Fleetwood Mac poured out of the speakers. Steph was sitting on the counter, champagne in hand, talking to Ivy, who was chopping up some strawberries. Jake was standing at the stove with his parents, gesturing at some caramel cinnamon rolls that were on foil, but Margot slapped his hand away.

Sam looked our way when we walked in. "They're here," he said with a smile that matched Drew's.

God, these people were wonderful.

Margot left Jake with a meaningful glare at the caramel rolls and back to him before heading our way. She pulled me in for a hug as soon as she reached me. "I heard you've had some travels this week." She stepped back and looked me over. I was struck by the clear affection in her gaze and lack of judgment.

I nodded. "Yep. I guess you could say I needed to sort out some emotional baggage."

"And it's sorted?"

"It is." My smile stretched across my face. I felt free.

"Good. Now let's talk about your online yoga classes. Are those going to become a regular thing? Because I told my friends about it, and they all have done the one you have up, but want more. They also wanted me to ask how to pay you for them."

I looked to Drew to see him standing with Jake and watching me with a look of amusement. We'd talked last night about how Kristine and I had decided to give the online yoga idea a go. Kristine was looking into what we needed to do to have a website for it and how to put it behind a paywall, though we were going to continue to have a class or two a month available for all without a fee. And of course the studio classes would continue, as was the idea of expanding into more local preschools and daycares. I was excited about the possibilities we had in store.

Returning my attention to Margot, I replied. "I'll have to let you know. We're working on it now."

"You do that." She patted my arm and looked to Drew. "We ready?"

Ready? I looked to Drew and Jake to see if they knew what their mom was talking about.

"Oh, this is going to be good," Steph said from her spot on the counter.

"It absolutely is." Ivy hopped up next to her as they both looked my way.

My heart began to beat harder, feeling like I was clearly missing something everyone else was clued in to. "Um, Drew?"

Drew came to me, wrapping his arms around my waist. "It's fine, Kate. I just asked Mom and Dad to pick something up for me before coming down today."

"I know..." He'd already mentioned that back at the apartment. Why did I still feel in the dark?

Drew looked to Sam and nodded. Sam, in turn, looked to Addie and whispered loud enough for us to hear. "It's time."

Addie began to bounce. "Let's go, Pop-Pop!" She took off toward the living room, Sam following.

Before I could even verbalize another question, I heard Ads pounding footsteps coming back our way, so I decided just to wait it out. I'd figure out what was going on in a minute. Drew moved to stand behind me, his arms around my waist, as we all watched the doorway.

And within moments, Sam and Addie appeared with a golden retriever puppy in Sam's arms.

I melted.

Looking to Drew, I whispered, "What's happening?"

He kissed me neck and said, "We're not wasting any time. That's what's happening. We agreed on this future thing between us, right?"

"Well, yes, but..."

"I want you to know I'm here for all your dreams. You said you'd always wanted a dog, and I told you I wanted one as soon as I knew I was settling someplace. My parents' neighbors had golden retriever puppies. When I overheard you telling the girls you wanted a dog, I messaged my mom, and she told them to hold one for me. She was ready this week and wanted to surprise you with her." He ran his nose along the underside of my jaw. "Thoughts?"

My heart was mush. That was over a month ago that he'd overheard me and decided to get this dog. A dog he didn't want until he was settled. A dog that we were, apparently, going to be parenting together because like hell would I ever be letting him go. I looked to Sam holding the puppy and let everything else go. "She's beautiful. Can I hold her?"

"Of course. She's yours."

"She's ours," I whispered as I moved toward the pup. Sam laughed as I scooped her up from his arms and held her to my chest. She was squirmy and immediately set out to lick my face, including the tears that were streaming down it.

I closed my eyes, soaking it all in as I sank to the floor with the pup in my arms. Drew was there and sat down with his arms around me. "You okay?"

"I'm better than okay."

"What's with the waterworks, then?"

I opened my eyes and looked at the puppy, then Drew, then his family all around us—Steph and Ivy with glasses of champagne and beaming smiles from the counter; Jake with Addie on his hip, Chief by his feet looking like he wanted to come over to investigate; and Sam and Margot near the stove, but with their arms around each other's waists, all here with us.

"I don't know if I've ever been this happy."

Drew smoothed his hand over the puppy's head, then turned my chin toward him. "I hope I can help you find this type of happiness from now on." He brushed a kiss across my lips. "Any idea what you want to name her?"

I looked down to the squirming pup in my lap and debated a few, but there was only one obvious choice. Looking from Margot to Drew, I asked, "How about Daisy?"

Drew closed his eyes and took a deep breath in before opening them and looking at me, joy shining through him. He nodded, then leaned past me to kiss the top of the dog's head. "Welcome to the family, Daisy."

As I leaned back into his arms, I soaked in the goodness. Welcome to the family indeed.

Epilogue

One Month Later

D*rew*

Shifting the leash into my right hand, I ran my left over my pocket, making sure I still had the small bag. I knew I did but needed to be reassured.

Damn, I was nervous.

Daisy and I stood against the side of the mansion, waiting for Kate to come out after using the restroom by the café. Today was Daisy's first hike here at Highland Woods. We'd worked for the past month to get her used to the leash and other dogs when we were walking. It was time to try the trails.

"Hey, Drew. Who do you have here?"

I looked to see Logan jogging over to join us. I'd gotten the job out here at the woods as their community outreach person at the end of February. Logan and I had spent the past month working on our plans for the spring and summer. He was a good guy, and I felt like I was finally where I should be.

Though, looking back to Logan, I couldn't help but notice the shadows under his eyes. I wondered what was keeping him from resting. From what I could tell, he'd built a staff out at Highland Woods that ran like a well-oiled machine.

"This is Daisy. Surely I've told you about her."

Daisy walked up to Logan to be loved on, which he immediately gave to her. Looking in my direction, he laughed. "Oh, I think I've only seen twenty or so pictures of this pup—"

"Wow, that's a low number for Drew." Kate joined us.

"—a day." Logan finished his original thought.

"Ahh, that's more like it," Kate said, shooting me a knowing look.

Yeah, I might be going overboard with our pup, but I wasn't apologizing for it.

"You all just heading out?" Logan asked as he stood from where he'd been petting Daisy.

"Thought we'd check out the bluffs," I said, working to keep my voice calm.

"Everything is just starting to bud, should be gorgeous..." His voice trailed off.

I looked to see what caught his attention and saw the back of Allyson walking in the door that was near the café.

"Excuse me, I need to—" With that, he took off.

Kate gave me a knowing look. "Allyson still won't spill. Says they're just friends."

I headed toward the trailhead. "Maybe they are?"

She knocked into me. "No gossip from Logan?"

"My lips are sealed." In all honesty, I had nothing but loved to torture her.

We fell into an easy pace, Daisy scanning the ground for anything interesting. As we walked along the trail, Kate ruminated on the houses we'd been looking at in town. We hadn't slowed down since we'd made things official. She'd been hard at work on her online classes as well as those in the studio. I'd started my job here and also worked with Jake and Sully to make some changes at the brewery to help with sustainability. And Kate and I continued to plan for our future.

We'd decided Highland Falls was the right fit for us and had been working on finding a house. Not too big, not too small. Kate was not about finding a starter home, then moving when we married and had kids. She wanted to pick the spot we could stay in and raise a family in now, and that worked for me. We'd just looked at a place two blocks from Jake and Ivy yesterday and were thinking of putting an offer in, which felt promising.

Alex was coming out in the next few weeks to visit. Jake, Sully, and Max gave me hell about it because of course they did. They swore that Alex and I were going to end up friends, but the joke was on them because we already were. Honestly, it wasn't that big of a thing; he was a great guy. We'd done several video calls since Kate had come back from her whirlwind trip across the pond. I could see how much they cared about each other, but it felt more like how I felt about Jake and Steph than anything romantic. I was excited to meet him in person.

As we made it down the trail, Kate was sharing her latest news from Betty. They'd also stayed in close contact since they'd met, but Betty had been traveling around Europe with a group of her friends, so no visit to Highland yet. I knew Kate wanted to spend more time with her and was hopeful that would happen soon, depending on the answer she gave me in a few minutes.

We reached the spot in the back of the park that was our favorite. A bench overlooked the river on the top of the bluff. The sky was a gorgeous blue, and the birds were chirping. Daisy's nose took her straight to the bench, just as if we'd planned it.

"God, I love it here," Kate said as she sank down onto the stone bench. "It truly is the most beautiful spot in the park."

"Wayland seemed to think so," I said in reference to the plaque on the bench that indicated it was someone's favorite spot, to sit down and enjoy it.

Kate closed her eyes and tipped her face to the sun. I took that as moment I needed and sank to my knee in front of her, pulling the ring from my pocket as I did. Daisy, like the best dog she was, sat on her butt next to me, tail wagging.

After a moment, Kate lifted her head to look for me, and her face registered a moment of confusion when she saw I wasn't standing anymore before she clicked in to what was happening and lit up from within.

I'd thought about preparing something to say but decided that wasn't needed and I was going to speak from my heart. Right now, I wasn't sure if that had been the best decision. My mind went blank until she leaned forward, a hand to each side of my face, and kissed me.

I took a breath and laid it all on the line. "Kate Ashley, I love you so damn much. I've only known you for three months, but I've never felt such a sense of certainty in my life like I do when I'm with you. When we met, I was so lost. You taught me about balance, about finding the strength I had within. And with you, I was finally able to see a path forward to a future that was more beautiful than I could have ever dreamed."

Kate had tears streaming down her face as she watched me with her hands pressed to her mouth, as if she was ensuring that she didn't start talking until I was done.

"I know it hasn't been a lot of time, but I don't need a lot of time. I know where our future is headed, and I'm ready to go there now. We can have a big wedding, a small one, or heck, we can elope. Whatever you want is what I want, here, now, and forever. Will you marry me?"

Kate slid off the bench to come right in front of me as she wrapped her arms around my neck, peppering my face with kisses.

"Yes, you crazy man, yes." Sliding back to the bench, she cupped my face in her hands. "I love you too, so, so much."

I stood to move next to her on the bench. "May I?" I asked, reaching for her hand. She gave it to me, and I slid the ring on. Thanks to some intel from Kristine, it was a perfect fit.

Kate gasped as she looked at it. "This is beautiful."

"I knew you wouldn't want anything big or something that would bother you during yoga. My mom gave me a ring from my grandma that had this opal and diamonds in it. I brought it to Melinda, the new jewelry designer in town, and she created this design. I thought it fit you." I felt like I was stammering, but trying to pick a ring had been nerve-racking, especially when I was having something designed especially for her.

"I love it." Kate looked from the ring to me. "And I love you. I'm so glad we both decided to start over in Highland Falls. Best decision we've ever made."

Daisy chose that moment to jump up and rest her paws on the bench between us and bark.

"Daisy agrees," I noted. "And wants to continue on our walk. Are you ready, the future Mrs. Spencer? Well, unless you want to stay Ms. Ashley. Steph would kick my ass if I just assumed you wanted to follow the patriarchal norms of our society."

Kate stood up, laughing, and reached down to pull me up. "Yes, she would, but this is one patriarchal norm I'm okay with. I cannot wait to be Mrs. Spencer, and the sooner, the better."

We headed off down the trail, and I wondered how quickly we could get married because every day with this woman was better than the last. Marriage, babies, and a life together in Highland Falls? Sign. Me. Up.

I wanted it all with her. And Daisy. There was so much good to come.

Acknowledgments

I cannot express the difficulty that I had getting this book out into the world.

This is the first book that has been written in its entirety since I started publishing. Let me tell you, friends, impostor syndrome is real.

This book shook my confidence again and again. To be honest, there were a lot of times that I figured Drew and Kate could stay in my brain and I could focus on teaching, parenting, and everything else that makes up my life beyond writing.

But they are insistent characters and I love their story. It spilled out, even when I tried to hold it back.

Even so, truly, my thanks, for this book being out in the world go entirely to my husband and a handful of amazing readers.

Thank you for reminding me again and again you love my stories.

Thanks to my therapist, to whom this book is dedicated. Drew's journey with anxiety is his own, but I definitely borrowed from my own experiences with it. I'm grateful that I finally reached out for help, and beyond thankful that I found a therapist I clicked with. If you're struggling with mental health, I pray you can find someone like Molly (or Jess!) and find some relief.

And final thanks go to my students. They don't read my books, nor do they know my pen name, but when this new group entered my class, several told me they believed they could write because I do. And I'm a sucker for life goals and dreaming big.

To my students - current, former, and future, this one is for you too.

All my love,

Kat

About the Author

Kat Ryan is a middle school teacher by day and a budding romance author in the free time she steals for herself. She loves to write about small towns, found families, strong women, and cinnamon roll heroes that love them. She's a sucker for a HEA and more than a bit of steam in the stories she writes.

Kat lives in the Midwest with her husband and her two teenage sons where she consumes a steady diet of coffee, chocolate, and romance books. And while her students and sons plan to never read the books she writes, her husband has and continues to cheer her on.

Want more from Drew and Kate? Subscribe to Kat's newsletter on her website, https://katryanwrites.com. All "extras" for each of Kat's book are linked in the newsletter that comes out every month.

Also by Kat Ryan

Coming Home

Finding Beauty

Loving Ivy

Follow Your Dreams

www.ingramcontent.com/pod-product-compliance
Lightning Source LLC
Chambersburg PA
CBHW051120190726

48290CB00006B/1622